# CAPTAIN CAUTION

First Printed . . . . . *November 7, 1934*
Reprinted . . . . . *November 16, 1934*
Reprinted . . . . . *December 14, 1934*

# CAPTAIN CAUTION

## A Chronicle of Arundel

# KENNETH ROBERTS

Doubleday, Doran & Company, Inc.
Garden City, New York
1934

PRINTED AT THE *Country Life Press*, GARDEN CITY, N. Y., U. S. A.

TO

L. T. R.

"It is a maxim, founded on the universal experience of mankind, that no nation is to be trusted further than it is bound by its interest; and no prudent statesman or politician will venture to depart from it."

—*George Washington.*

# CAPTAIN CAUTION

# I

CAPT. OLIVER DORMAN, of the armed merchant barque *Olive Branch,* of Arundel, ten guns and twenty-five men, stared calculatingly upward, quadrant in hand, his gray fringe of chin whisker seeming to point accusingly at the towering spread of canvas that half filled itself in the faint, hot air currents of the doldrums, only to go slack once more, as though every sail, from the vast courses to the small and distant royals, had sickened beneath the violent glare of the August sun.

What he saw seemed to leave something to be desired; for he fell to whistling soundlessly, and peered, as if hopefully, along the barque's broad deck, which wearily canted itself to every point of the compass in succession as the glassy surface of the ocean rose and sank in bewildering disorder. Heat waves shimmered upward from each of the five larboard carronades, and, more faintly, from the deck itself. Between the starboard carronades, the crew, barefooted and stripped to the waist, languidly worked at making spun yarn. They were screened from the sun by the foresail, as well as by a strip of sailcloth stretched from the foremast to the starboard ratlines; and as Captain Dorman eyed them, a seaman rose listlessly, dropped a bucket over the bulwarks, drew it slowly back and poured the water on his head and shoulders. Having done so, he gazed doubtfully into the bucket.

"It appears to me," he said, and so faint were the noises

of the barque in the oily calm that his voice came clearly to the quarter-deck—"it appears to me like as if somebody left a dead fish in this ocean."

Captain Dorman sniffed the air, as brackish, indeed, as though it rose from a dying sea. He grasped a spoke of the wheel and moved it a little against the grip of the helmsman, as if to feel the vessel's pulse; then turned abruptly toward the taffrail, where his first and second mates were busy on the day's reckoning with quadrant and latitude tables. Close by them, but sheltered from the sun beneath a patched skysail that served as an awning, sat a girl whose smooth black head was bent over a long and narrow book. She gazed from under arched brows at the serious face of the tall first mate; then moved a shoulder impatiently beneath the thin gray silk of the Chinese jacket that buttoned tight around her throat and fell nearly to the knees of the gray silk trousers below it.

"What do you make it, Dan?" she asked.

The mate plucked at the shirt that clung wetly to his broad chest. "Wait. I'll go over it once more."

She nodded pleasantly. "That'll make four times you've been over it, Dan. It's just as well we haven't had a breeze for a week or two; because if we had, you'd be going over it till suppertime."

He smiled at her. "I might," he admitted. "I aim to miss St. Paul's Rocks, and it's safer to miss 'em on purpose than by accident."

Captain Dorman moved beside them, mopping his face and wrists with a blue bandanna. "Now, Corunna," he said, "you tend to the book and let Dan'l tend to the sights."

She tossed her head impatiently. "I can take a sight quicker than Dan. I don't see he's any handier to do things

simpler and quicker than anybody else; and your telling me
again that he is, won't make me believe it. Just because he's
bigger than all of you together, you think his judgment's
better than mine, but if I can't shoot the sun in half the
time Dan Marvin takes, I'll eat the quadrant."

"Maybe so," Captain Dorman agreed. "Maybe you can.
You've had lessons from me and Dan'l and Noah and everybody else in Arundel that knows how to take a sight. I'd be
ashamed to own you as my daughter if you couldn't take one
as quick as any man. Only it just happens that what sights
are took for this barque are took by me and Dan'l Marvin.
We don't trust nobody's sights but our own. The only reason
we trust to your handwriting in the log book is because none
of us attended the Misses Hubbard's Academy for Select
Females in Waterville. No doubt you can write rings around
us, Corunna; but it don't seem to us we need any help in
navigating."

He thrust out his under lip and nodded severely at Daniel
Marvin, as if to imply that this was the proper way in which
to handle a select female—brusquely, that is, and with little
or no mincing of words.

Then he coughed, glancing at a slip of paper in his hand.
"What did you get, Dan'l?"

"South 4°; 29° west," Marvin told him.

Corunna Dorman lifted a shoulder in silent protest, but
dipped her pen in the ink bottle between the tips of her
Chinese slippers, bent her black head above the log book
and, with delicately upheld little finger, wrote across the top
of the page the words: "Remarks on board, Tuesday,
August 4, 1812."

"That's what I make it," Captain Dorman said. "How'd
you make it from St. Paul's Rocks?"

"I figure we're a good day's run from 'em, Cap'n Oliver, even with a decent breeze."

The captain hastily corrected a figure in his reckoning, nodded profoundly and tossed his paper overside. "That's about right, Dan'l." He handed the quadrant to Marvin, who replaced it in a triangular green box bearing, in white letters, the words "Elihu Marvin, Arundel, 1791."

Captain Dorman pursed his lips in sour contemplation. "Well, my mind's made up! There's something wrong. We ain't sighted a craft of any kind since we put into Pernambuco for water! Even the southeast trades, they've up and cleared out on us before their time. 'Tisn't natural!"

He raised his chin and moved his head, dog-like, as if striving to locate a scent. "There's a little air from the south'ard," he said to Noah Lord. "Get those yards squared around. We'll go off to the northeast."

Even as the second mate shouted the orders that started the half-naked crew from under the shelter of their strip of sail and set them to hauling at the heavy yards, Marvin stared doubtfully at Captain Dorman; and so, too, did the others; but the only one to speak was his daughter.

"Northeast?" she asked. "Have you changed your mind about going back to Arundel?"

There was something like bitterness in Captain Dorman's reply. "Northeast is what I said, and good reason too. We're a hundred and eight days out of Canton—a hundred and eight days!" He brandished a finger before Marvin's nose. "What you think your father would have said about a craft that took a hundred and eight days from Canton to St. Paul's Rocks? He wouldn't have called it a craft; he'd have said it was some kind of vegetable!"

"We had bad luck, Cap'n Oliver," Marvin protested. He,

too, raised his head and moved it from side to side, sniffing the hot and brackish air; and as he did so, the captain and the second mate followed his example, so that they seemed like puppets moved in unison by a single hand.

The captain's puckered lips became less sour. "I knew it," he said. "She's coming." In the direction toward which the three men stared, there was a faint darkening in the pallid expanse of sea.

"That shows you," Captain Dorman continued. "For a hundred and eight days we've done what we ought to do, and got nothing for it but a foul bottom. I reckon there's enough weed on us to fertilize Boothby's farm. As for the crosses we've had to bear, it's a sin and a shame!"

On the upthrust fingers of his left hand he ticked off additional complaints. "Tail of a typhoon off China; tail of some kind of a dod-rotted disturbance off Chile; druv back and druv back and druv back when we tried to round the Horn; blown two hundred miles out of our course off the Falklands; and now just laying here and rotting like a dead whale; and all because we always done what we was supposed to do! What I say is, it's high time I do different! High time!"

"Bad luck's bound to change, Cap'n Oliver," Marvin said. "She never stays anywhere forever; and I say let her go of her own accord. If we try to get away from bad luck, she's apt to move the same minute we do, and in the same direction. We might never get rid of her. Let's wait one more day, Cap'n Oliver."

"Wait!" Captain Dorman growled. "Wait! If we wait another day, we'll send down roots. . . . Hey! Look here, Dan'l!"

He seemed almost to prance on the quarter-deck as the

sails filled. Over the weather rail drifted a breath that had a perfume of the sea in it instead of the flavor of water laden with decaying things. The *Olive Branch* ceased her purposeless heaving and forged slowly ahead.

Captain Dorman sat himself beside his black-haired daughter, casting, as he did so, a somewhat dubious glance at the neat darns in the knees of her gray Chinese trousers. Daniel Marvin, staring down at father and daughter, found a singular resemblance between them—such a resemblance as might result from the labors of a Chinese craftsman if, having rough-hewn the kindly, rugged likeness of the captain, he should make another smaller carving, smoothing every line, rounding every contour, and making finer every feature until he had obtained the graceful figure of Corunna Dorman.

The captain turned his eyes from Corunna to Marvin. "You see, Dan'l," he said, "there's years when there's a southerly breeze over toward the African coast, contrary to Nature. Things being contrary to Nature up to now, we might catch it and move north on it till we meet up with the northeast trades. We might do worse than touch at the Cape Verdes for a breaming; then run for home with a clean bottom."

Marvin nodded impassively, raised his chin to the faint breeze and ran his hand along his neck to clear it of the moisture that made it as bright as the mahogany rim of the wheel. "I'll take the quadrant below," he said. "You through with the log, Corunna?"

She looked hard at him, but spoke to her father. "Dan thinks he knows better, father," she said. "He's getting the Marvin look around his ears." She laughed lightly. "If Dan owned the *Olive Branch,* he'd show us some sailing. I guess

Dan never heard that the longest way 'round is oftentimes the shortest way home."

"Now, now!" Captain Dorman protested. "A man's got a right to his opinion, Corunna. Eli Marvin wouldn't 'a' been so eager to have Dan'l come along with us as mate if he'd thought we'd try to hammer his opinions out of him; and if Dan'l goes as master of his father's brig next voyage, maybe he *will* show us. . . . Speak up, Dan'l, if you got anything to say."

Marvin shook his head. "It's not for me to say, Cap'n Oliver. It's only that I got a feeling against going off our course." He hesitated. "I woke up quick last night, as if there might be a change coming."

" 'Twon't do, Dan'l," Captain Dorman said. "If there'd been a change coming, I'd 'a' woke up myself. And there's no use fretting about going off our course! The way things are, we haven't *had* any course since I don't know when; and now look at us!"

The four of them peered to windward. The breeze, though faint, had freshened. The sickly pallor of the ocean had given way to something that lacked only a little of being sparkle. Astern of the *Olive Branch* stretched a long fold as if the water had been pale blue silk, caught on a bolt under the barque's counter and drawn into a ridge by a giant lying hid beyond the sea's curve.

Corunna Dorman closed the log book with a snap, picked up the ink bottle and rose to her feet, a sturdy, strong-shouldered figure. "It doesn't make any difference!" she said. "Not to Dan! This breeze has no business being here—that's what Dan thinks! . . . You'd rather lie in a calm, wouldn't you, Dan, than enjoy a breeze careless enough to be where it wasn't expected?" She turned and went to the cabin, pausing at the companionway to look superciliously at the three men and exclaim, "Shark-fin soup!"

Captain Dorman shook his head, seemingly baffled. "A woman gets to be a terrible nuisance on a vessel, 'specially in hot spells and calms. Every voyage, for the last three years, I've sworn I'd leave her ashore next time; and by gracious, so I would, if her mother was alive. Trouble is, there ain't anybody to leave her with. Most folks would try to make her feel like a scarlet woman because of knowing there was times when she wore those Chinese unmentionables of hers!"

"If you'd left her ashore," Marvin said calmly, "you wouldn't be getting shark-fin soup."

"No," Captain Dorman agreed uncertainly.

"It appears to me it might be more of a nuisance to leave her ashore than to have her aboard."

Captain Dorman eyed his mate blankly, his lips pursed in a soundless whistle. Marvin, silent and respectful, moved a broad shoulder suggestively toward the cabin. The captain emerged from his revery, cast a quick glance at the towering square sails on the main and foremast, ran his eye over the crew, gathered now around their mess kids between the starboard carronades, sniffed once more at the faint hot breeze; then, followed by Marvin, he scrambled down the companionway to his dinner.

# II

By MIDAFTERNOON the breeze still held, and the *Olive Branch,* with a bonnet laced to her gaff topsail and studding sails set on her main and foremast, held steadily on her course to the northeastward. At the break of the quarter-deck sat Corunna Dorman, her head bent over an intricate piece of needlework which pictured, in brilliant wools, the Holy Family seated beneath a fig tree and contemplating with what may have been suspicion the distant spires of Jerusalem.

Up and down the weather side of the quarter-deck paced Daniel Marvin, his blue-striped shirt and his bell-bottomed duck trousers, disreputable from countless washings, whipped against him by the hot winds from the northwest. When he turned at the break, an arm's length from Corunna, her eyes flicked upward at him, only to fall again to her work as he wheeled at the taffrail. He watched the sky; he watched the sea; he watched the helmsman. He watched the crew, forward, washing their garments by dragging them overside, attached to ropes. He studied the soft pitch, oozing, in spots, from the deck seams; he watched the set of the topgallant sails and royals; he watched the barque's wake, flowing out behind her, in small, endless folds. He watched everything, it seemed, except Corunna and her needlework.

Not even when she whispered, "Dan!" as he prepared to wheel for his monotonous journey to the taffrail did he look

9

at her, but only turned once more as if he had heard nothing.

At his next approach she stretched a hand toward him and spoke his name less softly. The hand, he saw, held a long needle, pointed firmly at his knee, and at no great distance from it.

"Ma'am?" Marvin asked. Moving to the rail beside her, he scanned, as if in eager inquiry, the swirling depths beneath.

"Ma'am!" Corunna said bitterly, but so faintly that even the helmsman could have caught no more than a murmurous sound. "Ma'am, indeed! You'd be careful not to commit yourself, wouldn't you, even if Gabriel was blowing his horn?"

Marvin's eye traveled from the water to the peak of the mizzen sail and back again, passing lightly over the face of the helmsman—a Maine Indian as tall, almost, as Marvin himself, and clad in knee-length trousers so voluminous that they had the look of a short fringed skirt. "Shipboard's shipboard, Corunna. There's always somebody to see what's happening. Plenty of time after we get ashore. And there's Cap'n Oliver: I wouldn't want him to have hard thoughts of me. A little patience never hurt anybody."

She drove her needle through the canvas background of the Holy Family and wrenched the yarn after it with such violence that it seemed to hiss. "You weren't worrying about what anybody might see that night off Rio." When Marvin remained silent, she looked up at him quickly and found him smiling.

"What's more," she persisted in a tone as peremptory as it was quiet, "you weren't delivering any lectures on the necessity of being patient—not *that* night! I don't even recall you making mention, that night, of waiting till we got ashore. And I don't seem to remember being addressed as 'ma'am'—not once! What was it you called me that night, Dan? I hope it hasn't slipped your memory!"

"It was dark that night, Corunna."

"Dark!" she exclaimed. "Of course it was dark! Does it have to be dark to make you stop behaving as if I had yellow fever? That's the way you've acted ever since!" She thrust her needle recklessly through the center of the Holy Family, rolled the needlework together, reached up to the bulwark and swung herself quickly to her feet. Something about the heel of her Chinese slipper seemed amiss, for she half turned to look at it; and in so doing her fingers, seeking support, caught at the hand with which Marvin held to the rail. Her arm pressed, as if by accident, against his side.

He stepped back to scan with sudden solicitude the spread of canvas above him. "Mind your helm, Steven!" he said sharply to the tall Indian. "Keep the upper sails full."

"You did it again!" Corunna whispered, when he turned to her once more. "A body'd think you'd be poisoned if you touched me! Didn't it mean anything to you—that night off Rio?"

"Don't be foolish, Corunna. We can't always have what we want as soon as we want it, and it's better we shouldn't."

"You mean you've changed your mind!"

"No," he said, "no. I don't mean that. I don't change my mind that easily."

"You do!" she insisted. "You have! If you haven't changed your mind, you couldn't keep away from me! You'd want to touch me, every chance you got!"

"So you find, do you, that all of us act alike?"

He laughed when she set her fists on her hips and stared up at him as if scorn at his words had robbed her of speech. "The way I figure it, Corunna, is that I'm sure enough about myself, but less sure of you. It's a long way home, and I'd dislike to have it said I'd taken advantage of a lady who's inclined to be hasty in her judgments."

"Hasty!" she exclaimed. "Hasty! I?" She drew in her breath slowly, almost as though it had been driven completely from her by his charge. "You seem to think I'm hasty because I'm able to make up my mind! Well, let me tell you this, Dan Marvin: It might be better for you if you had a little more of what you call hastiness in place of the patience you're forever preaching about! Patience! The Lord deliver us from your kind of patience, that won't let you do what you want to do till everything just suits you—so that you never do it because you die of old age before you're suited!"

Marvin glanced quickly at the Indian helmsman; then moved a little away from the angry girl.

"Hasty!" she exclaimed again, moving after him. "Who are you, I'd like to know, to pass judgment on my hastiness? Doesn't that just prove that you think you're better than the rest of us? You think your family's better! You think you're better because you invent new ways of doing things—yes, and because you're sizable enough to whip any man that might think to stand out against you. That's it, Dan: You're stuck up, like all the Marvins! They've always been stuck up; always thought they were better than anybody in Arundel, ever since your Aunt Phoebe marched to Quebec, and since your father helped that French duke to buy land from General Knox." She stamped her foot, seeming to flatten beneath it all persons of title as well as all Frenchmen.

Marvin shook his head. "I never noticed it, Corunna. Seems to me my father makes more of knowing your father and Steven Nason and this man's father"—he moved his head slightly toward the Indian helmsman—"than of having done Talleyrand a good turn. If he's stuck up, maybe he's stuck up on account of being first mate on your father's brig when he was young."

She fell silent, fingering the stitches that held together a rip in the shoulder of her Chinese jacket. "I suppose," she said at length, "that if these things were bright and new, you might——"

The helmsman interrupted her. "Dan'l," he said, "seems to me I caught a sight of suthin off the weather beam."

Marvin swung himself over the bulwarks and into the mizzen ratlines with an ease and lightness that belied his height and breadth of shoulder. Halfway up he stopped and stared off to the southeast.

"What is it, Dan?" Corunna asked.

"Get your father's glass," he said. "Tell him there's a sail to windward, and the wind's dropping."

She did as he ordered; then mounted the ratlines after him to sit on the crosstrees, clinging to his knee, while he focused the glass on the thick blue haze in the south, a haze so hot that it boiled and rolled like smoke.

Far below them, her father moved to the rail and looked upward, his round face, fringed with whiskers and gray hair, seeming to be balanced ludicrously atop of little more than a pair of shoes.

"What you make it out to be, Dan'l?" he shouted.

"Three sail," Marvin called down to him. "They must have caught a southeasterly breeze. One of 'em's headed straight for us. The other two, they're pointed more to the eastward."

Marvin lowered the glass and peered astern, past the limp, flapping expanse of the gaff topsail. The folds of the

wake had flattened into the oily, silvery surface of the sea—
a surface touched here and there by the small rufflings of
vagrant airs. Ahead of and high above him, the staysails and
the square sails on the mainmast hung limp and draggled;
while from among them came a thousand slappings and
lollopings as the staggerings of the barque in the renewed
calm set blocks and sails and sheets to bumping and lament-
ing in mid-air.

He went quickly down the ratlines, leaving Corunna to
follow or not, and gave the glass to Captain Dorman.

"Any sign of a breeze?" the captain asked.

Marvin shook his head. "Only the one the stranger
caught."

Captain Dorman adjusted the glass and leveled it. "First
sail we've sighted in a dreadful long time! Seemed as if
every seaman must have gone ashore and got himself the
cow and garden he's always talking about." He growled and
grumbled to himself as he watched the distant vessel, whose
topsail, topgallant sail and royal were now visible from the
deck of the *Olive Branch,* though the sails and yards and
masts wavered and quivered in the heat, almost like reflec-
tions dimly seen in agitated water.

"What you make of her, Dan'l?" the captain asked suddenly.

"I think she left the other two sail on purpose to have a
look at us."

Captain Dorman passed the glass to the second mate, who
stood silently beside him. "Let's hear what you think of
her, Noah."

Noah Lord studied the oncoming vessel deliberately.
"Brig: full sail," he announced. "Pretty heavy sparred,
she is. Pretty high hoist to her topsails, seems to me."

Captain Dorman's lips were pursed, and there was a gray cast to his face that may have come from the stifling heat that had again enveloped the barque. He made two turns the length of the quarter-deck, and in that time seemed to arrive at a decision. "Yes," he said, "they look high to me —high and heavy. Get out the sweeps! We'll sweep 'round and get to moving, so to take advantage of that breeze when it reaches us. No sense lying here like a bump on a log!"

The second mate ran forward, shouting to the crew as he ran, and in a minute's time six twenty-four-foot oars had been thrust through the sweep holes between the gun ports, and the sweating men were working the *Olive Branch* around to the northwest.

"Who'd 'a' thought," Captain Dorman said to Marvin —"who'd 'a' thought we'd strike anything off here? And I guess there ain't much doubt about her being something, with topsails that size! She ain't a merchant vessel; she's got some men aboard." He looked around him uneasily. "The Britishers, they'd be sticking to the West Indies— they and the yellow fever. It just don't seem reasonable to strike a thing like this, off in the middle of nowhere! There's something about it I'm taking a misliking to." He laughed with what may have been intended for carelessness, but to Marvin it seemed to be nervousness that impelled the captain to draw the folds of a blue bandanna handkerchief across and across his palms. "Some day, Dan'l, we may have to fight somebody, so's to remind 'em we got a few rights on their ocean."

Marvin nodded soberly. "We might," he said, "if we ever get half enough ships to do it, but it doesn't look as if we ever would."

Driven by the sweeps, the barque rocked slowly to the

northwestward. The brig, now astern, moved steadily closer, and before her the silvery blue of the ocean was darkened by the breeze that bore her on. The eyes of the three men moved constantly from the approaching brig to their own upper sails. At last the main topgallant sail and royal bellied a little, then slapped the mast.

The captain drew a deep breath. "There it is," he said. "Now we'll get it." The topgallant sail and royal filled again, and the topsail and the huge course seemed to come to life.

"We'll keep 'em sweeping," Captain Dorman said. "With the sweeps and the breeze, maybe we can show her a clean pair of heels. God knows what she is, but it don't seem likely she'd leave two other craft, just for a friendly call on us." He went through the motion of whistling silently. "We can't afford to take risks," he added. "She might be a Spanish privateer, or one of those damned Frenchmen from the Indies. They'd as lief cut our throats as eat a mess of greens, Dan'l! We'll have to load and double-shot the guns, my boy. Everything I've got on earth is in this barque! If the worst comes to the worst, we can cut up her rigging and get away when she hauls off to repair the damage."

From the brig, so close that her white streak was visible, wavering raggedly in the heat waves, there grew a small white blossom that bloomed and broke and drifted off in pale streamers, all in a moment's time. Down the wind there came a heavy thud, as if some vast horse, enraged, had driven a steel-shod hoof against a fragile wall.

# III

From the main hatch, Marvin, superintending the casting loose of the guns, as well as the bringing up of powder bags, six-pound shot, tubes, fuses and all the lumber that was necessary to the operation of the *Olive Branch's* small batteries, could hear Captain Dorman laying down the law to his daughter. "Go below," he told her, "and put off those heathen trappings. Get yourself into proper female dress; then hunt out a safe place below the water line, where you'll be off my mind."

Marvin had to listen hard for her answer; for her voice was low, with more entreaty in it than defiance. "One place is as safe as another," she told her father, "and I want to see what happens. I've been on the *Olive Branch* almost half my life since I was born in Corunna Harbor, and I never yet found a place safer than this quarter-deck. I'm not afraid of that brig. She's not as big as we are, and I don't believe there's anything to be afraid of, but if I have to be shut up below, where I can't tell what's going on, I'll die! I'm as much interested in this barque as you are! If there's to be any fighting over her, you'll need everybody you've got, and I want a hand in it."

As if overwhelmed by her flux of words, Captain Dorman looked desperately aloft and then astern, where the brig, thrusting thin white ribbons of foam from under her heavy bow-sprit, was little more than a mile away. He signaled to Marvin, who ran aft, pausing only long enough to remind the panting men to load with wads between the shot unless they wanted their guns to burst.

"Now, here," Captain Dorman told him, "she's faster than we are, though she wouldn't be if we had some of the sculch off our bottom. Anyway, she's bound to come up with us; and if she fires on us, there's got to be steps taken. We've run up the American flag, and she ain't got no right to fire on us, no matter who she is. If she does, she's a pirate, entitled to be treated as one. We're peaceable folks, going about our business. If she fires on us, we'll keep on going till she starts to yaw again, to bring a gun to bear; then we'll veer and come into the wind clumsy and slow, as if we'd given up. We've got just the breeze for it, Dan'l! There we'll be, Dan'l, helpless-looking as an old scow; and so she'll close with us. When she does, we'll fire with the upward roll and chop her masts and rigging to pieces."

Noah Lord nodded; but Marvin, his lips pressed tight together, stared silently at the oncoming brig.

Captain Dorman moved close to him. "Dan'l," he said, "nearly every cent I've got in the world is in this barque and her cargo. Maybe I did wrong to risk so much. I won't say as to that. What's done's done. If I get this barque home safe, I'll be a rich man. If I don't, I won't have a penny, and neither will Corunna. No pirate's going to stop me, not while I've got the say. I know what you're thinking. You're thinking what's going to happen if we don't chop her to pieces. Well, Dan'l, we got to, that's all. 'They cry unto the Lord in their trouble, and he bringeth them out of their distresses . . . he bringeth them unto their desired haven.'"

"These guns haven't been fired in a year," Marvin said slowly. "The men can't lay 'em or serve 'em properly."

Corunna came close to her father, a sturdy figure in her

jacket and trousers of gray silk, and stared at Marvin with what seemed to be almost oriental placidity. "They're going to be fired now, Dan, even if I have to fire them myself."

Marvin seemed oblivious to her words. "Why," he said thoughtfully, "there *is* a way! There *is* a way to lay 'em properly! I never thought of it before! We could hang a pendulum—a gangway pendulum—if only we had the time."

Captain Dorman sighed, a quivering sigh. "If only we had the time, we wouldn't need a pendulum, and we wouldn't need guns, either. Now, Dan'l, Noah and I, we'll tend to the two after guns. Take Steven off the wheel and put him on the bow gun, and you lay the two 'midship guns yourself. Wait for me to fire, Dan'l; then cut her up in the tops."

He stepped to the break in the quarter-deck and shouted to the sweating men who crouched close under the bulwarks. "Take it slow when you get your orders to veer," he said. "We figure on putting a fright and the fear of God into this craft, provided she needs it. When she's had her lesson, we'll clap onto the sweeps, get before the wind again, and be homeward bound as quick as you can say fish."

Behind them the brig yawed. To her mastheads rose the British ensign and pennant; and a moment later those on the quarter-deck of the *Olive Branch* clearly saw the orange flame that stabbed from the muzzle of her starboard bow gun, to be engulfed in the ball of white smoke that followed. There was a high thin screaming above the barque's weather beam—a screaming that ended when the shot, striking the water ahead of them with a thumping splash, sent a silvery cone of water high in air.

"British?" Captain Dorman cried incredulously. "Either

'tain't so, or she'll haul off when she sees we're willing to fight! They ain't so eager for war as all that!"

From the brig there came a hoarse shouting, indistinguishable above the small creakings of the barque. When the barque held on her course, another hail bellowed from the brig, following which her bow fell off again to larboard.

With that, the *Olive Branch* veered slowly to the westward. Less than a pistol shot away, the strange brig followed her example.

Marvin, tinkering with the elevation of his gun, saw Captain Dorman do the same—saw him prod and prod again at the quoin beneath the breech.

The captain stepped back to the lanyard, and in the same moment he seemed to twist and break and crumble—almost to fly to pieces with a thunderous roar. A burst of flame and smoke obscured the quarter-deck, and from the smoke came shouts and strangled cries. The captain's gun, Marvin saw, had burst.

As he ran toward the stern, he saw Corunna rise from her knees beside the heap of rags that had been her father. Behind her, Noah Lord moaned and clutched the bloody stump from which his lower leg hung by shreds and splinters.

She ran to the gun next to that which had burst, and it was there that Marvin caught her by the shoulders and held her. She strove to push him away, staring at him out of eyes as black as coals in her dead-white face. "The lanyard!" she whispered, in a voice that trembled and broke. "This gun hasn't been fired!"

"It's no good, Corunna! It's like breaking rock with your fists."

She struck him in the face and kicked at him. "Damn you!" she cried. "Fire that gun! Fire that gun! They've killed my father!"

He clutched the front of her gray silk jacket and dragged her, struggling and panting, to the mizzenmast. "Let go everything!" he shouted down the deck; and as he shouted, he slashed with a knife at the mizzen halyards and hauled down the American ensign that drooped from the mizzen truck.

She plucked at his arms and shoulders with fingers that scratched like claws. "You coward! You dirty damned coward!" she cried.

He caught her to him, pinning her arms to her sides, and looked at her quickly from head to foot. There were clots of blood on her paper-white face and her gray silk garments, but the blood, he knew, was not hers. Over her shoulder he saw that a boat had been lowered from the brig's after davits—a boat with a British naval officer in her stern sheets, and on her thwarts a dozen armed men. From near at hand there rose a steady moaning.

"Go to your cabin!" Marvin said. "Clean yourself and put on decent clothes! I want you back on this deck when that boatload comes aboard!"

She pulled against his arms like bent whalebone. It seemed to Marvin that her lips drew back from her teeth. "Damn you! Damn you! Damn you! You sneaking, cowardly turn-tail rat!"

He shook her as if she had been a folded staysail; shook her until her head sagged on her shoulders and her lips went slack. As suddenly as he had started, he stopped; her head fell back, and with the flat of his hand he struck her on the cheek. On her white face the prints of his fingers stood out with even greater whiteness.

"Noah Lord's bleeding to death!" he told her fiercely. "Get below, you little fool! If you've got brains, use 'em!" He dragged her to the companionway and thrust her into it. She stumbled and fell; then got to her feet and vanished toward her cabin.

Marvin ran back to Noah Lord, cutting loose and knotting the lanyard of his knife as he ran. He slashed the blood-drenched trousers from Noah's shattered stump, slipped the lanyard around it, pushed a belaying pin beneath the cord and rapidly twisted it until the cord, cutting deep into the leg, made an end of the crimson stream that flowed into the scuppers.

"Steven!" he shouted, his head bent over his sorry task, "Steven! Bring water buckets and a sail and two men!"

When, in five minutes' time, an English lieutenant in a wrinkled blue coat, soiled white ducks and a battered hat came over the side, a limp roll of canvas lay on the newly wetted deck, and Noah Lord, grayer than the rag of sail that covered the spot where his left foot should have been, was stretched motionless and seemingly lifeless in the shadow of the weather bulwarks.

The lieutenant was tall and young, with an air of having grown weedily in a space too small for him. His head was thrust forward, like that of a melancholy bird; his thin legs, half covered by soiled and shrunken duck trousers, gave him the look of a crane, stalking suspiciously at the water's edge. Marvin, watching him come over the rail, hitching at his sword to keep it from between his knees, was in doubt whether the redness of his face was due to the searing rays of the tropic sun, or to anger; but beyond question he was angry—so angry, indeed, that he forgot to demand immediately the name, destination and port of departure of the vessel he had boarded.

"By Ged," he said with no preamble whatever, "I should have blown you to pieces and left you to sink, and be demned to you for a lot of filthy Yankees!" His boarding party of eight men, in glazed hats, and shirts and trousers that might once have been white, dragged their cutlasses over the rail to cluster behind the lieutenant and peer at the wrecked carronade-slide and the blood-stained heap of canvas in the scuppers.

Marvin eyed the lieutenant calmly. "This is the American merchant barque *Olive Branch*. Her papers are in order. The only filth you'll find aboard this craft is what you've brought with you. What's your authority for this act of piracy?"

"Piracy!" the lieutenant ejaculated. "Piracy! Why, you ——" He gestured largely toward the hilt of his sword and frowned horribly. "His Majesty's cruiser *Beetle,* eighteen guns, and by Ged, sir, you're in luck, all of you, not to be shark meat this very moment. Why, demn you, sir, why didn't you heave to? You might have cost us a man! You're no better than madmen, all of you, always playing the fool—declaring war when you've nothing to declare it with, and now running from a cruiser that could knock you to driftwood with half a broadside!"

"War!" Marvin cried. "Did you say war?"

"A fool and deaf to boot!" the lieutenant said savagely. "D'you think it was a Maying party your clown of a Madison asked us to last June? A *conversazione?* My Ged! It's a pity all your carronades didn't explode, so to let a little light into you!"

Corunna Dorman stepped quickly from the companion-way and walked between Marvin and the lieutenant, her arms, tight at her sides, hidden in the billowing folds of a thin black dress. She swayed a little, staring at the lieutenant out of eyes like black flints. Marvin, watching her apprehensively, saw that one of her hands, deep in a pocket of her gown, clutched something, he knew not what. Filled with a sudden fear, he grasped her wrist. "Easy, Corunna!" he said. "We've been at war since June. At war! We've been at war with England!"

She turned a somber glance on him. When he released her, she lifted sad eyes toward the boarding party from the British brig. Her hands, obscured no longer, were clasped before her. "My father——" she said, and on the word her voice broke and failed. "My father——" She drooped toward the lieutenant, and with that he caught and held her.

"Great regrets, mem!" he said huskily. He cleared his throat and laughed in a way that he may have thought pleasant. "Didn't expect the pleasure—ah, Ged! Frightful pity, mem! Not for worlds, eh? Do what we can!"

She freed herself from the lieutenant's arm. "We knew nothing of it!" she said. "We left Canton in May. What had we—what made you fire on us—what——"

The lieutenant laughed ingratiatingly. "You'll come aboard the *Beetle,* eh? Ged, mem, a pleasure! We're for the Azores with our prizes—a slaver and a Frenchman, mem; and now you, thank Ged!"

He turned to Marvin. "Get your men into boats and over to the brig. You've got five minutes to collect your dunnage. Don't take too much or we'll pitch it overboard."

He turned back to Corunna. "Sorry—sorry to cause you the inconvenience."

## IV

Forty seamen and twenty scarecrow marines crowded close around the crew of the *Olive Branch* as they scrambled over the bulwarks and into the waist of the *Beetle* war brig, spurred on by the fractious voice and intemperate words of the *Beetle's* red-faced, thin-shanked commander, Lieutenant the Hon. Vivian Strope.

Lieutenant Strope himself followed hard on their heels, calling angrily for Mr. Benyon and Oddsly. Mr. Benyon, Marvin discovered, was a small pale child, attired in the white ducks, the glazed hat and the dirk belt of a midshipman. Marvin's discovery came about through being struck sharply in the small of the back and then brusquely elbowed to one side by Mr. Benyon in response to the lieutenant's call.

"Mr. Benyon," Lieutenant Strope said, "if any of you young gentlemen happen to know where there's a prayer book, bring it at once. There's an—ah—lady on the prize and we kent do a thing with her until we've fed the old man to the sharks in a manner to suit her! In this heat I couldn't remember a word of the burial service, by Ged, even if I knew the demned thing!"

The pale child saluted smartly and disappeared. His place was taken by the elderly, bald, disillusioned-looking sailing master in shrunken nankeen breeches and a gingham coat.

"Oddsly," the lieutenant said, "send ten men aboard the prize, with one of the young gentlemen in command—I think Mr. Jowkes. See to it, Oddsly, while I'm getting this

Yankee overboard. They tried to fight us, Oddsly, the demned ruffians. Demnedest nuisance of all, Oddsly, is that one of 'em blew his leg off! Demned well wish it had been his head! Can't put him with the prisoners, demn it! See to it, and search the prisoners; then clap 'em in the hold. And just bear in mind, will you, that we've got to close with the other two prizes before nightfall?"

Clutching a prayer book that Mr. Benyon had brought him, the lieutenant scrambled down into the boat once more; while a detail of marines, under the eye of the sailing master, searched Marvin and the crew of the *Olive Branch,* removing from them not only knives but even belt buckles, coins and every metal thing.

"Smartly, now!" Oddsly told them, when this was done. "You'll go under guard in the main hold and we'll stow your dunnage where it'll be safe. You'll be allowed on deck in sections, starting as soon as the hatch comes off in the morning. Settle your differences peaceably if you don't want a bullet in your gizzards. We're overburdened with prisoners, and the guards have orders to take no chances—not with such ugly brutes as you Yankees. Step lively, now!"

He stared arrogantly at the dejected group of seamen and jerked a thumb toward the hatchway. Marvin raised a protesting hand. "Leave us our dunnage," he said. "It's not right to clap these men under hatches half naked, as they are. They'll need clothes."

Oddsly's reply was contemptuous. "No they won't! Not here they won't! This brig ain't Buckingham Palace! The state bedrooms were overlooked when she was launched, and you'll find your quarters somewhat restricted." He laughed appreciatively at his own facetiousness and swung himself down the ladderway at the main hatch.

Marvin, waiting for the men to follow the sailing master into the darkness below, cast a look astern. The *Beetle's* crew had mounted to the carronades and the hammock nettings to watch the *Olive Branch,* wallowing under the brig's lee, her slack sails a bright pink from the setting sun. Between the shoulders of the British sailors, Marvin could see small figures on the barque's quarter-deck, and as he watched, a gray lump fell from the larboard rail, half turned in mid-air, struck the water with a clumsy splash and vanished as if it had never been.

" 'He bringeth them out of their distresses,' " Marvin quoted, thinking of kindly Captain Dorman and how he had come to stand close beside him, not an hour since, and speak of his and Corunna's needs. At the thought, Marvin laughed, but at the sound, which was more of a croak than a laugh, he licked his heat-cracked lips and passed his hand across his face, which seemed to him stiff. His eye ran quickly along the brig's armament—along the eight stubby carronades to a side, and the two long guns, twenty-four pounders, that had been run out of the larboard bow ports preparatory to raking the *Olive Branch* if the need had arisen. His shirt, drenched with perspiration, seemed to become even wetter when he contemplated what must have happened aboard the barque if those two guns had loosed their double loads of ball and grape at close range. He groaned aloud at the recollection of the words Corunna Dorman had spoken to him when, by his quickness, death and destruction had been averted. " 'Sneaking, cowardly, turn-tail rat!' " he repeated to himself. The words reformed themselves in his hot brain and spilled unbidden from his parched lips. "Cowardly, sneaking, turn-tail rat!" he muttered. "Turn-tail, cowardly, sneaking rat!"

The voice of the sailing master roared at him from the hatch: "Well, for God's sake! Are you coming along, or are you thinking of taking a berth in the gun room?"

"Could I have some water?" Marvin asked hoarsely.

"Come down that ladder," the sailing master snapped, "or you'll get a musket-butt behind the ear!"

Marvin descended the ladder hastily, stooped to avoid the beams of the berth deck, and moved forward to a second hatch. As his eyes became accustomed to the dimness, he saw, crouched on each side of the hatchway, two grotesque marines, looking, in that hot half light, like the guards of some dark inferno.

Out of a small square hole in the hatch protruded a ladder, and from the hole there came the sound of many voices, and a stench as evil as it was powerful.

"Down with you!" the sailing master said with what almost seemed like enjoyment. "We'll be at the Cape Verdes before you know it."

Seeing that there was no help for it, Marvin laid hold of the ladder to go down, but as he did so, a man rose through the hole in the hatch to block his way. He had a thin face, long and palely yellow, framed in lank black hair; a face that had, at no distant date, been cleanly shaved, but that was now shaded by a growth of black stubble. As he rose higher on the ladder his garments were revealed to be as darkly gray as a Quaker's coat. He glanced quickly at Marvin from under an eyelid that drooped heavily, but spoke to the sailing master in a hoarse voice that seemed to Marvin to have a singularly pleasing resonance.

"I believe, sir," he said, "that unless you let some of us on deck, you'll have a pile of corpses on your hands to-morrow."

"You know the rules, Slade," Oddsly said brusquely. "Nobody goes on deck when we're hove to, or in chase of a sail. It's nothing you can't stand. You mustn't judge white men by the blacks you've carried."

Slade looked carefully at the sailing master, tilting his head backward as though to see him more clearly from under his drooping eyelid; and Marvin saw that the grayness of the man's shirt was due to a crust of mud upon it.

He turned to Marvin then. "You're joining us, I think. Lurman Slade, if you'll permit me, captain of the *Graceful Kate* brig."

"Slaver!" Oddsly said scornfully.

Again Slade tipped back his head to stare at the sailing master. "You repeat yourself," he said. "I think this gentleman probably understood your first reference. He's not an Englishman!"

He smiled and nodded at Marvin, backing slowly down the ladder; and Marvin, after a final glance at Oddsly's grim features, followed Slade into a hot, foul blackness that seemed to rise about him like the steam from a witch's cauldron; then to close over his head as he descended.

He stood, Marvin felt—for in the darkness of the hold he could see nothing—on a tier of water casks that had been covered with a layer of mud, so that a second tier of casks might be placed in it and prevented, by its stickiness, from shifting. The stench of the place caught him in the throat and the pit of the stomach, as if those outraged organs fought silently against the unendurable; and the uneasy swaying of the brig seemed suddenly to sweep off into enormous arcs that momentarily threatened to become dizzying revolutions. He caught at the collar of his shirt and heard it rip in his hand; then, choking, he turned and fumbled again for the ladder.

A hand caught him by the arm. "No use to go up," Slade's hoarse voice told him. "The marines push you back. Lie down here between us. This corner of the hold is the officer's mess, anyway."

Dripping with perspiration, Marvin did as he was told, only to find himself wedged tightly between Slade and a hulk of a man whose outthrust shoulder, arm and hip had the feel of a seaweed-covered ledge. He groaned and heaved as Marvin pressed against him; but when Slade, leaning over Marvin, softly said "Argandeau," the hulk of a man was gone as quickly as though he had silently exploded. A moment later he spoke softly from above them: "Somebody call me?"

"I did," Slade said. "You'd sleep through hell, if you had to go there."

"Ah," the soft voice said, "you don't wake me to tell me about hell, I hope!"

"Why, no," Slade said. "I woke you so you'd give our guest some room."

"Ho!" Argandeau said. "So the Griffons took another! Soon we begin to be crowded, I think."

Against the dim light that filtered through the hole in the hatch Marvin saw Argandeau mount two steps up the ladder. "Mr. Griffon!" he called mildly. "Ho, Mr. Griffon! Rig the wind sail! I feel we are under way!"

A sentry's face appeared at the hatch. "Oo the 'ell you calling Mr. Griffin?" he demanded truculently. "We bloody well had enough of your Griffining!"

"Yes, well, you rig the wind sail," Argandeau said. "We choke to death here in this black sewer."

He came down the ladder, crouched beside Marvin and felt for his shoulder. "They are all Griffons, the English," he declared mildly, "with ugly, hairy faces like the hunting griffons of the Vendee. Similar as to whiskers, but less dependable and less aristocratic parentage. This ship of yours, what was she?"

"Barque *Olive Branch,*" Marvin told him. "Three hundred and thirty ons, twenty-five men, ten six-pounders, of and for Arundel, from Canton."

"Six-pounders!" Argandeau exclaimed. "Good for nothing but shooting flying fish! Why you run from this cruiser? Don't you know she can knock you into fireplace wood?"

"I thought you were asleep during the chase, Argandeau," Slade interrupted.

"Ho," Argandeau said carelessly, "I hear in my sleep. I hear, even, that although you decide to fight and run, you do neither. Pfoo! Bang! And in one minute you are here, eh?"

Marvin cleared his throat. "Yes," he admitted uncomfortably, "yes. The only gun we fired blew up, and there was——" He checked himself. "There were important lives aboard. I don't mean my own particularly—I mean—I think —if there had been more time—I mean, I could have rigged a pendulum in the gangway. Even through the smoke I could have cleared her decks if I could have rigged a pendulum. With a pendulum we could have fired from an even keel, always. It was too late when it occurred to me—a pendulum——"

His voice died away. The silence that followed was broken by a faint, hoarse laugh from Slade. Marvin felt Argandeau's hand on his shoulder. "Yes, yes," the Frenchman said soothingly. "You have had an experience! I understand quite well! You rest now, and I speak to you of my *Formidable*. You say in English *Formidibibble*, I think, eh?"

"*Formidable!*" Marvin said wearily. How did you come to call her *Formidable* when she wasn't?"

"No, no!" Argandeau murmured. "You be quiet. Do not speak of pendulums, or of anything, even. When word arrives in any port that Lucien Argandeau approaches in his *Formidable,* the ladies of that port, they flame with feeling! In every place—even in Martinico and Hispaniola —the girls cheer for the *Formidable* when she come, and weep for her when she go! For me they flame; for my *Formidable* they scream in exultation. She is gallant— swift like the frigate bird—swifter! Swooping on her enemies like the hawk, piff! In her I would fight any vessel, sailing in circles about those too large to take; laughing at them, ha-ha!"

"Yes, and here you are!" Marvin told him wearily. He buried his head in his arms and thought again of the words Corunna Dorman had spoken to him.

Argandeau was silent for a time. "I know what you feel, young man," he said at length. "You are sick, here in this cesspool. You think of your clean ship! You think of your home! You remember some sweet rabbit who has held you close—close! Your life drips out from you, here in the mud! You are all despair, eh?"

"I can stand it," Marvin said.

"Pooi! Of course!" Argandeau agreed. "On the sea, noth- ing is hopeless. We know that—we who have seen men washed from a ship's deck into eternity by a wave, only to be washed back again by the next."

"Got any water?" Marvin asked.

"They bring it to us soon. You listen, now. I tell you about Lucien Argandeau, because I have pleasure in speaking American, and I like very much your people. You notice my speaking of American, eh?"

"Yes," Marvin said numbly, "you speak very well."

"But of course! I am friends for three years with a beautiful rabbit from Boston. You know Boston?"

The words came slowly into Marvin's mind. "A rabbit? You were friends with a rabbit?"

"Ha-ha!" said Argandeau, "a stylish rabbit, very neat, very affectionate; a true angel, so that when she speak of returning to Boston, I say she go back to heaven."

"Oh, yes," Marvin murmured drowsily.

"Yes!" Argandeau sighed gustily. "I learn from the best of dictionaries—the sleeping dictionary. I have had a pocket full of them. *Epatant et pas chère, comme on dit, à Paris!* There is that about me, you understand, that is irresistible to rabbits! Now look: I tell you more about the brave Lucien Argandeau and his beautiful *Formidable*. In all the world, under my command, no vessel sail so fast. M-m-m-m-m-m! Like a bonito, she go Wheesh! Wheesh! Here, there, and then gone! Pfooi!"

At the hatchway above there was a stir and rattling. A faint breath of air, still hot, but less foul than the nauseous steam that filled the hold, lightly touched Marvin's face, so that he knew a wind sail had been rigged. Argandeau's voice, droning out of a black void, fell soothingly on the ear. Marvin, dozing presently, dreamed that there were pleasant sounds, even in hell.

# V

IN THE fetid hold of His Majesty's war brig *Beetle* there were close onto one hundred prisoners, forty-two of them Frenchmen from Argandeau's privateer schooner, thirty of them an unsavory lot from Slade's dark brig, and the remainder from the *Olive Branch*. Once a day one-third of all this sorry company were called from their filthy cavern, each man guarded by a marine with bayoneted musket. One by one, like dangerous beasts, they were herded and prodded upward, staggering and blinking, to the deck, where they were packed into a long-boat amidships and, ringed by sentries, allowed for a little time to rid their lungs of the effluvium that had poisoned them below.

So heady and so sparkling was the air, after their long breathing of noxious gases, that it mounted in them like wine, some becoming ill or dizzy, and others waggling their tongues as if, Argandeau said, they had been spliced with whalebone.

For two days the face of Argandeau remained a gray blur to Marvin—a gray blur from which emerged soft-voiced scurrilities concerning their captors, the English Griffons, and endless references to the rabbits—all of them rabbits of unrivaled beauty—who had succumbed to his charm in a hundred ports. Not until the second day after his capture was Marvin permitted to clamber up the ladder, preceded by Slade and followed by Argandeau and something more than a score of prisoners.

Accompanied by a marine as by a shadow, he went forward to the main hatch and emerged at last on deck. The sun beat down out of a pale sky, and the brilliance of its rays were so like an explosion in Marvin's eyes that he covered his head with his arms as he stumbled into the longboat amidships.

"Excuse, please," Argandeau said. "I hold your arm because it is easy to fall against carronades or something when you come from that place."

When he could bear the light at last, Marvin cleared the moisture from his cheeks with hands that seemed to him strangely unsteady, and peered aft in the hope of seeing Corunna Dorman on the quarter-deck. The stern was screened from him, however, by the swelling belly of the main course; and as Argandeau pulled him down on a thwart of the long-boat, he turned to look for the first time at his new acquaintance.

He saw a man who seemed, by comparison with himself, almost short—a man whose shoulders sloped downward from his full throat as those of a bottle slope away from its neck; so that it was hard to say where his neck ended and his shoulders began. The shoulders sloped in turn into arms that reached almost to his knees. His ears were small and delicate as those of a child, and his short black hair grew in a widow's peak on his forehead with something of the appearance of a woolen wig.

All of him—face, hair, ears, arms, hands, shirt and trousers—was blotched and crusted with mud from the water casks on which he had lived and slept. All in all, there was that about him that suggested an ape strangely erect, but an ape none the less.

Marvin looked quickly at the other prisoners, who, urged

forward by their guardian marines, were clambering into their long-boat, and saw that all of them were equally smeared with mud. He looked down at the hand with which he had rubbed the moisture from his eyes. That, too, was gray and mud-caked, and it came to him that his own appearance was no more agreeable than that of the others.

Marvin cast an eye aloft and around the horizon. The sultry breeze still held in the southwest. To leeward were a barque and a brig, and far back on their lee quarter, very faint, a sail. The barque, he knew, was the *Olive Branch;* the brig, therefore, must be Slade's *Graceful Kate* and the distant sail the *Formidable.*

"What's this craft doing without studding sails or royals?" Marvin asked. "It must be they're waiting for your schooner, Argandeau."

"Well, of course!" Argandeau said softly. "These are Griffons, sailing these vessels. Look there, at that poor *Formidable* so far astern she is no more than a small white flea! She sail twelve, thirteen knots, any day I have her. Put me on her quarter-deck and she run around this brig, pfoo! Like that! I am caught, it is true, but on a lee shore —yes; it is something that could happen to anyone, eh? To Surcouf; to Duguay-Trouin, even!" He glanced at Marvin. "Of course, I am not Duguay-Trouin, but be assured that if I had lived in the days of Duguay-Trouin, he would not have been ignorant of me!" He sighed pensively; then patted Marvin's hand. "Ask anybody in all South America, wherever you will. They tell you at once, 'But of course! Argandeau sail twice around Hispaniola while any Englishman trying to get from Dover to Calais!' Fourteen knots, whenever I take her out; but the Griffons, they cannot get more than eight, not ever. For me, she is a swan; for the Griffons, a dead skate. I tell you these Griffons do not know about sailing. They are nothing but mutton dealers and boot polishers, all loaded into vessels— nothing else! Nothing at all."

"That's right!" Slade said. "A lot of good stable boys were spoiled to make the British navy."

As if to prove Slade's assertion, tackles creaked behind them. Marvin saw the foot of the main course slowly rising. "Look there!" Argandeau laughed. "We take off more canvas, so to wait for my *Formidable*. I believe these Griffons cannot get even six knots from her!"

With the rising of the mainsail, Marvin turned again to the quarter-deck, which had become fully visible to the occupants of the long-boat. Forward of the cabin scuttle sat a woman, partly obscured by an awning; but from her dress of black silk and the brilliantly colored needlework that moved rhythmically in her lap, Marvin knew her to be Corunna Dorman. He half rose from his thwart: then, remembering the plight in which he was, sank back again.

Before Corunna stood Lieutenant Strope, though Marvin was able to see nothing of him save a pair of thin shanks protruding from abbreviated duck trousers. Yet they turned and postured, these legs, so that Marvin, in his mind's eye, saw Strope bending over Corunna in what he must have thought a position of fetching grace. From time to time, as the duck-trousered left knee thrust itself forward at a more acute angle, the rhythmic movements of the needlework were interrupted; and Marvin knew that Corunna's hands were idle so that she might more readily listen to the speeches of Lieutenant the Honorable Vivian Strope.

He stared around him with something approaching desperation in his eyes; and the sight of the noisome, filthy crew that filled the long-boat seemed to him, for all the cruel clearness with which the morning sun exposed them, as unreal as the solemn absurdities of a fearful nightmare. His glance fell on the tall Indian, Steven, and he thought, even while he noted the dead appearance of his copper-colored skin and long black hair where the gray mud had caked on it, that this was never the same Steven with whom he had so often gone into the marshes of Arundel to hunt black ducks, but a Steven out of a dream.

"You are shaking," Argandeau said. "I think it cannot be the wind, which is cooking my nose like an egg after the days I have ripened and grown white in the dark. I think it must be the sight of that rabbit there on the quarter-deck, eh?"

The Indian, catching Marvin's eye, put his hand to his chest. "Dan'l," he said, "I wish I could get me something for this ache."

Marvin rose to his feet and spoke to one of the marines who stood in a watchful circle about the prisoners. "Get an officer," he said. "I want to speak to the quarter-deck."

The marine stared blankly; then burst into a guffaw of laughter.

Argandeau whistled shrilly, close beside Marvin's ear, and gesticulated wildly. It was the infant midshipman, Mr. Benyon, to whom he gesticulated and whistled, and after a moment's hesitation the child pushed his way between the marines to stand staring palely at Argandeau as though staring at a strange animal in a cage.

"Your lordship," Argandeau said, while Mr. Benyon fingered his dirk and dropped his under lip, "your lordship knows how it is the custom on all civilized ships, that the people or the prisoners of the ship may at will present their complaints or compliments to the quarter-deck."

"Complaints?" the boy asked. "You want to make complaints?"

"Your lordship is a seaman," Argandeau continued, "and can recognize the barbarity that led one of these dog soldiers to do nothing but yell with laughter when my friend"—he placed his hand on Marvin's shoulder—"asked to speak with your noble commander."

The boy looked severely at the marines who towered about him. "That's no way to act!" he said. "Wha'd you want to laugh for? You ain't on this king's brig to laugh! You better look out, or I'll make you laugh out of the wrong side of your mouth!" He turned importantly and, like a petulant child, jostled the marines from his path.

"Sugar!" Argandeau sighed. "It catches them all, both little and great, if you know the sugar they prefer!"

Five minutes later Marvin was marched to the quarter-deck by a marine; and there he stood alone, as shabby a figure as could be found in any gutter, while Lieutenant Strope hung over Corunna, crooking first his left leg and then his right leg as he murmured to her. Rage grew in Marvin as he watched the black-haired girl, with her head bent low over her woolen Holy Family, and the Englishman who hovered above her—rage at an officer who could countenance such treatment of his fellows.

In spite of his rage, he had no eyes for Strope; he looked at Corunna, though she had no look for him in return. Yet, as he watched her, she stirred uneasily and flushed; then, while the lieutenant still addressed her, she stabbed her needle through her square of embroidered canvas, rose abruptly and went to the lee rail, to stand and stare at the three small sail that swam mistily in the blue haze to lee-ward.

The lieutenant peered after her; then turned sulkily to Marvin. "What is it you want?"

"Sir," Marvin said, "one of our men is sick. He needs looking after. I'd be obliged, sir, if he could have some attention."

The lieutenant thrust out his head, like a crane in a marsh pool at the sudden movement of a minnow. "Sick? What's the matter with him?"

"An aching chest," Marvin told him.

"Oh, indeed!" the lieutenant said. "What a pity!" He suddenly became bitter. "This is a war, you fool! We haven't the time to hold the hands of those with hangnails and bruised knees! A sore chest, for Ged's sake! D'you think I have so little fever among my own men that I must bother with malingering prisoners? Get back where you belong and take up no more of my time with your demned Yankee notions!"

"Sir," Marvin persisted, "the food is bad and the water's worse. We're choking, all of us, and the bread's solid with weevils."

"Well, what of it?" the lieutenant exclaimed, in a passion. "Do you think we can draw up to a bread shop in mid-ocean and lay in a fresh supply?"

"No," Marvin said, "but you could put us aboard one of your prizes, where we'd be able to breathe. Why, you feed your hogs better than we're fed; yes, and treat them better too."

The lieutenant's lips tightened and he laughed unpleasantly. "I wonder," he said, "what England would do without America to point out her shortcomings! Let me tell you this! You're like all the rest of your countrymen! You need a taste of the cat to improve your manners!"

There was a shout from the maintop. Losing all interest in Marvin, the lieutenant glared peevishly upward.

A seaman hung over the maintop nettings. "Sail on the lee quarter, sir!" he bawled. "Astern the French schooner!"

Strope thumped his fist on the weather rail. "Be demned and be demned to that French tub!" he cried in a reedy voice. "Turn up all hands and about ship! There's a sail in chase of the Frenchman!"

The waist of the brig straightway became a turmoil of thudding feet, shouted orders, the creaking of blocks and the shrilling of boatswains' whistles.

"Prisoners below!" the lieutenant added. "Get 'em under hatches and be quick about it!"

He went to the lee rail and placed his hand gently on Corunna's arm. She moved impatiently beneath his touch, and to Marvin there seemed to be a trace of moisture at the corner of her eye.

The lieutenant stared at her vacantly; then turned quickly and vanished into the companionway.

To Marvin, hemmed in by the turmoil of sweating seamen and grotesque marines, there was something crushed and forlorn about that figure on the quarter-deck—a figure that seemed to droop and waver in the blinding glare. In one small fleeting moment, he knew, he would be forced once more into the filth and stench of the *Beetle's* hold; and in his desperation he felt his heart must burst unless he could tell her how he grieved for her, and get from her in return just one word to cherish.

Hoping to be unnoticed in the tumult, he stepped beyond the mainmast. "Corunna," he said huskily, "Corunna——"

She turned a haggard face to him. Her drooping shoulders straightened. Her glance, hard and bitter, slipped past him to the mud-stained prisoners clambering from the long-boat; to the tall Indian, stooped with his wracking cough. Then her eyes stabbed sharply into his, and in them Marvin saw a look of terrible reproach and more terrible contempt—a look that said, as clearly as any words, "You did this! Coward!"

"Corunna——" he said again huskily.

The butt of a musket struck him between the shoulders. "Garn!" the marine cried furiously. "Garn below!"

Marvin stumbled forward, and Slade caught him by the arm. "Back to hell with us, eh?" the slaver captain said, and laughed. "You look like a man that's dead, and buried, too; but cheer up. There may be more than us in hell to-night, my boy! It's in my mind that something's coming down the wind and may be playing Yankee Doodle!"

# VI

THE LADDER had been drawn up through the square hole
in the hatch, and around the hatch coamings were stationed
four marines to make the security of the prisoners doubly
sure. Below the hatch, in the blackness of the sweltering,
reeking hold, there was a hubbub such as Marvin had never
before heard; for the prisoners, tense from the lack of
knowledge of what awaited them, screamed their hatred of
British ships, British officers, British methods and British
seamanship in language as foul as the air they breathed.

"If we had a belaying pin!" Marvin told Argandeau. "If
we had anything at all, we might get ourselves out of this!"

"Ah, yes," Argandeau agreed, but with no conviction in
his voice, "yes. And if we had a belaying pin, it would
be myself who would be the first man to lead such a sortie.
It would be unpleasant for the first three, four or five men
who would ascend with me, but I would hearten them with
my cries, and always they would say to themselves, 'Argandeau! Hah! Argandeau is with us,' and so——"

Marvin sighed deeply. "Well, we haven't any belaying
pins."

"No," Argandeau agreed. "And so, since we have no belaying pin, would it not be better to go quietly to sleep?"

The bed of mud quivered beneath them, and from overhead there came an angry, muffled crash that set the thick,
hot air to crawling on their faces. The cries of the prisoners
died away, to be replaced by the noisy silence of a ship—

the creakings and groanings of bulkheads, far-off thumps and rattlings, and above and through everything the chuckling and slapping of water against thin walls of plank.

"Now we find out something," Argandeau said softly. "The Griffons have spit out a pill."

"In that case," Slade said, "the stranger couldn't have run. She must have gone to work on your schooner."

"I fear it!" Argandeau said. "It would be like attacking a kitten whose leg has been broken—so easy!"

There was a quick change in the sound of the water that lapped against the brig's sides. The noise of slapping became a rushing swish; the vessel straightened, hesitated, seemed to hang motionless, and then tilted in the opposite direction.

"Yes," Argandeau continued. "What you say is true, Captain Slade. The stranger did not run. She awaited the approach of this Griffon's nest we're in: then she maneuvered. In no other way can our change of course be explained. If the stranger had not maneuvered, our English captain would have kept straight on. Yes, yes! And certainly the stranger would never maneuver against this brig unless he considered himself faster and better. No, no! If he were small and not confident, he would betake himself elsewhere, and in a straight line, without maneuvering! He would go quickly to a smaller tree in order to sharpen his claws." He sighed. "Observe, my friends, how the mind of a Frenchman is clear and logical, even in a moment of stress! I sweat with doubt and uncertainty: yet my imagination moves swiftly and unerringly, eh?" He grunted. "But none the less, I sweat! I, Lucien Argandeau, I am all brain and sweat! It is the waiting that causes the sweat, you understand: the waiting and the darkness, here in this Griffon kennel—this stinkpot. This waiting in a dark hole, I do not like! In the daylight, I care for nothing. I snap my fingers at a shipful of lions, pfoo! But to be caught so, in blindness! Bah!"

He rose suddenly from his place beside Marvin, seeming almost to bounce silently to his feet, and stood beneath the square opening in the hatch. "Yes," he said. "It must be that they have piped to quarters. And they have done something more. They have sent that rabbit from the quarterdeck. They have sent her below, to protect her from splinters and grapeshot. What a pity it is that I, Lucien Argandeau, am not free to comfort her! She is frightened; but the most frightened rabbit becomes calm, like a peaceful swan, when Lucien Argandeau comforts her. It is one of my talents—one of my smaller gifts."

Marvin and Slade rose from their places to stand close beside him. "How do you know they've sent her below?" Marvin whispered. "What did you hear?"

"I heard a rabbit!" Argandeau said. "That is something I make no mistake about, ever, because I have had great experience. I would not hear her unless she had come down the ladder."

"How did you know she was frightened?" Marvin asked.

"Rabbits are always frightened," Argandeau said calmly. "Also, this one is weeping, and she said to someone, 'Let me alone! Let me alone!' If you will listen, maybe you hear her."

"Hoist me up," Marvin said. "Let me climb on your shoulders."

"If you're thinking of trying to go up," Slade said, "you're mad! You'll get a bayonet in the face and they'll clap the grating on the rest of us!"

"Hoist me up!" Marvin repeated. "She's not frightened! Nothing ever frightened her. There's something here I don't understand."

They took him on their shoulders, steadying him by clutching his knees. He crouched just below the level of the hatch, listening. Beneath him the voices of the prisoners again swelled to a wild tumult of shouting. Marvin turned his head from side to side, striving to catch some sound from Corunna, but he could hear nothing save the cries of his comrades in misfortune, the lapping of the seas against the *Beetle's* bends and a rush of feet from the deck above.

Argandeau shook him impatiently by the ankle. "What you think you are doing up there? Picking coconuts?"

The words had scarcely left his lips when Marvin pitched sideways. The three of them fell in a heap. In the darkness of the hold the whole world seemed to reel and stagger. "Take care!" Argandeau said, and though his voice was gentle it almost echoed in the hold's dark stillness. "Guard yourselves! We luff to, and now will come something! Those who rest against the planking, move clear, unless you wish broken bones!" He quickly repeated the words in French.

Beneath them the brig steadied, only to burst at once into a paroxysm of gigantic jerkings and tremblings, accompanied by a thunderous roar. She had, Marvin knew, let off her broadside, which must mean that the *Beetle* had come to close quarters with her adversary; for he had seen that the bulk of her guns were carronades, useful only at short range. His muscles ached from the tightness that had come into them—a tightness that grew ever greater as he waited for the enemy vessel to let off her broadside in return.

Into his mind there came a picture of the Arundel

marshes, empty and silent within their walls of spruce and maple, and of a marsh hawk dropping with outspread claws on a helpless animal that could neither fight nor run, and so lay flattened against the marsh, waiting. He thought, too, how for years there had been glib talk of war in the shipyards and taverns of Arundel and a hundred other towns; and it came to him that not one of those who talked had ever thought of such a war as this—a war in which men lay in the dark and hoped that death would pass them by.

"Do you think they sank her?" he asked Argandeau, and he hurried his words, to get them out before they should be smothered and lost in the crash of the stranger's guns.

"Ha!" said Argandeau, and to Marvin his voice seemed somewhat breathless. "Not with carronades! You know what I think?" He made a faint sound of protest in his throat, as though he found some slight discomfort in the caked mud on which he rested.

"What?" Slade demanded, and his voice trembled with irritation. "Say it, damn it!"

"What I think——"

Again the mud beneath them jerked and shook, and continued to do so irregularly, as though the brig had burst into a spasm of gigantic coughs.

Slade laughed harshly. "I should say they *hadn't* sunk her. That's random firing! That means the stranger's closing with us, and it's every gun crew for himself!"

"What I think," Argandeau continued gently, "is that this stranger has one large long gun, and is maneuvering to rake the Griffons with it."

There was silence again in the hold. Marvin pulled desperately at Argandeau's arm. "Hoist me up again," he said. "I've got to try to see—to try to see——"

Somewhere astern, Marvin heard a grinding smash, the sound of timbers violently rent, and the heavy roar of a long gun.

"Piff!" Argandeau exclaimed. "Close, that one!"

The sound of cries came into the hold, and the spongy spatter of musketry fire. Marvin rose to his knees, only to be thrown down once more by the clangorous shock of the *Beetle's* broadside. The long gun of the enemy vessel bellowed a second time, so close that it seemed to Marvin he could almost feel the brig's planking bend before it like a beaten drumhead. Prisoners scrambled and tumbled over him, to stand cursing and screaming beneath the opening in the hatch.

Argandeau grunted. "God be praised!" he said. "They are aiming that pill bottle at the deck, like wise men! I tell you this, too: If they come closer, they will give their pills by hand instead of from the bottle!"

In Marvin's throat there was a taste of brass, and his tongue seemed to him to lie as thick and lifeless in his mouth as the salt-hardened sole of a sea boot. What he was passing through, he told himself, could not be real; like evil dreams that he remembered, it had the semblance of something that would never end; of something so dark and so terrible that his strength and his wits had deserted him together, leaving him panting and palsied.

The brig lurched suddenly and pitched forward—a small movement by comparison with the hammer blows of her broadside; but to the *Beetle's* miserable human cargo it brought an even deeper silence than the guns had brought.

Argandeau caught Marvin by the arm. "They board!" he whispered. "They have turned on this brig and outsailed her, and they have laid her aboard at the stern. Ah, my God!

Now I sweat indeed! Compared with this, my other sweating was no more than the perspiration of a flea!"

The uproar that arose on the *Beetle's* deck came to them like the closer and closer raging of a storm. Above the continuous rattle of small arms they heard the howling of men, the shouts of officers, the shrilling of whistles, the beating of a boarding drum, and a rush of feet like the scuttling of innumerable giant mice.

And there was something more. From the opening in the hatch above Marvin's head there came a girl's voice—the voice of Corunna Dorman. To Marvin it seemed to weep and to implore, as if in a frenzy of fear.

"Here!" Marvin shouted. "Here!" He would have risen to his feet but for Argandeau's grip on his arm.

"Softly! Softly!" Argandeau said. "Something drop down in here! Who has that thing?"

He was gone, then, from beside Marvin, but through the continued uproar from above, Marvin could hear him calling: "Who has that? Give me! Give me!"

"It came through the hatch!" Slade told him, his voice shaking a little, as if from cold. "I heard it strike."

Argandeau's soft voice was close beside them once more. "This is something wrapped in the clothes of a rabbit!" he told them. "I tell by the odor! Ah!" He exhaled ecstatically. "Wait now; I am unwrapping! Ah! Ah! Knives—three knives! . . . Wait, now! . . . Four—five knives; one pistol! We have one pistol; five knives!" He took Marvin by the shoulder with a hand that trembled. "You know about throwing the knife, eh?" he asked.

"I never tried," Marvin said. "I'll stick to my fists."

"Fists!" Slade cried derisively. "What good are fists!

Give me one of those knives! I've thrown a knife since I was a baby!"

"Now wait!" Argandeau said. "I am very fine with the knife—very well and very quick! You ask any man in Hispaniola!" He paused, seemingly to listen to an outburst of hoarse cheering from above. Hard on the heels of the cheering came another thunderous roar from close astern.

"Hear me now," Argandeau ordered. "Come close, all who can. I want the red man from the captured barque."

"Steven," Marvin said.

"I'm here, Dan'l," said a voice from the thick dark.

"Yes," Argandeau continued, "Steven and Aubert and Jonneau and Marvin."

Voices answered, close at hand.

"Listen, now," Argandeau said, "and see that this is told correctly to those who cannot hear. We have knives here. Four tall men will make a ladder, and we will go up and take this stink-pot from the damned British. You hear me?"

A rumble of voices answered him.

"Yes," Argandeau said, "whoever is trying to take this brig has been beaten off once, but will try again; and if you do not want to rot here in this hole, frying with heat and eating filth and choking, you will come up and help us. On deck there will be dead men, and wherever there are dead men there are weapons to be had for the taking. I go up—I, Captain Argandeau of the *Formidable!* When the English see me, they will be weak with terror! You understand? I go up first with Captain Slade. When we say come, step quickly on the shoulders of these four tall men, and there will be an end of this hell."

Marvin felt himself pressed against a group of men. "Lock the knees and brace the feet," Argandeau said. "Slade and

I, we carry all the knives. Hold us at the height of your shoulders until we have drawn ourselves up; then push up the others. You understand? Throw them! Do not delay. Soon there will be the ladder for the remainder; ropes also."

"For God's sake," Slade protested, "stop talking!"

"Come, now!" Argandeau said. Again the vessel lurched and staggered forward. Far above them burst a storm of shouting and musket shots. Marvin hooked his knee inside Steven's, bracing his other foot against the flooring of caked mud. Slade, breathing heavily, stepped on their knees, then on their shoulders. Marvin saw his head against the dim grayness of the hole in the hatch, and beside it the bullethead of Argandeau. They crouched there silently, steadying themselves; then rose upright together. Marvin felt Slade's feet press hard against his shoulder, and knew that he had thrown a knife. Immediately there was another quick pressure: then a sharp downward thrust as Slade leaped upward through the hatch.

A man fumbled at his arm, caught at his hair and went on up. Sweating, Marvin seized another, and another. There was a thudding overhead; the hatch came slowly off and the ladder slipped down past Marvin's face. Marvin threw himself at it and scrambled panting into the half light of the berth deck.

# VII

MARVIN, followed close by Argandeau, scrambled silently into the glaring sunlight and uproar of the brig's gun deck. A sweating marine, close by the hatch coaming, spat a bullet into the muzzle of his musket and turned, as he rammed it home, to stare wide-mouthed at the mud-smeared scarecrows rising in his rear. Marvin's fist struck hard against his jaw. His open mouth and eyes snapped shut; his neck stretched, rubber-like; his body rose as if to balance on his heels. Argandeau reached forward quickly, snatching the musket from his nerveless hands. The marine fell heavily beneath their feet.

On the quarter-deck a squirming throng of men struggled like animals packed tightly in a cage, howling and roaring as they fought. Jets of smoke stabbed from their pistols; cutlasses rose and fell spasmodically among them.

Over their heads was thrust the bow and long jib boom of a towering schooner, the tip of the boom lodged and tangled in the *Beetle's* mainsail. At the schooner's main peak the American ensign fluttered in the burning southwest breeze.

Half-naked men ran like ants from the schooner's bow, cutlasses in hand, to leap from the high bowsprit into the dense mass beneath. In the rigging of the schooner were men with muskets, jerking about like jumping jacks as they fired and loaded; while the ratlines of the *Beetle* were filled with marines whose muskets spat smoke and pale flashes at the teeming deck of the enemy vessel.

At the taffrail, Lieutenant Strope held himself above the struggling men by clinging to the schooner's dolphin striker. Thus sustained, he thrust and hacked with a reddened saber at the men who hurled themselves, their faces contorted and their torsos adrip with perspiration, among the British seamen.

A marine, clinging to the foremast ratlines, spied the mud-stained horde emerging from the hatch and raised a faint, thin cry of warning. In the very moment of its utterance, Argandeau threw the knife that lay along the palm of his right hand. It passed through the ratlines with the swift flight of a swooping bird and buried itself in the glistening breast of the marine, who ceased his outcry to spread his arms apart and stare down in blank amazement at the knife hilt. So staring, he toppled slowly backward and vanished soundlessly below the bulwarks.

One man, and then another, turned from the press that swarmed and milled at the break of the quarter-deck, to stare in horror at the swelling array of prisoners; then, shouting hoarsely, pulled at the arms of their fellows. Marines leaped from the ratlines, wrenching at their cumbersome swords.

"Haul down! Haul down!" Argandeau shouted. Swinging his captured musket by the muzzle, he leaped toward one of the advancing marines and brought it against his head with such force that the wooden stock split.

Almost from between the legs of the advancing Englishmen darted the diminutive Mr. Benyon, clutching in both hands an enormous horse pistol. "No quarter!" he screamed. "No quarter!" He snapped the pistol in Marvin's face and, when it missed fire, strove to hurl it at him. Over-balanced in the attempt, he sprawled ignominiously on the deck. Marvin lifted him by the belt and tossed him backward, over the heads of the yelling prisoners.

"Haul dawn! Haul down!" Argandeau bellowed again. With the stockless musket he smashed the arm of a man whose cutlass was swinging toward his head. "We kill all! Haul down!"

Armed by now, the shouting prisoners hurled themselves on the English who, falling back before the sabers, gun rammers, muskets and belaying pins wielded by these mud-caked figures, were pressed into a mob so dense as almost to prevent the use of weapons.

"Haul down!" they roared. "Haul down!"

Empty hands rose in the air beyond Marvin. "Quarter!" cried an English voice; and the word was repeated here and there like the drops of a rainstorm; first slowly, then with a sudden burst.

There was a movement of the blood-red ensign at the *Beetle's* mainpeak. "She's struck!" Marvin cried. "Belay! She's struck!"

Beyond the upraised hands of the *Beetle's* men, Marvin saw the thin, stooped figure of Lieutenant Strope. His hat was gone, his face the color of canvas fresh from the storeroom. The single epaulette on the shoulder of his coat was shorn in two, and the arm beneath it hung useless. He shook the hilt of his upraised saber at the men who reached with eager hands for ensign halyards.

"No!" he shouted, in a voice that quavered and broke. "Put it back! I say no! I say no!"

A seaman on the bowsprit of the enemy schooner caught at a stay, swung forward and brought down a cutlass on the lieutenant's unprotected head, shouting angrily, as he did so, *"Tais toi!"* The lieutenant slipped from Marvin's sight; and amid an ecstatic screaming that seemed to him almost feminine, the British ensign came down on the run.

Marvin turned quickly to push his way through the howling prisoners toward the hatch from which they had emerged, when he was caught by the neck in an embrace so violent that he could think of nothing save that there was further fighting to be done.

"Ah, ah, my brave child!" Argandeau shouted in his ear. "Don't we make these Griffons wish they have not rubbed mud into the beard of Argandeau, eh?" The Frenchman whirled him about, took his face between two sweaty hands and kissed him on the lips. "I see you hit that gentleman like a horse kick! I take you to fight with me anywhere! Ha, ha! We serve the Griffons mashed and *en brochette,* eh? You with the fist and me with the knife, no?" Holding Marvin by the shoulders still, he danced lightly before him; then kissed him again with fervor.

Marvin pushed him away. "Where's Corunna?" he demanded.

"He means the rabbit!" Argandeau cried. "Why have you not told me she is yours? Ah, but she is more pigeon! A true pigeon! You know where we are this minute—now, if that sublime pigeon had not helped us? We are down there in that stink-pot with mud in the ear, and nothing to look forward to but mud in the other ear! Oh, but Holy Christophe, Marvin, there is a pigeon whom I would be willing to acknowledge as the mother of my children!"

He drew up his shoulders, then, and smiled affectionately. "Why you look hangry because I make a graceful compliment?" he asked. "I tell you there are women who have sickened and died for lack of one kind word from Argandeau! Not more than one hundred times in my life have I paid such a tribute as I have paid to your pigeon! In Hispaniola men go for miles to look with admiration at a rabbit of whom Argandeau has been known to say that he would be willing to acknowledge her as the mother of his children."

"We don't need to go into that," Marvin said.

As if to himself Argandeau murmured, "He means I may think about his pigeon, but must never say what I think!" He shook his head despairingly, then added, "You wish now to know the whereabouts of your pigeon? Well, look there!" And he pointed to the hatch where Slade, bending so low that his long black hair fell forward over his face, was at that instant helping Corunna to the deck.

"Why," Marvin said, with bewilderment in his voice, "why, he didn't fight!" He stepped toward the two at the hatch, only to be stopped by Argandeau once more. "Wait one little minute!" Argandeau ordered. "You do not please anyone by saying he did not fight, because he did. Oh, yes! He is very agreeable man with a knife; not complete artist, like me, but I think very good—very well!"

The tumult on the *Beetle's* quarter-deck grew louder and more shrill; and Argandeau, turning to cast a quick glance over his shoulder, stood staring at the man who picked his way almost daintily along the bowsprit of the victorious schooner.

He had an air of fragility to him, this man, that seemed to come less from his stature than from the snugness with which his cream-colored small clothes fitted around his slender waist and hips, and from the dark shadows beneath his black eyes. His face was palely brown; his head held high by the tall stiff collar of his fine blue coat.

"Look here at this!" Argandeau murmured, with a quality in his soft voice that turned Marvin's eyes from Corunna's flushed face. "Here is something wonderful! Out of this American schooner arrives one of the great men of France!"

Argandeau took Marvin by the arm and hurried him toward the quarter-deck. On the bowsprit, which hung like a suspended sword above the conquered British brig, stood the fragile, shadowy-eyed man, staring down at the howling, blood-stained throng who cheered him, and at the dead and wounded who lay among them and ringed them round. He spoke brusquely to those beneath, and at once dropped lightly to the deck to stand beside the body of Lieutenant Strope.

"This brave gentleman," he said in a penetrating, nasal voice, "is dead! Who commands here?" He looked sharply about him; then nodded slowly at the young officer who stepped forward. "I am Captain Diron," he said. "Private armed schooner *Decatur,* Charleston. I think I have been assisted in taking this vessel."

The young officer laughed abruptly, but there was no amusement in the sound. "If it hadn't been for that rabble," he said, moving his head contemptuously toward the vessel's bow, "we'd have cut you to pieces!"

Captain Diron studied him attentively. "Ah, yes!" he agreed. "No doubt!" The seamen behind him set up a growling, at which he abruptly wagged a finger in their faces. "Loysel!" he called. "Loysel! Be quick! Attend these English wounded and our own. Take what men you need! Mr. Safifth! Take charge of this brig and place her in order for the prize crew. Mr. Wasborn! Cast loose the schooner and lay her alongside."

Argandeau sniffed suddenly, and Marvin saw that although he was smiling almost proudly at this brown-faced, fragile captain, there were tears in his eyes and wet smears on his mud-incrusted cheeks. At the sound of the sniff, the eye of the *Decatur's* captain fell on Argandeau.

"So!" Diron exclaimed. "You are the one!"

Argandeau lifted an eyebrow and shook his head. "With the help of these lion-hearted men it was nothing, Dominique! A lark hunt!"

Diron came quickly to him and kissed him first on one cheek, then on the other. Someone among the silent spectators laughed loudly.

Diron stepped back from Argandeau and swept the crowded quarter-deck with a hard black eye. "Get forward, those without business here!" he ordered.

The seamen about them thinned like smoke before the wind, and as they swirled and scattered, Slade moved from behind them, followed closely by Corunna Dorman. At the sight of her, Diron whipped off his hat, held it tight against his breast and bowed abruptly, with a questioning side glance at Argandeau. "Madame," he said, "your servant! I am most unhappy I do not know sooner that——"

"Yes," Slade said hoarsely. "Captain Argandeau might have mentioned her before." He pushed back his long black hair with a sweep of his hand. "We'd be down there yet if she hadn't brought us knives."

Argandeau smiled pleasantly at Slade. "Piff! You touch me! It should have been my duty to tell this thing with my first breath!"

Diron bowed again to Corunna. "Then you are a brave lady, I think. I have been in debt many times, but never to one so young and beautiful."

She made him the shadow of a curtsy. "Why," she said, "you'll owe me nothing if you get back the *Olive Branch* for me. Did you retake her?"

"That barque?" Diron asked. "She was yours, that barque?"

Corunna nodded.

Diron looked at Argandeau, as if seeking denial of Corunna's statement. Finding none, he glanced uncertainly around the quarter-deck. Two of the *Decatur's* seamen raised the body of a British sailor from the scuppers, swung it over the taffrail and let it fall. The splash seemed to put a thought in Diron's head.

"But such sights!" he cried. "They must be painful to a lady!"

"No, captain," Corunna said quietly. "These people killed my father."

Diron held up a protesting hand. "It is necessary that I examine the papers in the cabin. You shall come there, where we can talk quietly." He turned to Argandeau. "Give me a few moments, my friend, and then we will speak fully together. I see now that it was your schooner we sank. Like a gourd, she was—so thin—and sailed by men who could contrive to foul her jibboom in her own staysails! I am sad about this!" He patted Argandeau on the shoulders, kissed him again on both cheeks; then beckoned to Corunna and walked quickly to the companionway.

"Corunna!" Marvin said. "Corunna!"

She turned to Slade, seeming not to hear Marvin. "You'll come with me, won't you, captain?" Slade, following her down the companionway, glanced up at Marvin from under his drooping eyelid with what seemed to Marvin like malicious mockery.

"Listen, my friend," Argandeau said, holding Marvin by the arm, "my *Formidable* is gone! Nowhere was there a craft so beautiful or so swift, and now she is gone!"

"It's too bad," Marvin said absently. "Too bad."

"I tell you, my friend," Argandeau said, "it is bad, yes; but not too bad. Nothing is too bad. If you lose a ship, you will find a better one. If you lose a woman, you have not lost the only woman there is. Look at me, eh? I am gay! That is why I am loved by my friends, by the rabbits, by everyone!" He pointed a foot delicately, flung up an arm and struck a pose. "We will visit now with my friend, Dominique Diron. For him, too, nothing is too bad. He is brave, like a lion; and why not! He has learned from observation! He served with me on the letter of marque *Superbe*. There was one time when we were surprised and attacked, Dominique and I, by two British cruisers. For three nights and two days we fight them off. We laugh and are gay. Ha! Ha! They cannot catch us—those two Griffons. We run the *Superbe* ashore and escape, all of us!"

"Yes, but this time they caught you," Marvin reminded him.

"Caught me?" Argandeau said. "Caught me? Who has caught me? Look at me carefully! 'Ah-hah,' you say to yourself, 'I behold Argandeau, who did not wish to remain caught, and therefore is a free man!' But come; we wash the mud from ourselves and go to see Dominique."

# VIII

THE CAPTAIN'S CABIN of the *Beetle* was hot as an oven, and almost as small. Diron, his coat stripped off, sat before the center table, whereon was a litter of papers. Beside him sat Corunna; and when Marvin saw how Slade hovered over her shoulder, as if fearful that she might topple from her locker unless guarded, it seemed to him suddenly that this cabin was not less dismal than the hold had been.

Diron smiled affectionately at Argandeau. "You have arrived at the precise moment," he said. "You have not been presented to this lady, she has told me."

Argandeau bent his woolly, close-cropped head in a quick bow. "But I have had a gift from her, only today, that will make her live forever in my heart. No, I have not been presented to her, but I know her well; she is so kind that I shall never find time to say to her how kind she is."

Diron opened his mouth in a soundless laugh. "As you see, Miss Dorman, a dangerous man!" To Argandeau he added: "Thanks to me, Lucien, you shall have the opportunity to try; and for you it should be a good affair. This lady has kindly consented to take you and your crew to France, together with my wounded and the English wounded."

"To France?" Marvin asked quickly. "She has consented to go to France?"

"She has been so kind," Diron said. "The whole plan has come into my head like that, Lucien!" He snapped his fingers, glancing from Marvin to Corunna and back again; then addressed himself to Argandeau once more. "I thought for a time of taking you back to Charleston with me, Lucien; but the Americans, they do not have enough vessels of their own for privateering. For every American vessel there are a thousand American captains. But in France there are many vessels; fast ones—more vessels than captains. You assist this lady to go there, then, and maybe she assist you to get another vessel."

"Just a minute, Captain," Marvin said. "I don't understand this talk of France."

Corunna looked up at him angrily. "It's not necessary that you should."

Marvin drew a deep breath. "Don't talk that way, Corunna. What's France to us? Home's where we want to be."

Slade threw back his head to stare at Marvin from beneath his drooping lid. "You must have heard what the lady said."

"Just a minute, Corunna," Marvin persisted, ignoring Slade. "You can't afford to rush into anything like this. As I see it, the way to go home is to go home; and it's no good to say it isn't necessary for me to understand about it. It appears to me, Corunna, that I'm responsible for you. I've got as much right as anyone to know what you're planning to do."

"*You're* responsible?" she cried, rising to her feet, her hands clenched and her face colorless. "*You've* got the right? I'll have you understand that I allow no squeamish boy to be responsible for what I do or where I go. And of all men, you're the last I'd let question my decisions."

Captain Diron leaned forward in his chair. "It is all so

'simple," he said candidly, "that I think possibly you make a mistake not to tell the gentleman. It would be a pity if he smelled here a mystery where there was none!" He smiled gently at all the persons in the stifling little cabin.

"You see," he said, stretching out his hand, palm up, toward Marvin, "I have sacrificed a great deal to take the *Olive Branch;* for if I had not wished the barque for myself, I would not have fought this war brig, and so lost several men and suffered grave damage. It is not the business of a privateer to entangle himself with enemy cruisers. The odds against him are too great. You see that, I hope, sir."

Marvin nodded.

"Of course!" Diron continued, as frank and open a gentleman in his speech, Marvin thought, as he had ever heard. "Of course! Therefore, it seems to me only reasonable that I should ask a small favor from this lady in return for giving back her valuable property. After all," he reminded Marvin mildly, "title to the *Olive Branch* passed to the British when they took her, and to me and my crew when we retook her."

"The taking," Marvin persisted, "was not all on your side. Some of the taking was done by us, at some risk to ourselves. Meaning no offense, I must venture to remind you that our American courts might be more than sympathetic to this lady, if she should present her claim against yours."

Diron waved his hand languidly. "I find your reference to courts distasteful. There is a flavor of commercialism about it. It is difficult to remember, at times, that such a thing as chivalry still exists." He coughed deprecatingly. "Now this favor I have asked; in reality I have asked for nothing. In reality I have done a favor to the lady by suggesting to her how to act. Look here; there are British cruisers on your American coast as thick as bones in a herring. Your barque is slow; and if you run for home, you are nearly certain to be taken by a British frigate. But the nearer you come to England, the fewer English war craft you will see, for that has always been the custom of the English—to harry the enemy in his own waters. Captain Argandeau will tell you this is so."

Argandeau placed his knuckles above his eyes, with the forefingers extended. "I would be willing to sail into any English harbor this minute," he said, almost with indifference, "and make horns at the Griffons!" He wagged the forefingers.

"Of course!" Diron exclaimed. "With all the English far from home, therefore, your barque can run safely into a French port, where there will be a ready market for her cargo. And if, on the way, you should be overhauled, you will have enough men aboard to fight off a heavy vessel."

Slade nodded thoughtfully. "We'll have enough men to *take* a vessel, if we should feel like it—enough to take more than one, if they're not large ones."

Marvin stared at Slade and half rose to his feet, but sank back on his locker when Diron tapped him on the arm. "You see," Diron told him earnestly, "there will not only be the added safety of the route, but there will be these two fine seamen, Captain Slade and my friend, Captain Argandeau, to assist the lady with their knowledge and advice. Captain Argandeau, he knows the coast of France as he knows his own thumb."

"I know it better," Argandeau said. "There is no part of it that I could not recognize on the darkest night, which is more than I can say of this." He held up a grimy thumb and with it polished an imaginary spot before his eyes. "There is no port in all France where there are not at least several people related to me—" he stopped; then added, with an ingratiating smile—"by marriage."

Diron raised his eyebrows and held out his hands. "What more could one wish?" he asked Marvin. "I think it is great good fortune for the lady and for all of you that you encounter us."

"I admit it," Marvin said readily. "Still, there are a few small points that I might mention——"

"Yes," Corunna interrupted, "you might! Of course you might! But you needn't! I consider myself fortunate to have the advice of these gentlemen, and I've taken it!"

"Yes," Marvin said patiently, "but what's Captain Slade doing aboard the *Olive Branch?* He's got a brig of his own —a slave brig. That hasn't been destroyed, has it?"

"Mr. Marvin," Slade said a little ceremoniously, "I think I must ask you to use another tone of voice when referring to my occupation. After all, Mr. Marvin, John Paul Jones himself saw nothing wrong in officering a vessel on the Middle Passage."

"Is that an argument, Mr. Slade?" Marvin asked. "You can't make me respect the Portuguese by telling me that Vasco da Gama hailed from Portugal!"

Slade's voice was harsher than his words. "Any man who's had experience in these waters knows that it's doing a kindness to yonder poor black men to let them exchange the cruelties and sufferings of Africa for the comforts of a plantation."

Marvin looked hard at Slade; then turned again to

Corunna. "Why is it he's deserting his own vessel to travel on ours? He's got owners, hasn't he?"

"He's traveling on the *Olive Branch* for good and sufficient reasons!" Corunna informed him. "I'll have you know that Captain Diron and Captain Slade are doing these things out of the kindness of their hearts, and to question them is outrageous!"

"I don't mean it so," Marvin said. "All I want, Corunna, is that you should give these things proper consideration. 'Tisn't in reason, Corunna, for Captain Diron to be asking favors of you for giving back the *Olive Branch*. She's yours anyway. He knows he couldn't keep the proceeds of her sale, because there isn't a prize court in America that would uphold him in it as long as you're alive to put in your claim."

Slade cocked his head on one side to look out from under his drooping eyelid. "A sea lawyer!" he exclaimed.

"'Tisn't so much that I mind going to France," Marvin continued. "What I mind is seeing you deprived of your freedom to do as you like when you need to do it. Here you're hampering yourself with promises you don't need to make, and weighing yourself down with a lot of wounded men, and you're setting off for a strange country to sell your cargo—if you get there—in a market that'll skin you if it has the chance."

"You are speaking of the French markets?" Captain Diron asked politely. "You have had unfortunate experiences with them, perhaps?"

"No," Marvin admitted, "but I never heard of a market that was in business for our benefit. There's another thing, too," he told Corunna: "You're entitled to hold any opinion of me that you wish, but you know my family, and you know that when your father needed help, he turned to my father, just as mine turned to yours when he needed anything. When all's said and done, Corunna, we're neighbors, and maybe that might still mean something to you. Now, I want no trouble with these gentlemen; but without meaning any offense, one of 'em's a Frenchman and the other's a slaver; and it seems to me, Corunna, that it's a strange thing when a girl from Arundel feels obliged to take advice from a slaver and a Frenchman—both of them gentlemen she never saw before."

"Pooi!" Argandeau exclaimed. "Now the slush bucket is kicked over!"

Captain Diron shrugged his shoulders. "This poor young man," he said, smiling at Corunna, "I think he does not know he is being so—what shall I say? We call it *gauche*. It is a fault of your countrymen, I fear."

"Oh," Corunna said, "it's shameful! To insult these gentlemen—how can you stand there and say such things of them—they, who only want to help me."

"Wait, Corunna!" Marvin begged her. "Can't you see it must be themselves they're helping? It *must* be! You're the only one who stands a chance of losing anything! Why, if Captain Diron was so anxious to help you, he could convoy you home, couldn't he, instead of sending you off to France, near to four thousand miles?"

"Of course," Captain Diron remarked pleasantly, "it might be disturbing for you if the young lady should be removed from your protection. I think it is possible you argue for your own benefit, eh?"

Marvin pressed his lips tightly together. "Couldn't you?" he persisted. "Couldn't you convoy us home?"

"You make me ashamed for you!" Corunna cried. "It isn't the first time!"

Slade's voice, it seemed to Marvin, set the chains of the hanging lamp to vibrating, so metallic was its harshness. "It's plain to see," he told Corunna, "that he considers himself your master."

Diron silenced him with a glance, and spoke courteously to Marvin. "Your question concerning a convoy, sir, is a fair one, but I have already answered it when I said that the *Olive Branch* is slow, and that English frigates are plentiful on your coast. You would hardly expect my schooner to engage a frigate. No schooner afloat would last five minutes, once she came within range of a frigate's guns."

"That's true," Marvin agreed, "but as you say, you fought the *Beetle* so you might get possession of the *Olive Branch,* and you must have ordered your prize crew to take her to Charleston rather than to France. Otherwise you would have made an argument out of it, I think."

Diron threw himself back in his chair, laughing heartily. "But you are suspicious, you Americans!" he exclaimed. "If you heard one of our French larks singing in the sky, you would say it was not a real lark."

"Well," Marvin said slowly, "I've never had much difficulty recognizing larks when I see 'em—or when I hear 'em. Some time ago I heard one of you gentlemen mention the fact that if the *Olive Branch* sets sail for France, she'll not only have enough men aboard to fight off a heavy vessel, but even to take a small one. That's a suggestion I'm able to recognize as easily as I recognize larks. It's a suggestion that the *Olive Branch* be used to make prizes of enemy merchant craft—or maybe of friendly ones." He looked hard at Slade, who tossed back his long black hair and coldly returned Marvin's gaze.

"If I'm not mistaken," Marvin went on, "that suggestion

came from Captain Slade. He knows that none of us aboard the *Olive Branch* has a commission or a letter of marque entitling us to capture, burn, sink or destroy any enemy vessel. If we should attack one, we'd be in danger of being hanged at the yardarm—every last one of us. What Captain Slade suggested is piracy. While I'm in command of the *Olive Branch* I'll allow no such thing—and with Captain Dorman dead, I *am* in command."

Captain Diron placed his hand on Corunna's arm, as if to restrain her. "No, no!" he said. "You do not understand. Here on this table are the papers of Captain Argandeau, you see. Here is his letter of marque, my friend, for the *Formidable*. With these papers the *Olive Branch* will be the *Formidable* if she has occasion to attack any vessel, and still she will be the *Olive Branch* at all other times, eh?"

Corunna shook off Captain Diron's restraining hand. "Yes," she said, and to Marvin her eyes had the hardness of agates, "and you have forgotten that I am the owner of the *Olive Branch*. Therefore I have made myself captain, with Captain Slade as first mate and Captain Argandeau as second mate."

"What did I tell you about the slush bucket?" murmured Argandeau softly. "Two mules together could not more completely kick it over!"

CORUNNA DORMAN, impatiently pacing the weather side of the *Olive Branch's* quarter-deck, watched the last boatload of wounded rocking uneasily toward her from the near-by *Beetle,* escorted amidships by lazy-seeming sharks that rolled their eyes upward at the long-boat like affectionate dogs. The wounded who had already made the journey, twelve of them, were ranged close under the larboard bulwarks, where they might have the benefit of the steamy, sweltering breeze. All about them was piled the dunnage of the seamen who had come aboard and now clung to shrouds and ratlines to see the last of the *Decatur* and the *Beetle;* while the litter resulting from the capture of the *Olive Branch* still cumbered her decks and gave her an air of slovenly dejection.

Corunna, looking around suddenly, saw Slade smiling gravely at her, one eye half hidden by his drooping eyelid. There may have been meekness and modesty in the way he quickly lowered his glance, but there was little of modesty in his words or voice. "You're in danger, ma'am," he said, "wearing what might put to shame an empress and a bride."

She turned from him and peered over the taffrail. "I want somebody in the main chains," she said; "somebody with pikes or boat hooks to watch that boatload of wounded. The sharks'll have 'em over before we know it. I'll be obliged if you'll see to these things without having to be reminded of them, Mr. Slade."

Slade's exclamation seemed to have penitence in it as he jumped quickly for the vessel's waist; but quick as he was, Marvin was quicker. Almost as though he had heard Corunna's words, he came up the ladder of the main hatch, glanced at the approaching long-boat, and at once swung himself around the main shrouds and into the chains, shouting for a sweep as he did so.

From Argandeau, at work with a crew on the wrecked carronade near by, there came a faint and abstracted humming.

> *"Aux filles de bonnes maisons*
> *Comme il avait su plaire,*
> *Ses sujets avaient cent raisons*
> *De le nommer leur père,"*

he sang softly. Corunna stared severely at his widow's peak of close-cropped hair; but seemingly he was oblivious to everything except the task in hand.

"Mr. Argandeau!" she said.

Argandeau straightened. "You need me, lady?"

"Yes," she said, "and I don't like the sound of 'lady.' You can call me Captain while we're aboard ship."

Argandeau bowed so deeply that his bullethead seemed lower than his knees.

"When these wounded men are aboard," she continued, "tell Mr. Slade to run up his jib and fore-topmast staysail and get under way. I want her kept north by west a half west. We'll pass to the westward of the Cape Verdes. Get the decks cleared and divide the men into watches. Then call the hands aft and send word to me. I want to speak to them."

"Yes, Captain," Argandeau said. "And Mr. Marvin? He is not an officer: therefore you let me choose him for my watch, perhaps. Then I give him lessons in many things." His gaze was candid. "When he has had a lesson or two from Argandeau, he will know how to throw the knife, how to be brave like a lion, how to make love so that every woman who sees him will pant for him." Modestly he added, "He has not had my advantages, poor fellow."

Corunna raised an indifferent eye to the clouds overhead. "I'm afraid Mr. Marvin must get along without your guidance for the remainder of this voyage," she said. "He's to be bos'n of this vessel."

"Ho-ho!" Argandeau said softly. "You put him where he must exercise that patience of which he is so proud, eh—nursing seamen and touching the hat to his betters! I think well! Very well!"

Corunna looked hard at him; then turned quickly and entered the cabin.

"Captain!" Argandeau murmured, skipping from the quarter-deck into the waist. "She is sugar cane! Captain Sugar Cane! With that to crunch, I would not recognize any other wife—not for a very long time!"

He swung himself into the main chains beside Marvin, who was splashing the twenty-four-foot sweep up and down beside the *Beetle's* long-boat as the last of the wounded men came over the side.

"Pull your front hair and say 'sir!'" Argandeau told him. "Maybe you think this is a French vessel, Mr. Bos'n, and that we are all equal, eh? All perfectly equal?"

Marvin stabbed with the long sweep at a gray shadow that flickered beneath the long-boat's stern. "Bos'n, eh?" he asked. "So she decided to take me down a peg!" The sweep rose from the water as lightly as a fishing rod, and fell again with a smack. "Well, it's all one to me," he continued, "provided she gets me to a place where I can do some damage to a little piece of England. I'm surprised she didn't make me ship's cook, so she'd never have to look at me."

"If she had, my friend," Argandeau assured him, "it would be what you deserve for saying to her that she must not do this and cannot do that! That is something I learn about rabbits when I am six years old and in love for the first time, or maybe the second. They are like men, disliking to obey orders; and because they are built with nerves in the brain that we do not have, they explode, Pfoo! inside the head, when they are forbidden to do this or that. If they are timid, they conceal the explosion; but later, when all is quiet, they take courage and do what they have been forbidden to do. If they are not timid, they snap the fingers in the face of those who forbid! Piff!" His fingers clicked contemptuously beneath Marvin's nose.

A hoarse voice came up to them from the turbulence of the main deck. "Isn't this a little early to begin criticizing a lady?"

Argandeau turned from Marvin and looked down into the upturned face of Slade. "Criticize?" Argandeau asked innocently. "I? I criticize a lady? Never! I learn from ladies—learn only. I think, Captain, you might do the same to good advantage."

There was a rasp to Slade's laugh like the bite of a saw on wood. "If I feel the need of lessons," he said, "I'll think about consulting you."

"You will escape some trouble by doing it," Argandeau assured him, "and you will also escape some trouble by getting this barque under way and standing on quickly. The

Captain, she told me to tell you: North by west a half west."

"West!" Slade exclaimed, "You mean east!"

"East?" Argandeau whispered. "Is it east I mean? Now I am confused! She said west, I thought; but perhaps, as you say, it was east. You must go quickly and ask her." He struck his forehead with his hand. "My God, what horror if it should appear that Argandeau could not repeat orders properly—that if he were told to raise the ensign, he would let go the anchor instead! Oh yes! You must hurry to the Captain and tell her it was not west, but east."

"We'll see about this!" Slade said. "Diron told her to make the Cape Verdes!" His drooping lid seemed almost to close over his eye as he stared up at Argandeau.

"Ah, yes!" Argandeau said thoughtfully. "Well, maybe she has forgotten what she was told. It is possible she does not realize that Dominique intends to share the captaincy of this vessel with her, even after he has sailed away in his own schooner." He smiled innocently at Slade. "Perhaps," he continued, "perhaps you should go to her and inform her that she has made a mistake: that she is wrong: that her orders have not been to Dominique's liking. Perhaps, before it is too late, you should even send word to Dominique that he must come aboard once more and put his orders in writing, so they may never again be misunderstood by absentminded ladies."

Slade peered over the bulwarks. The *Beetle's* long-boat, freed of her cargo, had pushed off from the *Olive Branch's* counter. A cable length away, the *Beetle* swayed lazily, her rigging filled with seamen busy repairing severed shrouds and stays; and behind her squat bulk the slender, raking masts of the *Decatur* towered high against the billowing pink clouds that hung above the steamy horizon. There seemed to be something of remoteness about the two vessels, despite their nearness, as though already they had forgotten the very existence of the *Olive Branch.* Slade ran his fingers through his long black hair, glanced uncertainly from Argandeau's face to the empty quarter-deck; then turned abruptly to the throng of seamen who were noisily sluicing from themselves the muck of their imprisonment in the *Beetle.*

"Set the jib and fore-topmast staysail!" he shouted hoarsely. "Man the lee fore brace! Slack away fore tack and stand by to swing the main yard!"

The *Olive Branch* fell off, the fore-topsail filled and she slowly wore into the northwest.

Corunna, Marvin saw, had come on deck, carrying a glass tumbler in her hand. She set it down carefully at the foot of the binnacle; then stood by the taffrail, staring back at the *Beetle,* her gray Chinese jacket and trousers dark against the glowing cloud banks beyond, and her smoothly combed black hair bound tightly in place by a thin red cord. Marvin jumped from the chains and ran aft. "Corunna," he said, "aren't you going to give 'em a gun?"

She turned slowly. "As bos'n of this vessel," she said, "I'll thank you to address the quarter-deck properly."

"Corunna," Marvin protested, "don't be like this, Corunna! You know there isn't anybody that——"

She moved away from him and glanced at the card in the binnacle. "Keep her so," she told the helmsman; then looked coolly at Marvin. "Give them a gun?" she asked. "It seems to me you're a little backward about guns! I think you'd better dip the ensign instead; that's more in your line."

He eyed her in silence, smiled faintly and moved to the ensign halyards.

She stamped her foot. "You think I'm pretending! You think I'm playing! Well, I'm not! I can sail this vessel as well as any man—better than most. I can fight the British as well as any man! Nobody hates 'em as much as I do, the murderers!"

Marvin, staring steadily at the masthead, carefully dipped the ensign three times, made fast the halyards and turned away. Forward of the main hatch he saw Slade, half concealed by the lumber amidships, staring at him; and the whiteness of that single eye seemed to Marvin to give the slaver's face a look of confident contempt.

Marvin turned back to her. "There's nobody like you, Corunna," he said. "You know how I feel about that."

"You had your chance," she reminded him.

He moved his hand vaguely. "You know how I feel," he repeated. "You're a woman, and women don't fight or captain vessels. There's something they haven't got, Corunna. They aren't hard enough, maybe. Maybe they do things too much from personal reasons. They're apt to be hasty, they're——"

She caught at his upper arm and half turned him toward her. "Let me look at you," she said solicitously. "I think it must be the heat that makes your head like this—all mixed and muddled. Why don't you put a little cool water on it, so not to hurt it permanently, trying to make it express all the things you don't know about women! Just belay all that, and step down to the main hatch and tell Mr. Slade to bring the men aft!"

She whirled and left him, to stand again at the taffrail, looking back at the brig and the schooner, already shrunken to the size of toys. Sighing, Marvin eyed the flatness of her back and the sturdiness of her shoulders; then went forward toward Slade.

For such a vessel as the *Olive Branch,* the throng of seamen who gathered at the break in the quarter-deck was as cumbersome as it was motley. There were a score of tall Yankees who had made up the original crew of the barque; another two score Frenchmen from Argandeau's schooner—short and swarthy men for the most part—and a jostling knot of shifty-eyed nondescripts from Slade's slaver. These last, Marvin decided, were sweepings from the foulest corners of the brown countries.

Sailors filled the waist of the barque from larboard to starboard bulwarks. They perched on carronade slides and clung to shrouds and backstays, scuffling and swaying and breaking into suppressed exclamations and hoarse, short bursts of laughter as they stared open-mouthed at the trousered figure of Corunna standing at the weather rail.

Slade pushed through them, mounted to the quarter-deck and spoke briefly to her, at which she advanced to the taffrail, set her hands on her hips and coldly eyed the grinning faces below.

"I'm the captain of this vessel," she said. "A few of you may have some difficulty getting that into your heads, but the sooner you get it, the better off you'll be. I've sailed in the *Olive Branch* for eight years. I know her better than any man alive, and I can get more out of her. I aim to bring all of you safe to land; and when that's done, I aim to fight the British for what they did to my father. I'd like all of you to bear in mind that if I hadn't brought knives and pistols to you, you'd still be rotting in the mud in the *Beetle.* I'll do the best I know how for all of you; and for your own good there's certain rules you've got to observe, whether you like 'em or not. Probably most of you won't like 'em, but this is going to be a healthy ship, and you'll do as I tell you.

"There's to be no fighting and no cursing. You'll get greens to boil in your food, and I want 'em eaten! You'll wash between decks every day, and you'll dry out, even if we have to build fires in the hottest spells. Mornings, weather permitting, you'll air your bedding; and finally you'll wash yourselves and your clothes daily, and put on dry clothes when wet. I aim to have no scurvy aboard this barque."

From the rear of the throng of seamen there came a shrill caterwauling in no way different from the cry of an irritated infant, and hard on its heels rose a great burst of laughter. Corunna stepped up on the taffrail and stared hard at the most distant ranks of her audience.

"Silence!" Slade shouted hoarsely.

Corunna swept him with fleeting, angry eyes. "Apply that word to yourself, Mr. Slade," she said. "This is my affair!"

She dropped from the taffrail, ran to the binnacle and picked up the tumbler she had left at its foot. With it in her hand, she ran down from the quarter-deck and pushed her way through the throng of seamen until she reached, in the back row, a sallow, shambling sailor with black eyes that squinted at her with a hard defiance.

"I heard you yelping because your insides are out of order," she said. "I thought somebody's would be, so I made this medicine! Drink it!"

She pressed the glass, two-thirds full of a dark liquid, into his hand.

"Me?" he said contemptuously; but casting a glance about him and beholding only delightedly unsympathetic faces, he became uneasy. "I ain't got no trouble with my insides, and I ain't goin' to——"

"Drink it!"

"Lady," he said, "I ain't done nuthin'."

"Captain!" she said. "Not lady—Captain! And don't lie to me about your insides! I heard you! Drink it or spend a week in the black hole getting well! Drink it! Every drop you spill you'll get a day black hole!"

The seaman took the glass helplessly and drank. Movements of his throat denoted repulsion. With the last swallow he choked; then began to mutter protestingly.

Corunna took the glass from him and looked at him thoughtfully, while his fellows, puzzled, shifted and drew a little away from him. He pressed one hand questioningly upon his stomach and with an expression of misgiving turned and walked in silence toward the knightheads.

"My father had respect and obedience on this vessel," Corunna said to the staring crew. "So will I! Jalap and tartar emetic's what that man's got in him for his cure—jalap and tartar emetic, and he'd rather have the smallpox! It'll last three days, and there's more where that came from for any other man who thinks there isn't going to be discipline aboard the *Olive Branch*."

# X

O F ALL the sea captains that Marvin had ever known,
Corunna Dorman, he made sure, was the most unremittently
exasperating. Often he watched her from the main topmast
crosstrees, to which he climbed whenever the opportunity
offered, not only because he feared that other eyes than his
own might be slow to catch the distant glint of an enemy sail
but also because he could view unseen, from this lofty height,
the comings and goings on the quarter-deck.

There had been times when, between the owl-like twistings of his head as he scanned the horizon, he wondered
whether Corunna's seamanship was a matter of chance or
of design. He had seen her work the barque with her shining black head bent low over the worsted likeness of the
Holy Family. Seemingly she never raised her eyes, except
to give an order; and more than once, when she was tacking
ship to gain an advantage from the shifting winds, he had
leaned far out to watch her, fearful that she would either be
too early with her commands, so that the vessel would not
come round, or so late that everything would be caught
aback and the barque put in irons.

Yet on each occasion Corunna, looking up from her
bright worsteds, as if by chance, had at the precise moment
called "Mainsail haul!" in a voice that came as clearly to his
ears as though she stood beside him; and each time the
ship had come about as smartly as a Baltimore pilot boat.

More exasperating than this to Marvin was the manner

in which Slade followed Corunna about the deck, hanging over her when she was busy with her needlework, and almost seeming to lie in wait for her whenever she left the deck to go below. Marvin, gazing down from the crosstrees, came to think of him as a swarthy long-haired spider, watchfully sidling about the center of his web in expectation of the moment when he might pounce with certainty.

Yet Argandeau, coming to sit with Marvin on the cross-trees, found nothing exasperating in anything Corunna did and nothing repellent in Slade's activities.

"This pigeon of ours," he told Marvin, "she is different from all pigeons and rabbits. Out of the thousands and thousands of rabbits I have seen, she is the only one who is able to seem always like a rabbit, even while doing the work a man should do. You have noticed this, dear Marvin—how a rabbit who engages herself to play like a man, or dress like a man, or exert herself like a man with the brain or the body, loses something out of herself, so that she is useless to look at? You have found it so, eh? In my early youth I discovered that I had no overpowering desire to gaze upon such a rabbit; and as for kissing—small choice between her and the binnacle!"

"I never noticed," Marvin admitted gloomily.

"But it is so!" Argandeau exclaimed. "Kiss one like that, and the next time you will ask for the binnacle! You must pay attention to women, and then you will see it is so! But with this pigeon of ours, she is somehow protected against that loss of something out of herself. I am conscious of her! I must restrain myself, so that I do not make myself desirable to her! I think it is possible that if I am not obliged to think continuously of other matters, very important matters—to think about how I shall get a privateer for myself when we are safely in France—I would give some thought to letting her be attracted to me. So little is needed. Pfoo!" He snapped his fingers. "Like that, I only need to let my consciousness of her become known to her!"

He peered earnestly to starboard and larboard, and glanced quickly at Marvin from the corners of his eyes.

"It is unfortunate," the Frenchman continued, as Marvin remained silent, "that I am unable to give my attention to this affair, if only to make it more difficult for Slade. I tell you, dear Marvin, I do not love him. Beneath that eyelid of his there is a look that means he is too easy in his mind about the future. I am not easy, and you are not easy, eh? Why should he be easy, this long-haired buzzard? Here is something worthy of our thought!"

Marvin laughed sourly and shook his head. "Corunna's from Arundel. She wouldn't consider a slave captain, not even if he was as handsome as George Washington. When the slave captain has a damaged binnacle to boot, she wouldn't look at him unless she had to."

"Pooi!" Argandeau cried. "You think beauty makes a difference with women? Or occupation? It makes no difference! I tell you it does not make so much difference!" Between his thumb and forefinger he plucked an imaginary atom from the air and tossed it carelessly from him. "It happens that I have been found captivating. I do not boast; I state the fact, claiming no virtues for it. These things are not talents; they occur! But it was not for my beauty that women of many countries have so frankly shown me their pining. It is because I let them feel my consciousness of them. Afterward, they find it impossible to keep me from their thoughts. Then, to gild those thoughts, I tell them magnificent lies of myself, and even more magnificent ones of themselves; for that is what rabbits prefer above all else. Ha! To make a rabbit believe you are a giraffe and she an eagless? 'Oh, rapture,' she sighs! I could be as ugly as those sheep in the pens amidships, but unlike them, I would have a perfume that would be intoxicating!"

Marvin scrutinized him carefully; then cleared his throat and resumed his study of the horizon.

"I tell you, dear Marvin," Argandeau continued, "it may be that you have had a thought to obtain this rabbit for yourself; and if it is so, you must be soon about it, because Slade is with her at all hours, telling her she is a great captain. In a little time she will consider him the wisest man in the world."

"What can I do?" Marvin asked. "I can't tell her she's a good captain, because it's against reason for a woman to be a good captain. Anyway, she thinks I'm a coward."

"Then tell her so!" Argandeau murmured. "Tell her you have been the greatest coward on earth, but soon will begin to be great because she inspires you. She is still a rabbit, you see, and must never be told the exact truth about anything. It is better that you do it than somebody else. Also, she is not a bad captain. I have seen worse. She is better than most English captains I have seen. It was a good idea she had, sending down the top-gallant sails and royals, so that we are sure to see any dangerous craft before we can be seen ourselves."

"I see nothing good about the idea," Marvin objected. "If we wake up some morning to find we've blundered into an enemy vessel, we'll have small chance of escaping."

Argandeau laughed and swung himself down onto the futtock shrouds. "She is ready for such a misfortune also. She has many other ideas for our safety. You believe what

Lucien Argandeau tells you, dear Marvin: Think less about how the rabbit will not do properly, and more about this Slade."

For a time it seemed to Marvin that Corunna's ideas would not be put to the test; for the *Olive Branch* came out of the blazing heat of the doldrums into the soft and pleasant cloudiness of the northeast trades, and slipped unmolested into the harbor of Las Palmas in Grand Canary Island for water, vegetables and such livestock as could be packed in her waist and between decks. From the Canaries she bore up, close-hauled, to the westward of Madeira; then set her course for the high shoulder of Spain and the Bay of Biscay.

It was in that vast funnel-shaped ocean lane, the narrow neck of which is Gibraltar, that Marvin, overseeing the dry holystoning of the newly washed berth deck on a cool October morning, heard a thumping of feet on the planks above him, together with a hoarse bawling for the bos'n.

Even as he swung himself over the hatch coaming his eye caught the gleam of a small white sail far away on the starboard beam; and from the look on the faces of the men who packed the bulwarks, staring first at the distant sail and then at the three figures on the quarter-deck, he knew as he ran aft that there was something about the sail that sat ill in the minds of all who had seen it.

Slade turned to him as he came to the break in the poop, lifting his head somewhat as though his drooping eyelid had shut Marvin from his sight. "Pipe all hands below," he said in his hoarse voice; "all but the original crew of this barque. They'll work the vessel, and the rest of 'em we'll put under hatches and batten 'em down. If we should be boarded, we'll keep 'em hid until the prize crew's aboard; then when we're well away, we'll off hatches, rise against 'em and retake the vessel."

Corunna, her telescope rested for firmness on a ratline, peered and peered at the distant sail as though Slade's words had found no lodging in her brain. Marvin stared from Slade to Corunna, and then to the far-off stranger.

Argandeau, close behind Corunna, spoke softly in her ear, eyeing Slade's back as he did so. "For such a cautious man as our bos'n," he said, "it might be that this plan would seem too dangerous."

Slade's laugh was as harsh as the scraping of a boat against a barnacled ledge. "Look sharp about it!" he commanded Marvin, and with that he turned from him to stand at Corunna's side once more.

Corunna lowered the telescope, glancing quickly at Marvin. "Why, yes," she said, "it might be, but it's got to be done, whether he likes it or not."

"Well," Marvin said, "I don't like it, and I'm not ashamed to say so. What will you do if she's a British cruiser, and she takes all of you aboard as prisoners?"

"She won't," said Slade quickly; "not if we don't fight her."

Marvin turned on him. "Why won't she? The British do any damned thing at all when they're at war! I never heard of anyone getting decent treatment from 'em unless their own ends were served by it!"

"Perhaps," Argandeau murmured, balancing himself on his toes—"perhaps this bos'n who is so free with his criticism is able to make a better plan, though I do not think so, because he does not have an intelligent look." He met Marvin's angry stare with the faintest lift of an eyebrow.

"There's nothing else to do but fight," Corunna said calmly, "and I somehow doubt that he likes to fight."

"Fight!" Marvin exclaimed. "How can we fight when we're too slow to board anything but a tub! What we might be able to do is scare 'em."

"Scare them?" Slade laughed contemptuously. "You'll make faces at them, no doubt!"

Argandeau nodded his head for emphasis. "Of all the people in the world," he said softly, "the English are the most cruel, but they are not easy to frighten."

"Maybe not," Marvin said, "maybe not; but I've never seen anybody yet that wasn't afraid of cholera!"

Corunna whirled to look at him, while Argandeau opened his mouth wide in a soundless exclamation. "Cholera!" she whispered. "Cholera!"

"Yes, cholera!" Marvin said. "What do you want to run from 'em for, once they've sighted you? It's as good as an invitation! Put about and run for 'em, and when we're within hailing distance, put me in a boat with two men to row and let me try it. If it doesn't work, you're no worse off than you'd be if you kept running."

"What?" Slade cried. "Why, she'd rake us with her bow guns before we had a chance to speak her."

Marvin studied him carefully. "It appears to me you're a little hasty in your judgment," he said. "She'll do nothing of the sort if we run down to her under half sail and at loose ends, yawing as if we had a sick crew and helmsman, and making signals of distress to boot."

Slade's laugh was as discordant as it was sudden. "It appears to *me*," he said, "that you're bound to have us taken!"

Corunna closed her telescope with a snap. "All hands about ship!" she said to Marvin. Marvin snatched his whistle from his pocket and went to blowing on it as if to blow the bean through the air hole.

Slade moved toward Corunna, who had taken her station at the weather gangway; but at the sound of a gentle laugh from Argandeau, he stopped. "Down with the helm!" she called. "Rise tacks and sheets!" With a creaking of yards and a slatting of rigging against fluttering canvas, the *Olive Branch* came about and bore off for the sail that now showed itself to be a ship with topsails so lofty that Marvin knew they could only be handled by the large crew of a warcraft.

Half an hour later, the *Olive Branch,* with everything lying aback, lay wallowing in the path of the oncoming ship, a wretched slattern of the sea with the French ensign half hoisted to her peak. There was a helmsman at the wheel, but he hung across it, more like a sack of meal than a man. In the shadow of the mainmast lay two still forms, and on the quarter-deck a single dejected figure sat as if helpless on a coil of rope. Off her starboard beam bobbed a small boat, in which two men rowed, while two others huddled in the stern sheets.

The ship, a frigate of thirty-eight guns, came past the boat and rounded smartly into the wind, to leeward of it, her starboard bulwarks studded with gun crews.

The men in the boat gave way, pulling wearily toward the ship.

A blue-clad figure on the quarter-deck bawled at them through a trumpet. "What barque is that?"

Argandeau rose in the stern of the boat, holding to Marvin's shoulder. *"La Petite Citoyenne de Douarnenez!"* he called back, passing his hand weakly over his close-cropped head.

"Speak English!" bawled the holder of the trumpet.

Argandeau turned to Marvin, seeming to hold him in conversation, and the small boat came rocking closer to the tall black cruiser.

The Frenchman turned to the quarter-deck again. His face was pale, and there was an unnatural redness to his lips. "I ask you, please, you give us opium."

There was a running on the frigate's quarter-deck. "Halt, there! *Arretez!* Get to hell out of here! Get around under our lee quarter! Lee! Lee!" The man with the trumpet waved it violently.

Slowly the small boat rounded the high windows of the frigate's stern and came up under her lee quarter. On his feet once more, Argandeau lifted a pallid and imploring face to the taffrail above him. "Two men die this day," he said. "Five have sick, very much vomit! Maybe we all die unless we get opium!"

"Well, what is it?" the blue-coated man shouted, his voice somewhat shrill. "You got cholera on that barque? Hey? What you got—cholera?"

"I think yes," Argandeau said wearily. "You give opium?"

"Sheer off, there!" the blue-coated man shouted. "Yes, we'll give you opium and laudanum! Here, clap onto this line! Hurry up with that line, there!"

A slender rope fell across the boat. Argandeau, crouched in the bottom, caught it and slowly hauled it in. Fastened to its end was a package. He rose to his feet as if to thank the frigate, but already her sails were filling and those on her quarter-deck too occupied, seemingly, to listen. Listlessly the small boat turned toward the *Olive Branch*. The frigate slipped rapidly to the westward—so rapidly that the figures on her quarter-deck quickly shrank to featureless dots. Argandeau scooped up a handful of seawater and dashed it over his powdered face and reddened lips.

"Ha!" he said softly. "For a consideration I will give Monsieur Talma, of the Théâtre Français, a lesson in acting, eh? Now I think we know how to come safe to France."

## XI

Racked by a southwest gale, the *Olive Branch* tumbled across the Bay of Biscay. In the cabin, Corunna, Slade and Argandeau bent low over a chart pinned to the cabin table and studied the ragged and inhospitable coast of France, while the bulkheads groaned and the hanging lamp plunged and jerked above their heads. Marvin, rewarded for his help in escaping the British frigate by the title of third mate, sat by himself on a locker.

"When I sail the *Formidable*," Argandeau said, "I come gayly from far countries; and Sweesh! I vanish into La Rochelle like an arrow, no matter what wind I have. I am indifferent to lee shores in my beautiful *Formidable*. Ah, ah!" He sighed heavily. "She mind me like a woman in the ecstasies of obedience to her first love. I have never been slow to make either vessels or ladies obedient."

"It was she, was it not, who went up in smoke?" Corunna asked dryly.

Argandeau made her a quick bow. "You interrupt!" he said. "I was about to say that I have not been slow to tell a woman what to do, once I learn what it is she wishes to do. Now I cannot tell what this barque wishes to do on a lee shore; and these lee shores of Normandy and Brittany, they are not affable. You look on this chart—how the head of Brittany thrusts itself out to sea! It is the head of a dragon, snarling at the ocean, eh? That is how she is, too—a snarler! Me, I would run into La Rochelle, but maybe you find it more comfortable to sail around the dragon's head and come in under the land at Roscoff or Morlaix. They have a drawback, those ports—they are close to England. For smugglers, that is good; for us, it might be bad."

"The closer to England, the fewer her ships," Slade said.

Argandeau raised his shoulder. "I hear Dominique Diron when he make that saying, and in return I make one of my own. Englishmen are where you find them. If it should be my business to fish for them, I would fish in any waters at all, and have better luck than those who say 'We will not fish in those waters, for the English never go there.' "

"I'd go into Morlaix," Slade remarked hoarsely.

"Morlaix is not bad," Argandeau admitted. "Me, I prefer Brest maybe, or Lorient, where there are guns to get under, eh, in case a frigate thinks she would like to come in to sit beside you. There are no guns in Morlaix."

Slade swept back his long hair. "But no frigate will ever make free with Morlaix," he said. "You couldn't get a frigate in there unless you floated her in on a raft."

"Do you know Morlaix?" Corunna asked Argandeau.

"Do I know it? In Morlaix I have five brothers-in-law—three of one family and two of another! To me it is like the face of my own neck, where I shave it each morning."

"And we'd have no trouble landing our cargo?" she persisted.

Argandeau laughed. "France and England, they are alike. Both countries are alive with thieves and politicians, which are the same things. Those who are not thieves or politicians are either smugglers, users of smuggled goods, fools or sailors. With a little money here and a little money there, you do as you like, eh?"

"Then it's to Morlaix that we'll go," Corunna said. She

looked ruefully at the elbows of her gray, water-stained Chinese jacket; elbows so crossed and recrossed by now with silken darns that they had the look, almost, of embroidered pads fixed to her sleeves. "And high time, too," she added, "unless I'm to do my sailing in a skirt with a band of grape shot sewed to the bottom."

Slade touched her arm gently. "All the finery in France," he assured her, "can be no more beautiful than this."

She shook her head and smiled; and almost to Marvin's horror it came to him that there was a misty softness in her eyes that had not been there since the day her father died. He rose so noisily to his feet that both Corunna and Slade looked around at him in disapproval. "I'll go on deck," he said. "Somebody's got to be there if the rest of you want to talk dress all day."

Argandeau, following him on deck, laughed softly at him. "I think you are all alike, you Americans—without subtleness with your women! Look now what you have done! You have barked at this rabbit, so she will move her nose and sit where she is, to show you she does not wish to be barked at! To me it is a strange thing, dear Marvin, that any woman in your country consents to become married to an American man, when even your language of love consists of barks and growls, eh? We in France, we are subtle! We hunt always for the heartstrings of a woman, and we play softly on them, so that she is moved to do our will. You should learn from—well, I will not say from whom, but from someone whose words of love are like the whispering of spicy winds among roses."

"No doubt!" Marvin said bitterly. "No doubt! Slade must have taken lessons from a Frenchman!"

Argandeau looked condescending. "Perhaps. He does very well, too, though one would never mistake the little chameleon for the superb tree he strives to imitate. However, ladies are sometimes pleased with those little creatures, the chameleons."

There was anger in Marvin's voice. "You mean she's pleased with this one now?"

"Well, she's taking her time to listen to him. No?"

Marvin made no reply to this inquiry; and the two men, one meditative and the other moody, began to pace the quarter-deck in silence.

The *Olive Branch* had rounded Ushant and stood off to the eastward along the brown-spined nose of the cruel dragon's head of Brittany before Corunna came on deck again.

"Why not say it?" Argandeau said in a low voice to Marvin.

"Why not say what?"

"What you are thinking, my friend. Eh? What's that? Why, that I was right about that damned chameleon!"

It was late afternoon of a chill October day when the barque skirted the tumbled rocks of Roscoff and, with her bulwarks and rigging studded thick with sea-weary sailors, ran close-hauled for the high-banked estuary at the end of which lies Morlaix.

When darkness fell she lay at anchor three miles up the estuary. The stone walls of the Château du Taurau were far astern and the lights of the Happy Horse cabaret winked at her from the near-by shore. She was one hundred and forty-eight days from Canton and—as even Marvin admitted—safe at last.

Corunna, coming on deck the following morning, found Marvin bargaining with the bumboat men whose small craft, laden with horse-meat, water kegs and newly-caught marine delicacies such as mussels and squid, were clustered at the waist of the *Olive Branch* like squash seeds floating beside a segment of their parent squash.

Corunna gazed contentedly aloft and about her. The *Olive Branch's* yards were squared; a brilliant sun shone on the deck, still damp from holystoning, and on the brass-work at which the crew still scrubbed. The estuary lay glassy blue in the morning calm. At the small end of the estuary the town of Morlaix nestled peacefully at the bottom of a deep cleft in the green French hills—a true haven, Corunna thought, from the trials and dangers of a troubled world.

Marvin, seeing her, came quickly to the quarter-deck. "If it's all the same to you, Corunna," he said, "I'd like to run out the sweeps and move a little nearer to the town. These boatmen say there's enough water closer in."

"What's wrong with this anchorage?" Corunna demanded. "Mr. Slade and I settled on it last night. Perhaps it isn't safe enough for you, but it is for us."

When Marvin was silent, she laughed scornfully. "You can't admit it, can you, Dan! Just because I'm a woman, you won't give me credit for doing what you said I couldn't do! You said I wasn't a captain; but I've brought this vessel safe to port, and no captain could do more. Yet you're too stubborn to acknowledge it!"

"No," he said slowly. "I'm not too stubborn. No man

could have brought her in smarter, Corunna. Your cargo's safe, and there's no sick aboard. It's a miracle, almost."

"A miracle!" she cried. "Why is it a miracle? Why can't you admit it was seamanship, and be done with it? Mr. Slade says——"

"What do I care what Slade says!" Marvin interrupted. "He'd say anything! Common sense ought to tell you that! If he'd captain a slaver, he'd *do* anything too! Anything!"

It seemed to him then that Corunna's smile had malice in it. "Wasn't it you, Dan," she asked, "who jawed so much, not long since, about women doing things for personal reasons? Maybe you dislike Mr. Slade, Dan, because he's kind to me; not because he's a slaver. And after all, Dan, there's worse things than a good slaver! Why, think how much better off the negroes are in the Sugar Islands than they are in Africa, killing and eating each other."

"Yes," Marvin said. "I've heard that before. Slade told me. That's how I know he'd say anything. He'd say a squirrel was better off in a cage than up an oak tree, where it might get hit on the head with a limb! If he says you're a captain, he's saying it to curry favor with you! Where's your common sense?"

"What?" Corunna cried fiercely. "You'll see whether I'm a captain or not!"

"How'll I see that?"

"Listen and I'll tell you," Corunna said deliberately. "As soon as this cargo's sold, I'm outfitting a privateer against the English, and Mr. Slade said he'd be proud to serve under me!"

Marvin stared at her, his lips pressed tight together. "You'll not do that, Corunna!"

"Won't I? Watch and see!"

"Well," he said doggedly, "you can sail a ship, but you're not a captain! You're a woman, and you count on it! You're going into a venture without being willing to pay if you lose! You're banking on taking prizes without doing any of the fighting yourself; and if you're captured, you're counting on being treated like a woman, instead of being sent to the hulks like your officers and crew."

She swallowed twice and drew a deep breath. "What if I am?" she said at last. "What else can I do? What can I do when you talk to me this way? You wouldn't talk to Mr. Slade the way you talk to me, because if you did, he'd have a knife in you before you knew it. Just because I'm a woman I have to listen to you. Why shouldn't I take advantage of being a woman when I get a chance—especially against those that killed my father?"

Marvin stared down at his knuckles and slowly closed and unclosed his left hand. "Corunna, there's nothing so hard to answer as a woman's arguments, mostly because there's no sense to 'em. I could tell you that nobody's a proper captain unless he forever runs more risks than the men he leads; but you wouldn't listen to me. As for not being willing to talk to Slade, I think I can dispose of that argument, even to *your* satisfaction. I've been promising myself to say a few things to him as soon as we reached a safe anchorage, and it looks to me as if now was the time. Will you call him up here, or would you prefer to see me drag him up?"

"Dear me!" Corunna said. "Dear me! You're mighty brave all of a sudden, now that Mr. Slade has gone ashore."

"Gone ashore!" Marvin cried. "Why, how *could* he go ashore?"

Almost as though he had popped, like a djinn, out of the water butt, Argandeau rose suddenly from under the break in the poop. "Somebody saying Mr. Slade went ashore?" he asked softly.

Corunna looked from Marvin to Argandeau and back again. "Why, yes. What's wrong with that? I sent him ashore late last night, after you had turned in, according to plan."

"You sent him ashore?" Argandeau whispered. "I am sorry you have not spoken to me about needing something on shore at such an hour. I would have been honored to go, eh? And maybe, in spite of having some relatives by marriage here who have a mistaken opinion of me, I think I should have contrived to be back on the ship by now."

"Oh, there was no question of returning quickly," Corunna assured him. "Mr. Slade felt that the sooner we started hunting for a privateer, the sooner we'd be able to set out against the British."

"Ah, yes!" Argandeau said, almost happily. "Mr. Slade reminds you of this, and so you send him. That is very nice, but it is a little pity he would not speak to me before he go, because I might tell him where to look for this privateer. I am surprised, too, that he know Morlaix so well as to be able to ask confidentially about such an expensive vessel as a privateer."

"Not in Morlaix," Corunna said. "That was why we thought it best for him to land at night. Then he could be well out of Morlaix before daylight, so that no official would detain him, and reach Roscoff in good season. He has acquaintances in Roscoff, I think."

"Ah, Roscoff!" Argandeau breathed. "It is too bad, if he has acquaintances there, that he was so eager we come here rather than to Roscoff!"

"Well, land alive!" Corunna exclaimed angrily. "It's beyond me why you should make such a mountain out of a mole hill! Why shouldn't he have friends in Roscoff?"

"Why shouldn't he have told Argandeau?" Marvin demanded.

"Good reason!" Corunna declared. "He knew you hated him, and that you'd do whatever you could to hinder his attempts to help me. And so you would, both of you!"

"He set off to buy a privateer," Marvin said thoughtfully, "so he must have had a deal of money with him."

"To *hunt* for a privateer, I said!" Corunna told him.

"But he must have had money to go traveling," Marvin persisted. "You didn't have any. It's all tied up in the cargo. You'd be needing money to get the cargo ashore and buy supplies. Perhaps he had enough himself; perhaps even enough to lend you some."

"Is that your affair?" Corunna asked. She strode to the larboard rail and marched up and down the deck, staring sternly at the small white houses on the far bank of the estuary and the little brown-sailed luggers that were slipping slowly out to sea before the vagrant morning airs.

Argandeau laughed gently. "By now he is in Roscoff," he told Marvin, "and there is nobody in Roscoff except all of the best smugglers in the world, by which I mean all of the worst ones; so we will hope that someone take him for a spy and stuff him in a brandy keg."

# XII

CAPTAIN SLADE in Roscoff, however, was far indeed from perishing, as the vivacious Argandeau desired, inside a brandy barrel; though it might well be of record that in his few hours of residence in that estimable town he placed within himself no inconsiderable quantity of the contents of such a barrel. His capacity was notable; no one who saw him could have guessed what he contained.

There was something disarming about his drooping eyelid; for when he tilted back his head to see the better, and smiled his quick and knowing smile, there was a look to him as though with the raising of the eye he lifted the curtain that hung before his mind, and permitted the world to gaze in on his sincerity and honesty. Even the hoarseness of his voice seemed proof of his candor; for on the face of it, no man would dare indulge in guile or fabrication in such rasping tones, lest his fraudulence be at once detected.

There was little indeed about the appearance of Captain Slade to inspire anything but amiability in those who saw him as he swung down the narrow streets of Roscoff on a warm October morning and entered the square that bordered the graystone inner basin. Clearly he was a somebody. There was distinction and urbanity in his bearing as he scanned the host of luggers, cutters and schooners that thronged both the inner and the outer harbors; and the rakish forward tilt to his fine beaver hat indicated a generous disposition and a well-filled purse.

It may have been the backward slant of his head that

made him seem to inhale with pleasure the somewhat powerful odors of Roscoff; it may have been the stout cane held so carelessly beneath the arm of his light blue coat that gave him his air of harmless affability; but whatever it was that did it, there was that about him which drew a tolerant growl from the swarthy Frenchmen who sat along the basin's rim, scratching themselves and looking resentfully at the cloudless sky.

Moving thus in an atmosphere of honesty and good cheer, Slade eyed a tall and narrow tavern fronting on the basin—a tavern whose signboard was blazoned with a round red object bearing a faint resemblance to the face of King George III, together with the words "Biftek Rouge." What Slade saw appeared to please him; for he swaggered jauntily through the door of the Biftek Rouge into a long room so full of men and of smoke as to give the impression that the floor itself was smoldering, and the men attempting to prevent a fire by sitting on it. The room buzzed with conversation when he entered, but as he stood by the small counter at the entrance, surveying the occupants, the buzzing died away and was succeeded by a heavy silence.

Slade laughed and cocked his eye at the fat woman in black who sat knitting behind the counter. "Brandy, madame," he said, smiling blandly at her small black mustache. "*Fine de la maison.*" He fumbled in the breast pocket of his coat and brought out a slip of paper. "You *savez cet homme ici*—Capitaine Henry Potter? Pottaire, eh?"

The mustached woman set a bottle and a tumbler before him; then studied the paper, front and back, without emotion. From a near-by table, a French sailor, gold earrings dangling on his cheeks and a canvas petticoat over his breeches, lurched forward to the counter and spoke quickly to the fat woman, who looked noncommittal, raised her shoulders to the level of her ears, and passed the slip of paper to him.

The Frenchman stared at it, scratching his nose. "No," he said at length, "that name means nothing in Roscoff."

Slade motioned to the fat woman for another tumbler, filled it for the Frenchman; then sighed and pondered, his lids downcast in vague regret. "Too bad!" he said. "Too bad! My friend Captain Chater told me Henry Potter worked regularly between Roscoff and Plymouth, and would set me across."

"You know Chater?" the Frenchman asked. He swallowed half his tumbler of brandy, shivered violently, and stared hard at Slade out of watery eyes.

"I knew him," Slade said. "He had the fever in Fernando Po. The damned fool wouldn't close his ports at night."

The Frenchman grunted. "Fernando Po!" he growled. "That is another thing, then! Strange Englishmen are not welcome in this town, but men from Fernando Po——"

Slade drew papers from his pocket, and as he waited for the Frenchman to examine them, he heard the humming and buzzing of the room mount again to its former violence.

The Frenchman pushed back the papers. "Yes, I will tell you. You know about Dunkirk?"

Slade shook his head.

"The Emperor Napoleon, he has turned over a section of the city to the English free traders, so that our poor country may take a few millions from the rich Goddams. All the time there are in that port five hundred sailors from across the ditch"—he jerked his head toward the Channel—"and if you go there, I think you find Pottaire." He finished his brandy, shivered again and pulled pensively at an earring.

"It's too far," Slade said. "Anyway, those that run out of Dunkirk wouldn't be going so far west as Devon; they'd be for Kent and Sussex. It's Plymouth I'm for."

Seemingly lost in thought, the Frenchman sniffed at the brandy bottle and pushed it toward the fat woman in black. "This Cousin Jacky is for export to England," he growled. "Spill none of it on your dress, lest it eat a hole. Give us a measure from the keg of '97."

Grumbling, the mustached woman produced a second bottle, from which the Frenchman poured two half tumblers.

"And," Slade reminded him, "I want to come back the same way in four days. I thought I'd pay in advance on this side, and leave the return money with madame here, to be paid when I come in again—paid with a hundred-franc bonus."

The Frenchman put an arm around Slade's shoulders and breathed heavily on his neckcloth. "Ah, but this is something we arrange at once. I am arrive here this morning, and I do not go back for four days, because every Englishman in the world either carries lace and Cousin Jacky, or wishes to buy it! There is the English of it for you! They make a law; then all of them work day and night to break it! Now there are so many of us that unless we take our turn, we bump into each other in mid-Channel! It is a hard thing for poor France that so many English should take the bread out of our mouths, no?" He patted Slade's shoulder and seemed to weep a little.

"It's tonight I want to go to Plymouth," Slade said.

"Yes, yes! But not Plymouth! Polperro, Yealm, Dartmouth, Cawsand, Looe—yes; every night there are luggers to those places, but not to Plymouth. Plymouth, it is too full of war vessels. Listen now to me. Here is what we do: Tonight four luggers go to Whitesand Bay, between Looe and Plymouth—two English and two French. I send you with an Englishman—Captain Vincent, cutter *Lottery;* he is very intelligent man. If there is something to be found out"—he raised his eyebrows suggestively—"by those fools in the army who are forever studying and daily growing stupider, Captain Vincent, he will deliver even a general anywhere in England in two days, entirely safe. You go with him to Whitesand Bay tonight and be nicely in Plymouth for breakfast; then in four days you come with a friend of Captain Vincent to Whitesand Bay once more, and we return here like two larks."

The cutter *Lottery,* laden with one hundred ankers of cognac, five hundred pounds of tea, seven thousand yards of lace and thirty bales of silk, ran due north from Roscoff on the night tide; and Captain Vincent, nursing the tiller of his swift vessel as easily with one hand as though he navigated a ship's dinghy in a canal, held Slade's gold pieces to the dim light of the binnacle; then stuffed them into the pocket of his breeches and cast a quick glance under the mainsail.

"You came to the wrong place for a Plymouth vessel," he told Slade, staring at him innocently out of clear blue eyes, "and if you wasn't a stranger, you'd 'a' knowed it. It takes money to shut up the Excise and Preventive officers in a port that size, and pay off a dozen revenue-cruiser captains to boot; and us little fellers, we ain't got it. It's only the big Scotch and French and Dutch and English companies that can pay that high for protection; and if we nose in on their preserves, it's a knife in the ribs or a bullet in the back, like as not, for those of us as does."

He spat over the side. "Of course, them that has to make port in all weathers, maybe they need protection; but White-sand Bay is all I need; no questions asked and labor plenty. You'll see 'em turn out tonight, with four vessels unloading! We pay 'em well; and every farmer and shopkeeper and blacksmith in the town, they'll be out to help; yes, and the women and children and the parson. And why shouldn't they, when it comes to that? What right's a government got to say a poor man sha'n't have his tot of Cousin Jacky, if so be he needs it!"

"It's all the same to me where I land," Slade said, "so long as nobody throws me into jail for being American. Going on an errand of mercy, the way I am, I wouldn't want to be branded as an enemy and all that." He laughed. "I'm no more an enemy of England than you're an enemy of France, but we'd both be hard put to it if it came to explaining!"

Captain Vincent nodded, gazing round-eyed at Slade. "Aye," he said, "I was thinking the same. It's likely you'd have no trouble, with your head cocked up on account of your eye, and so looking important and mean, like an English gentleman. It's likely you wouldn't; only there's no telling—there's no telling." He brooded for a time. Then: "You said it was Bristol you were making for?" he asked.

"To carry poor Chater's watch and seals to his mother," Slade said.

Captain Vincent nodded. "If I was you, I'd make sure. Better be safe than sorry, 'specially if you can enjoy yourself doing it. It'll cost some money, but you'll find it'll be worth it, more ways than one—that is, unless you got objections to traveling around with a young female."

"It depends some on the female!" Slade tilted back his

head to look at Vincent, and his teeth, as he laughed, were tight together, so that his laughter had more the sound of soft and eager breathing than of mirth.

"Well, I tell you," Vincent said, "this female's all right. She's young and she's sensible looking. Nothing flash about her, see; nothing to set people watching her all the time; nothing that'd oblige you to be fighting some young buck every few minutes to keep him from trying to cut her out; but she's sharp as a whip, and buffs better'n any female ever I see! Now, if you should get this female and take her around as your wife, she'd do all the talking, and nobody'd suspect you of not being an Englishman. Most Englishmen act tongue-tied when they're with their wives, anyway."

Slade cleared his throat. "I've had the same idea in mind for some time," he said frankly, "but I thought of visiting a house of entertainment where I could make a selection. I'm a little particular about my women."

"I'll tell you how it is," Vincent continued quickly. "There's plenty of females in Plymouth and Portsmouth and every other port nowadays, what with the men of the fleet to take care of, and the regular run of trade, and prisoners coming in to be looked after; but I tell you right now, you have to watch out for yourself! There's plenty in Portsmouth that'll stay with a prisoner fresh aboard a receiving hulk right out of the cable tier of a frigate, two shillings for a full night's work; but you know what happens if you take up with one like that!"

Slade laughed, a hoarse and racking laugh.

"Yes," Vincent went on, "but this female, she's nothing like that! There's admirals that've enjoyed associating themselves with this female, and haven't hardly been able to wait to get back off their stations so they could get hold of her society again. Admirals!"

The two of them chuckled.

"How's it sound to you?" Vincent asked.

"Not bad!" Slade said. "Not bad, provided she doesn't get to thinking I'm made of money. How much would I have to pay her?"

"I'll tell you how it is," Vincent said. "There was a few of us fitted up two houses in Plymouth—not the regular run, but high-class houses of entertainment. Some of the females we brought over from France for entertaining purposes, just the same as the Duchess of Portsmouth was brought"—they chuckled again—"and some we found closer home; but they're all of 'em ladies, fit to be presented at Court, or to spend a week visiting in Buckingham Palace. Now, if this female goes stepping off with you, it hurts the profits, as you might say; so you'd better pay me enough to cover that end of it, and then you can fix up with her. Maybe she'd come too high for you. Whenever she puts in considerable time entertaining a gentleman, she has to have two new dresses, one for day and one for night, and five guineas a day. Too much, ain't it?"

"Well," Slade said, clearing his throat, "if she's as shrewd as you claim, she might be worth it. How much would cover the profits?"

"Oh, call it five guineas," Vincent said carelessly.

Again Vincent examined gold pieces in the light of the binnacle; and after that, in the lurching and swaying cockpit, he whispered busily in Slade's ear until, dead ahead, a score of blinking, wavering lights marked the tumbled rocks and the sheltered crescent beach of Whitesand Bay.

# XIII

THE office of Admiral Sir John Duckworth, high above the dockyard at Devonport, looked out over the bewildering marine activities of the Hamoaze to the lofty wooded slopes of Mount Edgcumbe, beyond which lay Whitesand Bay; and Admiral Duckworth himself, stocky and formal in his high-collared uniform coat and spotless nankeen breeches, stared from the window at the swarming waters below, in which shore boats, bumboats, ships' boats, and lighters of every description scurried like beetles among the frigates, line-of-battle ships, hulks, ships repairing, ships fitting and ships under sail. Behind him, the hoarse voice of Captain Slade filled the room with a ceaseless and not displeasing hum.

Admiral Duckworth turned from the window suddenly. "As I understand it," he interrupted, "you want one-half of the sum realized from the condemnation sale, if, as and when this barque is cut out from some port unknown. I tell you at once, my good fellow, it won't do! It's too much!"

Slade shrugged his shoulders. "That's as you see fit, Admiral." He coughed. "I've heard there are ways in which vessels are ships when they enter your prize courts and sloops when they come out—though, of course, that's none of my affair. And I know your prize money is often divided oddly. Why, I know a case, and so do you, too, sir, where a British admiral received four thousand pounds prize money from a single vessel, while the seamen on his ship were given two pounds apiece. Of course, that's none of my affair either, but it's been done, and done often, where your admirals were concerned; and what's been done can be done again."

Admiral Duckworth stared at him coldly, but Slade only laughed.

"It seems to me," the slaver continued, "that the circumstances should make some slight difference, too. Here's a vessel that will be fitted out as a privateer against you, under a Yankee captain that—meaning no offense—can sail circles around your fastest frigates and sloops-of-war. It seems to me it should be a privilege for you to nip this little enterprise in the bud, no matter how much it costs you— a privilege and a patriotic duty."

"Dear me!" the admiral said in a light voice. "Lessons in patriotism to a British admiral delivered by a Yankee merchant captain whose position is—let us say—equivocal? Interesting!"

Slade tilted back his head and smiled up into the red face above him. "Don't take me wrong, Admiral! Don't take me wrong! It only seemed to me I ought to mention the saving to your country, seeing that you've objected to my reasonable price for the information. Why, here, Admiral; this barque and her cargo will sell for thirty thousand pounds. That's fifteen for government and fifteen for me; and if you send a schooner to cut her out, her officers and crew would consider themselves made men if they divided five thousand among 'em. There's ten thousand left for government. Or call it five thousand, and make a fast sloop-of-war out of the barque. All profit, Admiral! But if you don't get her, what then? Suppose she slips out and takes four or five of your merchantmen, as she will! As she will!"

Slade clicked his teeth together and laughed his soft laugh that sounded like quick strokes of a brush against stone. "You'll have the shipowners buzzing around the Admiralty's ears, crying for their lost money and cursing the navy for a kettle of old goats and younger sons, and that's all you will have!"

Duckworth walked up and down the room, glancing angrily at Slade. "It's beyond me!" he said at length. "I've done some fighting against your people in my time, and it was generally the other way around. Usually it was our people that went running over to yours, because of all your wild talk of freedom; but here you are, wanting to sell your own shipmates!"

Slade seemed hurt. "No, no! You've got it hindside foremost, Admiral! The barque belongs to a poor, helpless girl with no mind for business. She's fallen into the hands of two unscrupulous rascals, Admiral. If they have their way, it'll be no time at all before the girl's stripped clean and deserted in a foreign port. They'll take her barque for a privateer, and they'll take her money from her on the plea of refitting. It's that, Admiral, that's set me off on this. I do hate to see an innocent maid so fooled and misled."

The admiral looked at him and laughed.

Slade sighed softly and rose from his chair, smiling somewhat ruefully. "Well," he said, "it's no matter! I see you don't take to the idea." Hat in hand, he moved toward the door.

"Half a moment," Duckworth ordered. "If we go in after this barque, are you sure she won't be tied up at a dock? Won't be unloaded? Are you sure a cutting-out expedition could get to her?"

Slade set his gray beaver hat on the floor once more. "I

saw a French official before I came away. She'll be held at anchor, and won't break cargo until I return; and she'll cut out as easy as a rat hole out of cheese."

"Well," Duckworth said reluctantly, "we might arrange it."

Slade eyed the admiral thoughtfully, his drooping eyelid a pallid patch in his swarthy face. "You won't regret it! No: you won't regret it! And by the way, Admiral: there's one or two things I'd like to be sure of before the matter's considered settled. There'd have to be articles between us, stating clearly that I'm to receive one-half of the prize money resulting from the sale of the barque and her cargo, whose value is tentatively estimated at thirty thousand pounds; and that in case she's used for government service, I'm further to receive one-half of her value as decided by the prize court. Also an agreement that when the barque is cut out, the lady, if aboard, is to be set ashore before putting to sea. Also an agreement that the crew shall be taken for imprisonment to the hulks farthest removed from the port where the barque was captured. They're dangerous men, Admiral, and I want 'em put where there's no likelihood they'll cause the lady more trouble."

"Dear me! Dear me!" Grumbling, the admiral dropped down before his desk and scratched busily on a sheet of paper, while Slade watched him out of one black eye that seemed to glitter like a drop of ink in the sun.

The next morning this benevolent adventurer sat at an upper window of the *Swan* inn, tapping impatiently with a snakewood cane at his newly varnished boots. He cocked an eye at the curving streets of ancient Bristol and the forest of masts that edged the serpentine curves of the Avon as willows rim the banks of a meadow brook.

"Interesting, isn't it!" he said in his hoarse voice. "These English; they know how to do things! They put up a battery of church towers to catch your eye; and while you're busy looking at the towers, they run their slave ships right up to their own back doors."

He laughed the laugh that had the sound of bristles passing lightly over granite; then turned his head quickly. "Look here, my love! I've got business in this town, and I want you with me! Crowd on some canvas or you'll get something you aren't looking for!"

A small, brown-eyed, brown-haired girl came to his side, circled his head with a bare arm, rapped him lightly on the cheek with the back of a hairbrush and pressed his face to her bosom. "Now," she said, "don't tease!" She broke from him and went back to her prinking at a mirror; and Slade, watching her with a gleaming eye, was silent.

It was an hour later that the captain swaggered proudly from the narrow door of the *Swan*, his snakewood cane jauntily a-swing and at his side his lady, her small hand thrust demurely beneath his elbow; her eyes, sheltered by a snuff-brown bonnet, modestly cast down. It scarcely seemed that she could muster the courage to leave the side of her escort to ask even the smallest of questions of a stranger; but leave it she did; and while her apparent husband stood lost in admiration of the Norman tower of St. Peter's Church, she timidly begged a white-aproned wine merchant to direct them to Queens Square.

Then the decorous couple skirted the busy Avon, passed through the odors of wine, tobacco and leather that hung over the crowded High Street, and made their way into the quiet southern quarter of the city, where the squat brown houses of opulent shipowners were sheltered on three sides by the waters of the Floating Harbor. Here, while Captain Slade again seemed stricken speechless by the cold bronze scrutiny of King William III and his horse, or possibly by the sight of either the customhouse or the jail, his gentle companion hesitatingly inquired of a lofty footman where the residence of Sir Austin Braymore might be found.

It was not, indeed, until these two obviously estimable and virtuous folk had been admitted to the dim hallway of Sir Austin's home that Captain Slade regained his tongue; and the very manner of his regaining it was proof that he was pleased.

"Little devil!" he said, drawing his lady to him. "Every inch the bride! We came here as neatly as though we'd been brought up on the smell of fried eels!"

He peered past her at the elaborately carved love seat in the hall; then raised his chin, as if in haughty appraisal, to eye the cabinet in the near-by reception room—a cabinet of mahogany, carved delicately to represent a bamboo pagoda, rising to eaves that swept upward to still higher eaves, and thence to a stork at the top; a stork so graceful and so lifelike that it seemed poised above the cabinet, rather than mounted on it. Inside the cabinet were silver bowls and jars and milky plates, their centers blazing with heraldic designs in gold and blue and scarlet.

He bent his head to whisper close to the snuff-brown bonnet: "Make an excuse and stay out here. I'll see this gentleman alone; and after that, my love, I'll set you to playing the dear, fresh-wed little spouse once more."

A portly gentleman with a triple row of chins came

heavily down the staircase, wrinkling his forehead at the couple below him. "Captain Slade and ma'am," he said politely. "The name is not—is not——"

Captain Slade seemed almost to stand on tiptoe, so far back did he throw his head to see Sir Austin clearly. "I came direct from Admiral Duckworth," he explained.

"So, so! So, so!" Sir Austin murmured. "From Sir John! So, so! Pray step back here, Captain."

He turned toward the far end of the hall, but before Captain Slade could follow him, his lady had swayed and gasped a little, and to the distress of Sir Austin and the captain, declared timidly and sweetly that the journey had been a thought too much for her: that she would sit alone, here in the hall, if only Sir Austin would have the kindness to send a servant to her with a thimble of Madeira.

"Of Bristol milk, ma'am! Not Madeira, but Bristol milk! That's the wine to bring the color back to those soft cheeks!"

He hurried to the bell pull, hastened for the smelling salts and bustled about for a cushion to slip beneath the feet of this delicate little lady; so that when he was finally alone with Captain Slade in the small white-walled room at the rear of the house, he was short of breath from his hospitable exertions, and wheezed a little as he sat wide-legged before his visitor in a large wing chair.

"So, so!" he panted. "From Sir John! Ha-ha! Difficult post! Happy to think he thought of me!"

The quick rasp of Captain Slade's laugh brought a look of puzzlement to Sir Austin's face. "It just happened," Slade murmured, "that your name didn't come up. No, your name wasn't even mentioned."

Sir Austin clapped his fat hands on his knees and stared

in amazement. "Not even—not even—— Then to what, if I may ask, am I indebted——"

Slade turned his head and looked hard at Sir Austin from his one good eye. "Some little time before I saw Sir John, I ran into Fernando Po." He nodded brightly and added, "On business."

Sir Austin cleared his throat softly. "On business in Fernando Po? That is in Africa, is it not?"

Slade laughed a little harshly. "Seeing that the *Narcissus* was in the river when I was there, and that the *Venus* had cleared with six hundred and nine blacks three weeks before, you ought to know where Fernando Po is!"

He looked coolly about the small white room; got up, even, to scrutinize more closely the lady in the gown of shimmering brown whose portrait hung above a mantel of yellow marble—a mantel with a medallion chiseled by a master hand to show a dog, bone in mouth, staring at his reflection in a stream.

"H'm!" Slade said. " 'Lady, by Kneller'—best man you've got when it comes to white shoulders above a silk dress!" He sat down again and grinned into Sir Austin's still face.

"What happened," he continued, "was that Chater wouldn't close his ports at night. That's what you get for taking a man off the Channel and putting him on the Middle Passage. They know it all, they do, just because they've been able to run a few ankers of brandy past a handful of paid Preventive officers. Won't take advice! That was Chater! Wouldn't take advice! I told him what would happen if he didn't keep his ports shut, but he laughed, and it occurred!" Slade hissed jovially through his clenched white teeth, "He died of the fever."

Sir Austin drew a key from his pocket and fumbled, with helpless hands, at the lock of a mahogany cellarette that stood by his elbow. Slade leaned forward to take the key from the trembling fingers of his host. With a deferential smile he thrust it into place and raised the lid.

"Permit me," Slade said. He glanced mournfully at Sir Austin. "Your health, I fear, is not what it should be. It's the rich food, perhaps. Yes, it must be the rich food! A man your age can't be too careful about avoiding exertion or excitement. What can I give you, sir?"

"Brandy!" Sir Austin whispered. "A little of the brandy!"

Slade brought up a bottle with a fly-specked label, turned his head sidewise to examine it; then, puckering his lips in a tuneless whistle, he plucked two glasses from the rack. When he had filled one for Sir Austin, he sipped from his own, sighing gently as he rolled the liquor over his tongue.

"You'll be relieved to know," he at length continued, seeing that Sir Austin seemed content to sit silently, staring into his empty glass, "that I saved her for you. Yes, sir; I saved the *Narcissus!* When Chater was dying, the blacks rose, and if I hadn't been handy with a long knife, you wouldn't have any *Narcissus*. You'd have lost her, and everything with her—men, sails, spars, coppers and leg irons."

He shook his head reproachfully at Sir Austin. "You ought to give your niggers more space! There were ninety packed into the boys' room, and it was only thirteen feet, nine inches long. That's not enough—not for vessels as slow as your English tubs. Fifty days they take for the Middle Passage! You're bound to lose half of 'em when you pack 'em in like that! Sometimes it seems as though you English didn't have any sense at all! It's a wonder to me you're able to lay up a penny! Instead of suffocating so many, why don't you carry forty-five instead of ninety in your boys' room? They'd cost half as much, and you'd have next to no losses unless you struck bad weather."

"You don't know——" Sir Austin's voice failed him, so that he was forced to try again: "You don't know what you're saying!" He worked his lips from side to side, as if to free them of stiffness. "I won't listen to such things! I don't know what you're talking about!"

"No," Slade said, "I suppose not!" He brusquely drew a bottle from the cellarette and poured himself another brandy. As an afterthought he offered the bottle to Sir Austin, who seemed not to see it. "I suppose," Slade continued, "you also don't know what I'm talking about when I mention the *Narcissus* or the *Venus* or the *Delight* or the *Apollo!* Since you merely happen to own 'em, you naturally wouldn't have heard of 'em, or of what they're doing. That being so, I'll be glad to furnish you with something authentic. You'll doubtless be happy to hear the *Delight* landed four hundred and eighty blacks at St. Thomas on her last voyage, along with three tons of gum copal and twenty-two hundred double pawn cloths. That ought to mean fifteen thousand pounds in your pocket—fifteen thousand in addition to your profits in—ah—black ivory from the other three! Why, I doubt there's another slave trader in Bristol who can hold a candle to your fortune!"

He smiled in friendly admiration at Sir Austin, whose fat white cheeks seemed to be afflicted with spasms of trembling, as jelly shudders at a weighty footstep; and for a time they sat in silence, these two; Sir Austin clutching at his knees with plump white hands that shook and sweated, and Slade grinning up at the white shoulders of the girl in the portrait above the mantel.

Sir Austin, when he stirred, moved with the stiffness of a wooden man. His eyes were dull as those of a dead haddock. "Never!" he gasped. "It's not so! I deny it!"

Slade stroked his long black hair with the palm of his hand. "Before Chater died," he said, "I thought it might ease his mind to sign a writing for his family showing he wasn't in that business for himself. It mentioned he was working for you; and then—blast my absent-mindedness! —if I didn't go and forget to give that paper to the widow!" His eye glittered. "But to remedy that, and to fix up poor old Chater's reputation, I've arranged that the writing shall be presented to Admiral Sir John Duckworth and other responsible officials on a certain date unless—unless——"

Sir Austin rolled almost drunkenly in his huge wing chair. "By God, sir! You must have—— Why, damn you, sir! Chater wouldn't have done any such thing unless you held a knife to his throat! I mean to say—— I beg your pardon! Yes, yes! He might have been crazed by the fever! Crazed; yes, yes! Crazed! This damned calumny—why, my daughter—but there's no one would believe such a slander—— What? Of a man that put a window in St. Margaret's and that bishops are damned glad to dine with?"

"Dear, dear!" Slade said carelessly. "I fear the bishops may be upset when they learn they've been dining with the owner of slave ships!" He rose to scan again the portrait of the girl in brown. "This your daughter? She's in society, I take it; but probably her position wouldn't be affected by anything that happened to you—ah—would it, Sir Austin?"

Sir Austin pressed his hands together. "The jail's just across the square, Captain Slade, and the sheriff's a friend of mine! I might warn you to have a care how you speak loosely of me in Bristol, or elsewhere. Do you think any man in Bristol could be brought to believe that——"

Slade waved his hand languidly. "And would they never believe it of such good Bristol citizens as Standish Trevor and Sir George Batt and Cottrell and Foster Penhallow?"

Sir Austin's breath made faint popping sounds as it broke from his slack lips, and Slade's eye gleamed with satisfaction. "They're on the list," he said suavely. "Those names are there with yours, and the names of their vessels as well." He cleared his throat. "You're slow to make laws, you British, but when you make 'em, you make 'em too severe, to my way of thinking! Of course, we've got a law against importing slaves into America—had it before you made your law, because of the way you were glutting our markets with blacks—but our law's nothing like as strong as the law you passed last year."

With his tongue he made clicking noises of commiseration. "To think it's a felony in England since last year! A felony to deal in dirty blacks, when everybody knows your cane fields can't be properly cultivated by anyone but niggers! Yes, sir; a felony, and punishable with transportation! Why, sir, it just doesn't seem within the bounds of reason that if that document should fall into Duckworth's hands, you'd be torn from your family and that daughter of yours, and transported to Botany Bay along with common thieves and drunkards and diseased women!" His shoulders shook with silent laughter. "It might be, in time, your family could join you out there, if you behaved yourself. I think your family'd be permitted."

Sir Austin looked at him piteously. "I suppose you want something."

Slade drew from his pocket the paper he had received from Admiral Duckworth, glanced closely at it, and handed it to Sir Austin. "I want two things," he said, "and considering I saved the *Narcissus* for you, it's little enough. I want fifteen thousand pounds advanced on that piece of paper, and I want a vessel. I want the fifteen thousand pounds in cash, and I want it tomorrow. And when I say I want a vessel, I don't mean any vessel. I mean a brig, a fast brig—a fast armed brig. She's got to have fourteen guns at least, and two of them long guns—long 24's. She's got to have quarters for a crew of a hundred and forty, and she's got to be trim and taut and ready for sea."

"Preposterous!" exclaimed Sir Austin, and he blew out the word as if it burned his tongue. "Why, where would I get such a sum and such a brig? How could I——"

Slade fixed his one good eye on him fiercely. "I've made myself clear," he said. "That's what I want and that's what I propose to have! You know it's worth that to you and Penhallow and Cottrell and Trevor and Batt to be saved from Botany Bay! You can tell them for me they're on the list, and the list will be in Duckworth's hands if I don't get what I want—the money tomorrow and the brig within a month. You know as well as I do that Liverpool has enough fast brigs hidden away to fight every sloop-of-war in the British Navy! Where would you get it, indeed! Who should know better than you that there were two hundred and fifty slave brigs out of Liverpool less than ten years ago? Two hundred and fifty! Go there and get one! You've got the money and you've got the influence! You own slave ships, and Liverpool was built on the profits of the slave trade. A man of your influence can get whatever he wants in Liverpool!" His laugh was like the rubbing together of two bricks. "Doesn't the sheriff come here to dinner? Don't you have bishops to dine?"

. . . When at last Captain Slade emerged from Sir Austin Braymore's small white-walled study, triumphantly rolling his glittering black eye from the Turkey carpets on the floor to the silver in the great pagoda cabinet, his modest little lady was asleep on the love seat in the hall, the tips of her brown slippers barely reaching to the floor and her lips parted as innocently and sweetly, in her childlike slumber, as the petals of a rose.

She opened her eyes as he gazed down at her; then, after a cloudy moment, recognition came back to her. "You're a sweet man," she said—"a sweet man to stand and smile at me so kindly."

"My dear, I wasn't," Slade told her as she rose and they moved toward the door. "I was smiling to myself to think how vastly I bettered myself in so short a time. Five days —why, it's genius!"

## XIV

By FIVE DAYS Captain Slade meant the five since he had left the *Olive Branch* in the harbor of Morlaix, where that patient barque still lay with all her cargo, and a great deal of perplexity aboard her.

There were times when Marvin, eager to break bulk and see the cargo of the *Olive Branch* safe ashore, fell into such a rage that he talked bitterly to Argandeau.

"What's the matter with these Frenchmen?" Marvin demanded. "The crew of the *Formidable* went ashore long ago, and the English wounded have been safely put in jail, God help 'em, so that we're harmless enough; and we've shaken hands with a hundred officials and officials' clerks, and Corunna spends half her time on land, signing all the papers that anyone brings her; and we've paid money to every soul in Morlaix, I do believe! Everyone except the priest and the schoolmaster! Yet every day they think up another reason why our goods must stay under hatches! Why, they're worse than the Chinese, these Frenchmen!"

Argandeau raised his shoulders helplessly. "No, no!" he said. "You do not understand them. They have had many years of war, and many years of democracy, when every man claimed to be as good as every other man, but privately knew himself to be better; and now they have Bonaparte and a dozen spies to watch each one of them, so they must be careful, poor people."

"Careful!" Marvin exclaimed. "Do you call a thief careful when he makes you turn out the same pocket twenty times?"

"Eh, eh?" Argandeau cried. " 'Thief' is a strong word! The trouble is merely that some important man has not yet received what he should receive. He is afraid, perhaps, to tell us what he wants; or perhaps he is waiting to find out what all the others have received from us, so that he may be certain he will not receive less than any man."

"A body'd think," Marvin told him, "that we were their enemies, instead of helping them to fight the English. Don't they ever say what they mean? Are they always bowing and smiling and talking about friendship, and then doing everything they can to ruin us, like your idiot Admiral D'Estaing who talked so loud about helping us whip England in the Revolution?"

Argandeau examined him calmly. "I think you are excited, dear Marvin. It is true that D'Estaing was not a lion in battle and was something of a hen as a seaman, but if I had been in his boots, I would have won that little war for your thick-skulled countrymen in two weeks—maybe three."

Marvin reached over and caught Argandeau by the shoulder. "Of course! Of course! I am sure that it is so, my dear friend! How much easier it will be, then, for you to win an even smaller war with people even more thick-skulled!"

Argandeau lifted his eyebrows. "What is this you say, dear Marvin?"

"Go ashore!" Marvin exclaimed. "Go ashore and tell Corunna to stop signing papers; that you'll arrange this thing! We must make a start at landing this cargo today! I tell you I don't like lying here with no way of maneuvering, and not enough crew to fight off any gang of frog eaters that takes a fancy to come aboard. I don't feel easy. There's a change coming! If you're as good as you think you are, go ashore and make these Frenchmen stop squabbling over their pennies long enough to let us tie up to a dock and get our goods on land. Tell 'em we want less politeness and more friendliness."

Argandeau elevated his shoulders. "But we must be patient! These poor people will not understand if we are rude to them; and I am sure that when our little rabbit returns, she will have the permission to begin tomorrow or the next day to unload."

"So that's what you think, Admiral," Marvin inquired, with an exaggerated air of urbanity. "I scarcely knew you at first, but now you've finished speaking, I recognize the D'Estaing accent. How well I remember your skill at doing nothing, Admiral, when we needed help the most!"

Argandeau laughed softly. "Be quiet!" he said. "That tongue of yours, it is too busy! I'll do what you want! I'll see that rabbit of ours at the Hôtel de Ville in ten minutes and tell her I arrange to do what you wish, but only do it to save myself from the clacking of your voice."

Marvin watched him being rowed ashore. "Do not look so serious!" Argandeau shouted back to him. "Argandeau, he arrange everything! This afternoon you toss your cargo about, eh, and tonight we have fried eels and two bottles of brandy—maybe three! I bring them back with me!"

The boat moved in toward the wharves of Morlaix and the dismal-looking buildings of gray stone that rose steeply above them. Marvin, confident that Argandeau, brought at last to the point of speaking his mind to his countrymen, would be successful in his mission, went forward to the bow, where those that were left of the crew were dividing their time between the catching of eels and the exchange of hoarse pleasantries with the occupants of small boats engaged in the sale of onions, checked shirts, flatfish, apple brandy, red wine, lace and mussels.

With reluctance they abandoned their fishing, removed the hatch and fell to swaying bales on deck in preparation for the afternoon's unloading. Marvin, having put them to work, inspected the galley and the forecastle, examined the guns with a mind to having them scraped and repainted; then, still with the thought of painting in his head, went aft to the cabin to look for spots that would be better for a brushful.

The cabin was divided into two sections, and it was the smaller of these that Corunna still occupied. At its door Marvin hesitated, but only for a moment. There seemed to him, when he entered, to be something of Corunna about this small white room with its standing bedplace and its wide lockers—an air of sturdiness and crispness. Drawn over the bedplace was a patchwork quilt that almost glittered in the brilliance of its colors, and folded neatly on it lay her needlework—that worsted work of art representing the Holy Family gazing with suspicion at the towers of Jerusalem.

Marvin, touching it gingerly with his forefinger, smiled a little. From it there seemed to rise a faint fragrance of sweet grass and mallow, such as had come to him so often from the Arundel meadows on summer nights. He stared up at the ceiling and around at the white panels of this neat small cabin; then moved to the high locker against the after bulkhead—a locker with a Chinese courting mirror over it, and a swinging whale-oil lamp of pewter and copper, with small paintings of her mother and father on either side.

The painting of her mother, Marvin thought, would be Corunna to the life if, in place of the low black dress, edged at the neck with wooden-seeming lace, the portrait showed her in a stained and darned Chinese jacket with a collar that came high up around her throat and fastened with three jade buttons.

He slipped the oval frame from its hook. Through the tightly drawn black hair gleamed a white ear tip; the lips seemed to tremble on the verge of a smile; in the smooth column of the throat, as Marvin studied it, there was almost the beating of a pulse. He touched the pictured throat gently with his finger. The scent of sweet grass and mallow came to him again; and the face at which he looked softened and became charming, as had Corunna's on that night off Rio. He lifted it toward his lips, but before it reached them, he guiltily raised his eyes to his reflection in the mirror.

Reflected also in the mirror was the stern window, and through the mirrored window he saw, far down the estuary, a tall black schooner beating up on the rising tide from the Channel, close hauled on the larboard tack.

He quickly hung the picture in its place, turned to the window and examined the rig and cut of the distant vessel. Despite the briskness of the southwest breeze, she rode stiff in the water, heeling over so little that no part of her copper showed, if indeed there was copper on her. She was, Marvin felt, too large for a smuggler; and he knew, as well, that there was scarce a smuggler in either France or England but used either a lugger or a cutter in his trade in preference to a schooner.

She might, he told himself, be a French privateer; but it was doubtful, since her top-hamper was lacking in delicacy, his mind, for such a vessel. Even at that distance he could see, from the spread of her ratlines, that she carried more shrouds and backstays than Diron and Argandeau would consider needful; and it was plain that she was rigged for strength rather than for great speed. Furthermore, she showed no colors, which seemed to him unusual for a vessel entering a home port after a cruise.

Vaguely uneasy, but more curious than uneasy, he took Corunna's telescope from the rack beside her bedplace and went on deck, where a score of bales had risen from the hold to clutter the amidships section. Increasingly uneasy, he mounted to the mizzen top and focused the glass on the schooner, which had come about on the far side of the estuary. She was pointing downstream from the *Olive Branch,* but from the set of the tide it appeared to Marvin that when the stranger next came about, she would be abreast of the barque.

Through the glass he could see guns on her deck, which was nothing strange; and her ports were closed, with no crews to be distinguished near the guns, so that she looked peaceable enough. He was a fool, he told himself, to be disturbed over a harmless merchantman, running home, no doubt, with rum and sugar from Martinico; and with that he polished the lenses of the glass with a fold of his shirt and stared even harder at her.

From far behind him he heard a hail. A boat, he saw, was bobbing toward the *Olive Branch* from the direction of Morlaix—a boat with three men in it. As he looked, the man in the stern sheets rose to his feet, pointing and waving toward the oncoming schooner, and hailed again. Marvin saw, with a faint trembling in the pit of his stomach, that the man was Argandeau. What it was that he shouted Marvin could not hear, nor did he need to hear.

His thoughts churned in his head, like wheels spinning in butter. "If I can pile her up on shore," he thought, "she's safe. If I try to run her ashore, but don't have time, I'm making it easier to lose her." He cast a quick glance at the schooner. To Marvin, the mile-wide estuary seemed to have shrunk in size; the white cottages on the far shore, so distant until now, must, he thought, have drawn near to stare critically at him. The schooner, pushing a milky wave before her, had swelled beyond all reason. Already half across the estuary, she seemed to tower above the crinkled water like a giant among schooners.

He jumped into the rigging. "All hands tumble up!" he shouted. "Get axes! Cut the bow anchor cable! Cast loose the main and fore-topsail!"

He rushed, spiderlike, down the ratlines; then leaped to the helm, putting it hard over and lashing it there. "Jib and fore-topmast staysails!" he shouted. "Crowd 'em on!"

The waist and bow of the ship seemed alive with movement as the remaining men of the crew scurried over the bales and into the rigging to get sail on her.

Slowly the gray walls and roofs of Morlaix moved to starboard; and the tall Indian, Steven, came up over the bows, in his hand a cleaver from the galley, so that Marvin knew the bow cable had been cut.

He called the Indian aft. "When they've got sail on her," Marvin told him, "wait till she points for the bank. Then cut the stern hawser and jam her ashore. Ram her in anywhere! Get there! No matter how!"

The tall Indian flicked the cleaver into the deck. It stuck there, quivering, handy to his grasp. "What is she? A lobster box?"

Marvin shook his head and vanished down the companionway. The *Olive Branch,* pushed by the southwest breeze, moved slowly against the incoming tide, hesitated, as if caught on a sand bar, while the loosed sails shivered noisily but to no avail.

Argandeau scrambled over the starboard bulwarks. "Haul!" he snapped. "Haul those yards around! Never mind that schooner! Haul!"

He looked quickly over his own shoulder. The schooner was on them—so close that her long white jib boom had the look of threatening the reluctant barque with a lashing; so close that Argandeau could see the moving lips of a whiskered seaman who leaned over the bows, a cutlass gripped in the fist that rested on the bulwarks.

The tall Indian at the helm jumped to the taffrail, slashed the stern hawser and hurled the cleaver at the towering schooner. The *Olive Branch* surged sluggishly toward the brown rocks that lay a half cable's length ahead.

"Dan!" Argandeau called. "Dan!"

Marvin burst from the companionway, spilling an armful of cutlasses on the deck.

"All hands aft!" he shouted, snatching up a cutlass. "All hands aft to stop boarders!"

"No good!" Argandeau told him. "We don't make it!"

"No!" Marvin shouted. "They can't do it! Hold 'em off!"

"No good, dear Dan," Argandeau repeated. "They cut us out. Look here, what they do!"

The schooner shot past the *Olive Branch's* stern, veering swiftly as she did so. Her bulwarks, Marvin saw, were packed with intent red faces, and as she veered, blue-clad men in shiny black tarpaulin hats swarmed into the fore and main chains and ratlines—twenty of them, thirty of them.

She slipped between the *Olive Branch* and the haven of brown rocks. Her broad walls of canvas hung over the barque, seeming to Marvin to cut off from the *Olive Branch* all sun and light and air. Then she closed in; and even while Marvin waited for the rasping lurch that must come when she laid the *Olive Branch* aboard, there was a growling call of "Boarders away!" from her stern. The bulwarks of the schooner spouted men, who hurled themselves into the *Olive Branch* like gargantuan blue locusts.

Argandeau caught Marvin's arm as a dozen British seamen converged on the quarter-deck. Two of them darted by Marvin. One went to the deck with the Indian; the other put the wheel hard over. Over the shoulders of the Britishers, Marvin saw that his crew, taken front and rear by the English, had dropped their weapons. Four of the seamen jumped suddenly at Marvin and Argandeau. A pistol butt struck Marvin's wrist and the cutlass fell from his hand.

The blue-clad Britishers, hitherto silent, burst into uproarious talk and laughter. "Easy as pickin' gripes!" one of them shouted. A sour-visaged officer, old enough to be an admiral, went to the *Olive Branch's* larboard rail and hailed the schooner's quarter-deck. "All clear, sir," he called to an elegantly uniformed youth who stood by the schooner's wheel. "Shall we run for the Nore?"

"What about the female?" the youth demanded pettishly. "Bring her up where we can see her!"

The officer turned on Marvin and Argandeau. "Where's the female that's supposed to be captain of this barque?"

Argandeau raised his eyebrows. "Female?" he asked. "How does it happen you think we are supposed to have a female captain?"

The sour-faced officer took a quick step forward and

swung the flat of his cutlass against Argandeau's upper arm. "Where is she, you swab?" he demanded.

"She's ashore," Marvin said quickly. "Is Captain Slade aboard your schooner?"

"Slade!" Argandeau cried. "Ah, my friend! You've hit it! How else could these British have known we lay here worth the taking, and could be taken? How else would they have heard we have a female captain? Slade! Yes; Slade! But we shall not find him on their schooner! He would not risk that Argandeau, in chains, should yet find means to bite him to death!"

The sour-faced man turned to the rail to hail his youthful commander. "Ashore, sir! They say the female captain's ashore!"

The younger man laughed. "Ah, that's where the admiral said she was to be put! Nice of her to save us a bit of trouble! Sorry to miss her, in a way, what? First American that ever did anything right, to my knowledge! Sorry to miss a freak like that!" His voice became crisper. "Get right along," he called. "Take the barque to Sheerness, but not a foot farther, Cropsey. We'll go up to Chatham together."

The *Olive Branch,* manned by her British captors, sheered away from the schooner, which ran rapidly down the estuary ahead of them.

"Nah, then," said the sour-faced officer to Argandeau and Marvin, "we'll just clap you and your questions abaht Captain Slade into the cable tier! Captain Slade, eh? Well, if he's one of you hole-and-corner Americans, you'll probably meet up with him in the hulks, where all of you belong!"

# XV

From the courtyard of the *Queen of Scotland* tavern in the town of Morlaix there emanated at all times a powerful odor of badly cleaned stables, venerable wine casks and cheese; and when the sun appeared—as it infrequently did —above the chimney pots and jumbled tile roofs that surrounded the court, a singular penetrating fragrance of pickled herring rose in waves from the seemingly immaculate stone pavement of the court, and passed through the closed windows in the tavern as readily as though every window had been thrown open.

Since the sun shone brightly on this clear October day, and since, as a result, the fragrance of pickled herring was strong in every room in the *Queen of Scotland,* but particularly strong because of an opened window in the small fourth-floor room numbered "44," it seemed strange indeed that Corunna Dorman should sit huddled in a corner of that dim and cheerless chamber, staring fixedly at a knot in the floor—a knot around which the soft wood had been worn away by the restless feet of countless vanished guests.

From the roundness of her eyes, there seemed to be little doubt that she had seen all of the knot there was to see, but long minutes passed, and never once did she look up— not even when her black cloak, which hung in the center of a wall, moved jerkily and swayed from side to side, as if the evil spirit of the room, maddened by the smell of herring, had taken violent possession of it.

The cloak fell at last, revealing a small hole in the wall over which it had hung; and at its fall Corunna rose to pick it up and hang it over the hole once more. Having done so, she stood silent beside it, holding to the cloak's hem and staring with round eyes at nothing whatever.

She seemed, almost, to have lost her hearing as well as her vision, for when a light knock sounded upon her door, she still held to the cloak and stared fixedly into space. When, however, the knock was repeated and a woman's shrill voice called, "Open, please, lady!" she turned quickly to the door, dragged a chest of drawers from before it and snapped back the bolt.

The woman who entered was short and fat. Her fatness spread outward from her bust, so that her shoulders had the look of being pressed upward by it, her eyes squeezed half closed by the surge of her enormous bosom, and her vast hips and thighs spread outward by the weight they carried. She breathed heavily and peered past Corunna into the room.

"You eat nothing! Why not you come down? I give bread and *chocolat,* and you need not think of *monnaie*—not yet."

"Yes," Corunna said. "Thank you. I think—I think I——" She stopped, swallowed hard, and contented herself with saying "Yes" once more.

The fat woman pushed past her into the room, jangling a cluster of keys attached to a brass ring, and stared at the large and elaborate bed. Her half-opened mouth had the look, in that enormous face, of a sort of buttonhole. She darted a quick, suspicious look at Corunna. "Don't you sleep sometime? You don't like this bed?"

Corunna reached out to her cloak and drew it to one side, revealing the hole beneath. "I slept in the chair."

By a movement of her eyes and upper lip, the fat woman

gave the impression of raising her shoulders. She went to the hole, stooped a little and squinted through it; then, applying her lips to the aperture, she violently shrieked a veritable explosion of syllables. When she turned back to Corunna, she wagged her head solemnly. "Nothing! Think nothing about this! All rooms have these holes, and all men look through! What you expect?"

As broad and solid as a hogshead on two boulders, she stood and examined Corunna with scrupulous attention; but Corunna, again staring wide-eyed at the protruding knot, seemed oblivious of her presence.

"You don't know no way to get *monnaie?*" she asked at length. "You don't have no *bijou*—no ring, maybe?"

Corunna shook her head.

"You don't know some friend in Paris, no? In Boulogne? In Lorient? Maybe in Brest or Nantes, eh? In Brest and Lorient come many Americans in lettres of marque. Maybe you go there, and you find a friend who take you in America, when you kiss him nice."

Corunna looked up quickly at the fat woman, opened her lips; then closed them again and fell to staring at her clenched hands.

The fat woman jingled the keys on the brass ring and dropped her voice to a confidential whisper. "Is here an *avocat* who is think you can get *monnaie* from the government in Paris because you bring wounded men here on that poor ship the dirty British had the audacity to seize from you. Eh! What a terrible thing for our beautiful city of Morlaix that those English should be so sly and so bold as to come into our very harbor in such a manner! Now perhaps the Emperor will give us some fortification worth something! *Hélas!* But it will not do you much good, poor little one! What you need, my child, is a protector. Come, you let me speak to our *avocat!* I will arrange it. You permit me to hint to him that you can be persuaded to go with him to Paris, and he will become eager. Oh, yes! When they are old, they are easily inflamed!" She placed a pudgy finger beside her nose and smiled craftily at Corunna. "It will be a good affair for both of us! He is good man—old and kind. I think he would be gentle, and you like his protection very much."

Far below them there was the sound of a slamming door, and of a stir—a throbbing pulse that somehow seemed to bring new life into the stale and tainted air of this ancient tavern.

The fat woman surged past Corunna and stood listening at the threshold. A burst of speech came up the darkness of the stairway, together with the noise of quick footsteps —footsteps that drew rapidly nearer.

The black bulk of the listening mistress of the *Queen of Scotland* shot through the doorway, plucked from her place by a violent hand, and where she had been stood Lurman Slade, slender and neat in his fine blue coat, his head thrown far back so that he might see clearly into the room, and a look of deep concern on his thin brown face.

"Corunna!" he cried hoarsely. "My poor Corunna!" He went to her quickly and took her by the shoulders. "My dear! I've been in a torment to reach you! If ever I'd known——"

He looked into her brimming eyes; then drew her suddenly against his breast, cupped her face in his hands and kissed her tenderly.

She drew a deep and quivering breath, like a child who

has borne a heavy weight of suffering; then clung eagerly to him.

"You're here! You're here!" she said. "I didn't know—I was afraid—I thought you might never come! It was terrible! It was terrible! They were here, and then in a second they were gone!" She shook her head wearily.

Slade kissed her eyes and held her tight. "Never come!" he whispered. "You thought I might never come! I'd have come to you across the whole world, my sweet—my little sweet!"

She leaned backward in his arms to stare at the walls about her. "Why," she said, "it's been like an awful dream! Everything gone—everything swallowed up, and not a word from anyone! Not a word!" She shivered.

Slade took her hands in his and kissed them; then led her to the one poor chair and knelt beside her. "My heart was like lead in me when I left you," he told her softly. "Like a stone, it was! I could hardly eat for thinking of you! I came to you on the instant the news reached me. With all my heart in the search, I was seeking for the ship that would be your privateer, happy that I was working for you. Then, at a tavern in a little town I heard by chance of the cutting out of the *Olive Branch,* and thank God I did hear! And so I am come to you!"

"Yes," she said. "I'm glad you've come. I need somebody."

"Aye," he assented gravely, "you've needed somebody a long time, Corunna—somebody that could protect you from your own simple trust in people. I don't think you yet know," he added, "how the barque was taken."

"Why, by the British!" she said, wondering. "They came in——"

"Aye, so they did," he agreed, looking at her pityingly. "In Roscoff it's known how the British did it, Corunna. Aye, they know who helped to do it! I blame myself! What a fool I was! I'm like you; I'm not suspicious either, dear. I never dreamed he was anything but a coward—a sulky country coward! He's a cumbersome lout, half giant to the eye; and I was simple enough to think him an honest one, all brawn and no cunning."

Corunna stared at him. "What do you say?"

"You ask me what I say, Corunna? I say what's incredible; much harder for you to believe than for me, though I thought I knew him. My dear, I sha'n't blame you if you can't believe it. I think there was a time, before you knew me, when you liked him very well."

"Marvin?" she whispered. "Why, yes, I did!"

Slade touched her shoulder gently; he looked kind and wise and good. "I knew. I understood, because from the first I understood you. I knew you'd been very close to giving your heart to him, my dear, and that but for some vital flaw, some ugly defect in his character he'd betrayed to you, you would have given it; and so you'd have been lost to me. Isn't that so?"

"Why, yes."

"I knew," he said in a low voice, full of pain; then smiled, as in a lover's noble forgiveness. "Thank God that's past, and you *did* see that defect. It's your having seen it for yourself that makes it easier for me now to tell you how that base metal in him runs through the whole fabric of his character, so that he could do what every man in Roscoff knows he has done."

"Knows he has done——" she repeated uncertainly. "Lurman, you're telling me——"

"See here," he said. "I don't want to tell you. Do you think me a man not too proud to put a defeated rival in a false position?"

"No." She swallowed. "But Marvin—Dan Marvin! Marvin!"

"Marvin," Slade burst out bitterly, as if the truth leapt from his lips despite him. "Good God! Why, he handed over the *Olive Branch* to the British without a blow, either for you or for his ship! Without a blow! When he lay in the black hole with us, didn't he try to slip out to traffic with 'em? I never told you this before, Corunna, but he did! Why, you must have seen him currying favor with the commander of the *Beetle*, on the pretext of obtaining medicines for a common seaman! Medicines! Good God! I don't know what scheme he has, but you saw he was forever against anything that meant fighting the British. Oh, aye! The dog would ever keep his record clean with them! Forgive me if I'm bitter, but when I think what he's done to you, I forget you once held him for a friend."

"To me?" she said. "You think Dan Marvin would——"

"Corunna! Corunna! How did the English know just where to come and what to do? Why, my dear, there's not a man in Morlaix, aye, or Roscoff either, who doesn't know the *Olive Branch* was delivered to the British by her officers —and for a consideration. Do you think that Marvin couldn't have run the barque safe on shore if he'd had a mind to? Pah! You know better yourself! You're too good a seaman not to know. I wish to God I'd struck him dead at your feet, before he should have done this to you."

She rose suddenly and went to the window, where, square-shouldered and flat-backed against the pale October sunlight, she stared down into the noisome courtyard below.

"How could they know?" she asked faintly. "How could all these people know that Dan sold his soul to the English?"

Slade sighed, and his sigh seemed freighted with compassion. "Such things are always known, Corunna." He shook his head sadly. "Always, my dear."

"But he didn't want to come here in the beginning! He said the way to go home was to go home."

"Yes," Slade assented, "and when you overruled him, he was sour and sore, and now he's paid you for that overruling. You asked me how these people knew. Corunna dear, it's life and death to every smuggler on the coast to know what goes on in the British Navy to the last detail; and they *do* know, believe me! They know Marvin sold the *Olive Branch* to the English, and they know he'll not only get money in return but a British commission to boot."

"Ah, he wouldn't," she whispered.

"He'll have a commission from them if he wants it," Slade insisted, "and most of them here think he'll be a wise man to take it. Aye! They say he knows that America, with only fifteen cruisers, can make no stand against England with her thousand ships of war, so that England must win, and America be a colony of England's once more. That being so, Marvin will not only have money but he'll keep his lands in America, and be high in favor with the British as well." He shook his head and cocked his eye at Corunna. "Yes, he's a cautious man," he reminded her. "I think I've heard you speak of that, my dear; but now we both know, to our cost, it was something more than caution in him."

Corunna seemed to choke, looking down into the courtyard. "No!" she exclaimed. "No!"

Slade came close beside her. "My dear," he said softly, "we none of us know what's in a man's mind, and I could almost forgive him for turning against his country, if so be those are his principles. It's what he's done to you that I shall never forgive. To turn from a woman more beautiful than any Queen on her throne, and with the brain of a Decatur or a Nelson—that's what shows him in his true colors!" He touched her hand gently. "To think he left you here as destitute as any beggar in the streets! Left you here without a cent, without a ship, and, so far as he knows, without a friend!"

He turned her about, so that she faced him, and took both her hands. "Well, let him go! It's nothing to lose a vessel! It's nothing to lose money! If I had you, there'd be nothing in the world, no matter how poor I was, that would keep me from whatever it was you wanted and needed." He kissed her fingers.

"All my life I've paid no attention to women," he went on. "Now that I've seen you and felt the touch of your hands and the softness of your lips, I'll hate all women but you for the rest of my days."

She smiled faintly and shook her head.

"It's so!" he insisted. "Why, tomorrow we could set off for Paris; and before you can have bought yourself a dozen gowns, I'll find a way to get you a vessel, and have half of Paris at the feet of the fairest bride in all France."

His voice was that of a loving friend who brings a brave gayety to battle the despondency of his beloved. Tears seemed about to rise in his eyes—tears of love and pity— yet he smiled upon her in a valiant encouragement, and his hand came upon her shoulder with the touch of a hearty comrade.

"Eh, Corunna? We'll up and at 'em! Here's a pair of us

that can look misfortune in the face. Now we're together, not all the bad luck in the world—no, and not all the sneaking treachery of those we'd love to believe in, neither!—ah, my dear, not all the evil in the world can keep us down!"

Thus he swept her away.

# XVI

IT WAS not discomfort that weighed heaviest on Marvin, as the violent Channel seas racked and rasped him against the harsh coils of the cable in the airless, wedge-shaped den of the cable tier, nor yet the lack of humanity in the British who had him in charge, but the almost certain knowledge that it must have been Slade who had sent His Majesty's Schooner *Sparrow* to cut out the *Olive Branch* from the harbor of Morlaix, and the even greater certainty that Corunna, by this sudden and overwhelming disaster, had been left penniless and friendless in France, with no person to whom to turn save Slade himself.

He groaned, ill at ease mentally and bodily, and prevented by the deck above from rising even to a sitting position. "You could have stayed there," he reproached Argandeau. "You *should* have stayed there!"

"You think too much about this, dear Marvin," Argandeau told him gently. "When those smugglers come running, to me in the *Préfet's* office, doing me a kindness by saying that this schooner is a Griffon—a Griffon who had already cut out one other vessel from Morlaix and two from under the batteries of Dunkirk, and must therefore intend wickedness to the *Olive Branch,* what can I do, eh? You know who I am in Morlaix? I am the brave Lucien Argandeau! Can I say to them 'Pooi for your Englishman! I stay here and do nothing about him!' Can I say that? Not if I wish to remain the celebrated Lucien! No, I must say, 'Hah! The perfidious English! Lucien Argandeau will show them something that will make them laugh out of the wrong mouth! He will go out alone and dispose of them! Thank you very well!' Another thing, dear Marvin: There was a chance, eh? —a chance that if we were quick and fortunate, we could have got her ashore, so that this Griffon could have done no cutting out. Then your rabbit would have had money, and we could have shown the British some cutting out of our own!"

He was silent, and Marvin as well, so that they heard nothing in the darkness of their lurching, coffin-like inclosure save the smashing and rattling of the seas against the bows.

"To show the British something!" Argandeau whispered yearningly. "There is nothing else I want any more! Women and wine are pleasant, but I have had a large share—so large a share that to count the favors ladies have shown me—— Eh! Can a man count the glasses of wine he has had? Only the English are a flame in my head. Nowhere can I get money for a privateer except through you or your rabbit, dear Marvin!"

His voice was as soft as the murmur of a gentle wind among small leaves. "It was apparent to me that if your rabbit was deprived of the *Olive Branch*, she also lost the power of purchasing a privateer for me or for anybody else. Therefore I was obliged to devote my efforts to saving the *Olive Branch*. Observe the clarity of my thoughts, dear Dan! We French are logical above all other people; and when you say I should have stayed ashore to look after your rabbit, you are not logical! By the stomach of the Supreme Being, I did not even wait to go into the next building and tell her what was happening in the harbor. While there are

Englishmen alive, I could not stay my feet! No, no! Argandeau to the fray! Well, it was done, and now I grieve about your rabbit. I am sorry we have not tossed a knife into Slade before he made this trouble, but I am sorrier that we have lost our chance to privateer. These English, dear Marvin, there is nothing in the world like them; and now I wish nothing in this life except to be in a fast vessel again, so that I can rip their seacoast from end to end!"

"Slade must have gone to Roscoff and crossed with a smuggler," Marvin murmured, seeming to have heard none of Argandeau's words. "If I'd got sail on her two minutes earlier—if those damned Frenchmen had let us haul in to the dock——"

"If!" Argandeau protested. "You are stuck full of 'ifs!' You will 'if' yourself into a sickness! You did everything very quick and with no slip. No man could do more. Duguay-Trouin, he could not have done more. Tom Souville could not have done more. My soul! Argandeau himself could not have done more! You dwell too much on this! You must sleep, eh? Sleep will wipe out the regrets that are false. You listen to me! In Spain, when I am younger, I learn Spanish from a Spanish lady, very beautiful. She teach me a proverb for everything in the world. 'An "if" in the mind is as bad as a *banderillo* in the hide of a bull,' she say. Also, she tell me, 'Two hours' sleep is better medicine than two hundred years of tears.' Whatever she wish to prove, she can prove with a proverb."

There was an end, at last, to the dizzy gyrations of the hole into which they were packed, and the prisoners, foul with the slime of the cable tier and sore from head to foot because of the bed of wet and stinking rope on which they had lain interminably, clambered weakly up the companion-ladders to find the barque hove-to under heavy skies in the lee of the crowded dockyard of Sheerness, at the mouths of the Thames and the Medway, and under the guns of two lowering forts.

The gray-faced officer watched them brought on deck; then, with a faintly sour smile, he warned them against shouting or the making of unnecessary noises if they wished to enjoy the benefits of the open air.

Doubtful concerning the quality of the smile, Marvin pressed forward. "With your permission," he said, "we'd like to take our private belongings with us—our clothes and some small articles."

"What articles are those?" the aged lieutenant asked.

"There's the picture of a lady in the small cabin——" Marvin said.

"No such thing!" the lieutenant snapped. "There's no picture of any kind on this vessel! If there was, it would do you no good to take it; there's no room for such trumpery on the hulks."

"Our clothes——" Marvin again ventured.

"Clothes!" the lieutenant exclaimed in disgust. "There's nothing I'd call clothes aboard this craft! Nothing but dirty Yankee rags! I suppose you'll be trying to say you had something wearable, and that these men of mine stole them! You'll be provided with clothes aboard the hulks, so let me hear no more drivel about your filthy duds!"

Marvin shivered. His muscles tightened until his back and his neck ached from the strain of them. Argandeau tapped him on the shoulder and sighed gently. "I tell you they are a flame in my head, these English!"

Two hours later, followed by the ironic cheers of the

English seamen who had cut them out from Morlaix, they were packed into the waist of a government tender, with boarding nettings at both bulwarks and a squad of marines before and behind them; and thus guarded, they bore off to the westward, into the curving channel of the River Medway—a river with flat low shores and a wealth of mud banks from which there rose wisps of mist, smelling of decay.

It was near dusk of that gray October afternoon when the tender, rounding a wide bend in the river, came into an expanse of water so broad that it had the appearance of a lake. Ranged along the center of this lake, and bulking mountain-like above the flat expanse of water and the low fields beyond, floated fifteen structures that seemed to Marvin to have the look of giant coffins, but coffins sadly misshapen by pipes and platforms and warts and knobs that protruded from them in a thousand places and at a thousand angles.

"So there they are." Argandeau sighed. "There are the hulks, that have been more terrible to France than any hell." He drew a deep breath, and then another. "Breathe deep, dear Marvin, while you can. There are Frenchmen in those coffins who have not breathed pure air for six long years."

The tender drew abreast of the rearmost hulk. She was, Marvin saw, the defaced and dirty remnant of what once had been a ship-of-the-line—of what once had been more beautiful, with her tiers of gun ports, her symmetrical sweep of hull, her glistening paint, her towering masts, her web of rigging and her cloud-like spread of canvas, than any other structure fashioned by the hand of man.

Argandeau growled faintly in his throat. "Look!" he

said. "Look how she is old and sick, I think with leprosy, and so squats there in anger, wishing never to move again! It is a sight to make a seaman weep! They are cruel to everything, even to their ships, these Englishmen!"

Pale vapors oozed from the countless pipes that were thrust from the sides of the soiled and dreary hulks, vapors that coiled and drifted downward like a mournful fog, so that the tender moved along the melancholy fleet through an acrid veil of smoke.

She drew close to a hulk near the middle of the line; and to the crew of the *Olive Branch*, silently staring from behind the boarding nettings that had been raised between them and any possibility of escape, came the shrill babble of unnumbered voices. A platform encircled the hulk three feet above the water; and on the platform two sentries rattled their muskets and challenged sharply.

"Tender *Primrose*, of Sheerness," bawled a hoarse voice from the tender's stern, "wiv twenty-four Amairikins, cut out of Morlaix by schooner *Sparrow!* Consigned to *Crown Prince* hulk by orders of the Transport Office!"

High up in the lofty stern of this miserable vessel a window swung open, and from it peered a face with a babyish look to it—a look as though the person to whom it belonged had lived long, but never grown up. The features seemed pinched together, as though the eyes and nose and mouth, in infancy, had been seized in a ruthless hand and compressed until they had become fixed.

"Are they washed?" this face called down angrily. "Have they had a bath?"

"Yes, sir!" shouted the hoarse voice from the *Primrose*.

"Send them up!" called the angry voice. "But if they hadn't been, back they'd have gone to Sheerness! See you remember it, my man! You bring any more dirty Yankees to this hulk, and either you'll take 'em back to be washed, or wash 'em on your own deck!"

The *Primrose* swung against the landing stage, whence a long, canvas-sided companionway ran up to the high bulwarks of the *Crown Prince*. The boarding nettings were lowered, and the captain of the tender motioned the prisoners toward the hulk.

"You heard what he said!" he growled. "If you don't aim to be soused in the Medway with a rope round your middle, stick to it you been washed!"

They mounted the companionway, and the tall Marvin, coming over the top of the bulwarks at the head of the line of seamen, found himself looking down into an oblong space that seemed to him the size of the floor of a fair-sized barn. Beyond a loop-holed wall at one end rose a drab and dreary forecastle, from which smokepipes protruded like pins from a pincushion. Armed sentries stood behind the wall, and marines moved about on the forecastle itself, so that Marvin knew the forecastle belonged to those who guarded the prisoners. Beyond a similar wall at the other end rose the structure that had been the quarter-deck; and in his quick glance at it, Marvin saw it was still sacred to the ship's officers; for the pinch-faced man, dressed in a uniform too tight for him, stood silently at the break in the deck to watch the prisoners come aboard.

The space between the quarter-deck and the forecastle was a-swarm with men—more than Marvin had ever before seen packed into such a space—and from these men there rose an odor so strong and penetrating that it caught at Marvin's nostrils and his throat and sickened him.

The garments of these men were shredded and tattered.

Through wisps of cloth showed skinny ribs: pipestem arms: bony shins and thighs. Such was the emaciation and pallor of this sorry crew that they had the look of skeletons who, by some devil's dispensation, had risen from the dead in rotted grave clothes for a reunion in this purgatory of the sea.

Yet there was nothing skeleton-like about their actions; for they posed and pirouetted when Marvin came down among them. They capered insanely before him, flinging their arms about, moving their shoulders, screaming unceasingly in shrill and womanish French. A thousand hands, it seemed to Marvin, were stretched forward to pat his back; to touch his arms: his shoulders. *"Les Américains!"* he heard them cry. *"Les braves Américains! General Madison brave homme! George Vasington brave homme!"*

There came into his head the thought that war made strange bedfellows, and that a common cause could unite men of widely different races. In that moment he felt a movement against his thigh, and as his glance dropped toward it, he thought he saw the flicker of fingers drawn back with the speed of light. He clapped his hand to his pocket; then turned quickly to the men from the *Olive Branch*. "Keep tight hold of your money!" he told them. "They got mine!"

Argandeau came close up beside him and spoke in French to the jostling throng around them. What he said was said softly, and took not long in the saying, but the words had the hiss of a whiplash. The ragged Frenchmen fell away before Marvin, so that a lane was opened through them. Suddenly silent, they stared at one another and at the Americans with eyebrows raised, and with hands and shoulders that protested their innocence more clearly than any words. Yet in their eyes Marvin seemed to see amusement, and even something of malicious mockery.

He scanned their faces sharply. Rage filled him at his loss, but in addition to the rage there was almost a sickness at the knowledge of his pennilessness; for without money, he knew, a corpse would have less trouble in rising from its coffin than he would have in escaping from this hulk to go in search of Corunna and of Slade.

An irate voice put an end to his attempt to find, among those pallid countenances, the face of the man who might have robbed him. "Here!" the voice shouted. "Here! Where do you think you are? Get back here where you belong!" It was the voice of the pinch-faced lieutenant; and, Marvin, recognizing a dangerous childish fury in the sound of the words, hastened through the jostling Frenchmen to stand close under the high poop on which the angry lieutenant stood.

He was, Marvin saw, a man approaching fifty, a plump man whose arms and legs were oversnug in an ornate uniform which had the air of having been made for a woman. His hands, resting on the carved rail before him, were smooth and white, and heavy with rings.

"Good God!" he shouted, stamping his foot angrily. "Twenty-four more! Over three hundred of you damned contrary Yankees aboard this ship already, and now twenty-four more of you wretched contentious creatures! You there—you tall man! What was it you stopped for? You spoke to someone! You've brought a letter to one of these prisoners! I won't have it! I'll put you in the black hole! I'll cut off your rations! I'll——"

"I've done nothing!" Marvin interrupted. "Nothing but try to find the man that picked my pocket."

The lieutenant, slack of lip, stared dully at him; then burst abruptly into laughter. "Listen to that, Sugden!" he cried, turning to a small man who stood humbly beside him, his eyes downcast and a long book beneath his arm. "There never was an Amairikin in this world that wasn't always talking about money or claiming he was badly treated! Pocket picked! 'Pon my word, Sugden, that's positively convulsing! Tomorrow he'll have something to say about the food. Tough meat, or weevily bread, most likely!"

Sugden laughed, a raven's croak, and looked, grinning, at Marvin. "Most likely," he agreed.

"I warn you now," the lieutenant told Marvin disdainfully. "There's no sympathy on this ship for whiners! Whine and escape! Whine and escape! You ought to have that motto on your flag along with the bars you've already put on it. One of you's worse than a thousand Frenchmen! I'll remind you now that those who try escaping from this hulk get the black hole! Don't forget it! Give your names to Sugden; then get over with the rest of your brave Amairikins and let them find room for you on the lower deck, if they can. If they can't, it's not my fault!" He turned and minced away.

Sugden set down Marvin's name, vessel and other matters in his long book. Another clerk tossed down to him a limp hammock, a bag of chopped rags and a blanket that had the feel of being woven from string. Behind him the Frenchmen were dragging hammocks from an airing-stage and disappearing beneath the hatches. He heard Argandeau supplying Sugden with astounding information—name, Lucien Argandeau; nationality, American; residence, Boston; wife, one wife; children, no children.

Before he could protest, he felt a touch on his arm and

whirled to see a man no taller than a cabin boy—a spare young man with a face of extreme gravity and crinkly side whiskers the color of corn-silk after a frost. He wore an overcoat so long that it was near to dragging on the deck.

"Newton," he said, holding out his hand to Marvin. "Matthew Newton of Salem. Matt to some and Newt to others, but answer to both. Pressed aboard the *Poictiers 74*. Got put in here for not fighting. Enemy, I am. Dangerous enemy! Bad and dangerous! Now I'm President of the Lower Deck for a month. Come on forward." He nodded his head toward the bow. "We got a law—no Americans allowed aft of the main hatch when there's other Americans coming aboard."

"So you won't be robbed?" Marvin asked doubtfully.

"Oh dear, no!" Newton exclaimed. "We haven't anything to steal! It's so none of us'll lose his head and tell that fat snake Osmore what we think of him. If that should ever happen, he'd starve us to death, innocent and guilty alike."

He turned briskly and led them forward to the Americans.

## XVII

THREE hundred and twenty-seven Americans, Newton told them, were already quartered in the lower battery of the *Crown Prince,* and now there would be three hundred and fifty-one to pack in with their hammocks, like herring into a barrel. Above them, in the upper battery, he said, there were three hundred and nine Frenchmen, privateer officers for the most part; while below them, on the orlop deck, slept another two hundred and sixteen of the Frenchmen, known as *Raffalés* and *Manteaux Impériaux*—men wholly lost and abandoned, who sold their very food and rags for money with which to gamble, and so went naked, except for single cloths which swarmed with insects, even as the imperial mantle of Napoleon swarmed with bees.

"So here we are!" Newton said. "We can't spread down onto the orlop deck, because no decent men could live within sight or sound or smell of the *Raffalés;* and we can't spread up with the officers and the bourgeois, because no American can get along with 'em." He eyed Argandeau and grinned. "No offense," he said. "Maybe somewhere there are better Frenchmen than those we've got aboard this hulk, but here there isn't one we can trust: not even the captains. They're mean, all of 'em, in small ways."

"No offense, to me," Argandeau said quietly. "I am a little tired of the French equality that is no equality at all, and the French liberty that gives Frenchmen no liberty except that of remaining in English prisons all their lives. For a time I shall try being an American—Lucien Argandeau, of Boston. These French, they are what you say because they believe that all is fair in love and war, and they can prove to you that life is nothing else—war and love. It is of course true that the French are, as they say, the most logical of all people on earth; but recently I have come to think that the simple truth is preferable to French logic."

Newton stared at him doubtfully, shrugged his shoulders and led them to the main hatchway. They descended its single ladder to the upper battery deck, where dim distances were filled with the upflung arms of Frenchmen, hanging their hammocks; then went down another ladder to the lower battery deck, where the Americans, crouching beneath the massive planking of the deck above, crawled about with upturned faces, seeking the numbers chalked beside their hammock-hooks.

"It's too late for shifting hooks," Newton told them. "You'll have to sleep on the deck, between two lines of hammocks. You get a powerful lot of fleas down there, and it might be you'll be stepped on a few times, but you'll have better air. Tomorrow we'll squeeze these folks together, and you can sling your hammock amidships."

Marvin, close on Newton's heels, dragged his hammock as best he could through the shifting, jostling, noisy mass of men. Newton's hooks, he saw, were in a corner, near a barred porthole and a latrine; and even as Newton made fast his hammock-rope of spun yarn to the ceiling, a chain rattled loudly beside him. The port fell shut with an echoing thud. An angry roar of protest rose from the men around them.

"Drat 'em!" Newton cried. "You'd think they were afraid we'd chop ourselves in pieces and squeeze through the bars of the ports if they were left open after dusk!"

One by one the other ports along the lower battery slammed shut with a rattle of chains, and on that crowded mass of prisoners there descended a blackness that seemed to Marvin to thrust itself into his ears and press against his eyelids.

"Bring a light here!" Newton shouted. "There's twenty-four men got to sleep on the deck between No. 1 and No. 2 rows in the northwest quarter." A sulphur spunk flickered into blue flame near Marvin, then yellowed as a candlewick took fire.

"Get your hammocks in place," Newton urged the men from the *Olive Branch*. "Anybody caught with a light gets three days black hole on half rations, so all candles are doused if we have word from above that anybody's coming."

The hammocks, Marvin saw, formed a continuous layer of canvas between deck and ceiling, the edges of each hammock touching those on either side. Here and there, in this gigantic slit of a room, the dim light of a candle glowed palely. Stowed in their hammocks or squatting beneath them, the prisoners gabbled and shouted, the chorus of their voices striking on Marvin's ear like the muffled outcry of innumerable sea gulls.

" 'Tisn't anything you can't stand," Newton told him, thrusting his head over the end of his hammock to look down at him. "When I was pressed onto the *Poictiers*, me being supercargo of one of my father's brigs and fresh out of Harvard College, I thought I'd die in a week, what with the terrible food, and the slave drivers they called officers, and the workhouse mongrels in the crew. But my goodness alive! I got fat on it! I'd have got fat on it even if the captain hadn't made me his secretary. Give a man fresh air and a little work and enough food to fill his stomach, no matter what the food is, and he'll get along."

To Marvin it seemed as though the air had suddenly been heated by a giant stove. It had the feel, he thought, of an animal's breath—the breath of an enormous beast that had preyed on carrion—and with the thought, a black depression filled his brain, so that the realization of his lamentable state came fully to him. In his mind's eye he saw Morlaix once more, cold and drab at the end of the narrow estuary, and as distant as those far-off Chinese cities that seemed less real than dreams. It was, indeed, like a figure in a dream that Corunna trembled in a sad perspective before him; a figure remote and small, and surely beyond the reach of one who lay, like these unfortunates, half clothed, half fed, and only half alive.

"I suppose he will," Marvin responded at length, becoming aware that Newton was contemplating him curiously.

"Yes, he'll get along," Newton repeated. "Now, you take these men here on this deck; they're in prison for nothing, all of 'em. Every last one of 'em, nearly, is in the same box I am. They were hauled out of American ships by British press gangs before the war broke out, and made to serve aboard British cruisers—hell-ships, they're called by some, and 'hell-ship' is the proper word for 'em. When the war came on, they said they wouldn't fight against America. That's all—just wouldn't lay a gun against a Yankee craft. For that they catted us, the bloody lobsters; whipped us like balky horses; chopped our backs to hash, and threw us into these hulks, so that we came into 'em feeling pretty bad— pretty bad!"

Newton laughed mildly. "If we were felons, we'd have better treatment. If we'd murdered our mothers, we'd be put in a prison ship, same as this; but we'd have more room and better food. The British never put more than four hundred criminals in a prison ship; but we're more than criminals. We're prisoners of war. We won't fight for 'em; so they jam as many as nine hundred of us into each hulk—us who never did anything to 'em."

He laughed a laugh so mirthless that it ended in a cough. "Not yet we haven't done anything to 'em, but some day we will!"

He stared down at Marvin unwinkingly. "I give 'em credit!" he said. "They did what they could to keep us just barely breathing. They underfed us, so they could make money out of our food; and they gave us no clothes to wear if so be our clothes wore out; and worst of all, they took our air from us at night; but it hasn't killed us—not any of us! We're alive, all of us!"

He studied Marvin's face intently, and seemed, even, to measure his great body with his eyes. "It's easy to see you've had enough air and plenty of victuals. You look as if you could stand some punishment—swim ashore, even!"

"Swim ashore!" Marvin exclaimed thickly. So heavy had the air become that Newton's hammock, dimly seen above him, seemed to have descended on his chest. The mere act of breathing had grown to be a labor, and there was a ringing in his ears—a ringing broken by short silences that must, he told himself, be sleep, but that seemed more like lapses into a poisoned stupor. He shook his head to free it of the rank fog that enveloped him, and into his mind came the sallow face of Slade, its drooping eyelid giving it an expression of malicious triumph.

"Swim ashore!" he repeated. "I'd swim a hundred miles to get to shore and to France!"

He moved to rise to his feet, but his head struck the bottom of Newton's hammock and he fell back again.

Newton disappeared, and his hammock sagged as if he had lost interest in the subject. "Well," he said, "sweet dreams! I'll see you in the morning."

It seemed to Marvin, staring up with hot eyes into the dark, that he was caught in a tomb. Through the web of noises that surrounded him he could hear Argandeau close beside him, squirming and scratching.

"In some circumstances it is a terrible thing to be too alluring," Argandeau sighed. "I think all the fleas upon this *Crown Prince* hulk must be females, because I do not believe that anybody else but me is receiving attention from any of them."

At seven in the morning, the ports were raised and the gratings removed from the hatches; and Marvin, shouldering his hammock and bedding, followed his fellow prisoners up the ladders to be counted. In the dusk of the day before, the French prisoners had seemed miserable, but the naked creatures who came up into the brilliant sunlight of that October day were purely horrible. To Marvin, waiting his turn, after the counting, to stack his hammock on the covered platform over the main hatch, they had the look of vicious and repulsive animals as they scuttled down the ladders again to their den on the orlop deck.

Newton came to him through the press of prisoners. "Here," he told Marvin, "come up on the forecastle. I want to show you something."

Marvin, drawing Argandeau with him, followed the small swaggering figure in the overlong greatcoat as it bustled forward and mounted nimbly to the high forecastle, from which a reek of smoke rose through a score of pipes. Four marines in threadbare scarecrow uniforms growled glumly at Newton as he stopped before them to strike an attitude that had something of the heroic about it.

"Ho!" one of the marines exclaimed. "'Ere's the bloomin' hactor! Well, we ain't got nuffin' for yer! No tobaccer; no ole clo'es; no needles ner thread ner nails ner nuffin'!"

Clasping his hands before him, Newton raised sad eyes to the speaker's face. "Pity!" he whispered. "Have pity on a pore unfortunate woman turned into the snow with her two tender children"—he gestured dramatically toward Marvin and Argandeau—"by an unnatural and inhuman father, with never so much as a sup of rum or a measly piece of twist to hearten them against the bitter winter winds! Ah, my children! My pore, pore children! Ah, the pity of it, to see them waste before my very eyes for lack of the barest necessities of life!" He seemed to sob and droop.

One of the marines snorted. Another said angrily, "We ain't got none, I tell yer!"

"Ah, say not so!" Newton cried. He drew himself erect and thrust a hand into the bosom of his greatcoat. "None! None! In all this broad demesne, no single piece of twist! No twist in all this royal throne of kings, this sceptred isle, this earth of majesty, this seat of Mars, this other Eden, demi-paradise, this fortress built by Nature for herself against infection and the hand of war, this happy breed of men, this little world, this precious stone set in the silver sea, which serves it in the office of a wall or as a moat defensive to a house, against the envy of less happier lands,— this blessed plot, this earth, this realm, this England! No twist! Good God, no twist in England!" Passionately he struck his brow with his clenched fist, and staggered.

"Oh, 'Ell!" one of the marines growled. He drew a fragment of rope tobacco from his pocket and reluctantly handed it to Newton, who examined it suspiciously, dusted it against the front of his coat, and suddenly bit off the larger part of it. He returned the remainder to the marine and, deaf to his hoarse outcries, herded Marvin and Argandeau to the starboard bulwarks.

"Now we're all right," Newton said. "Those lobsters won't bother us, for fear of losing the rest of their tobacco. Still, it's best to talk low and keep your eyes open."

The three of them stared out over the wind-swept waters of the Medway. Ahead and astern extended the long line of soiled and misshapen hulks, each one attended, as though it had spawned during the night, by a small fleet of vegetable and supply boats. Along the main channel of the river, between the hulks and the windmills and neatly hedged fields, moved brigs and ships and sloops, bound to or from the docks of Chatham.

Newton turned an uncertain eye on Argandeau. "There's some situations that require frank speaking," he said to Marvin. "Now I've got nothing against this French friend of yours; but what I've got to say is important; and if anyone should be careless enough to blab, it might be the death of us."

Marvin nodded. "What you've got to say can be said before Argandeau or not at all. He's here himself because of helping me try to stay away. If I get out, he gets out too."

"All right," Newton said hastily. "All right! That's understood. Now look here." He spat negligently at a passing supply-boat. "Opposite this hulk, on shore, is a village. See it?"

"We see it," Marvin said.

"All right," Newton whispered. "That's Jillingum, that village is. Spelled 'Gillingham,' but pronounced 'Jillingum,' the way they do here. To the right of the village there's two windmills. In line with 'em, and fifty yards off shore, there's a mud bank. See it?"

Marvin nodded.

"That bank runs all the way along this reach, out of water most of the time. Sometimes only a little out. Could you swim that far at night in cold water—real cold water?"

"Easy," Marvin said.

"The mud in those banks is like glue," Newton remarked. "You go into it pretty near up to your middle. That's the trouble with getting to shore—if you swim as far as the banks, you're pretty tired, on account of having to carry things with you; so when you strike the mud, you can't get through it, sometimes. Sometimes, when the ports are opened in the morning, we see men in the mud, dead. The British leave 'em there all day—two days, sometimes—so they'll be a lesson to the rest of us." In a thoughtful voice, he added: "The crows eat 'em."

The three men stared silently at the square green fields and the slowly turning windmills, toy-like against the clear sky.

"Well?" Newton asked.

"Well what?" Marvin demanded.

"Do you think you could get through the mud?"

"Why, I'd have to," Marvin said.

"Men have got through it, no?" Argandeau asked.

Newton nodded. "Three out of five got through it a month ago—Americans. Frenchmen have got through it, but mostly they were new men—privateer captains. Tom Souville got through it four times, and reached France twice, but he was captured three times and brought back."

Argandeau laughed silently. His close-cropped black head wagged gently from side to side. "Tom Souville!" he exclaimed. "When I am a young man in Calais, I have taught Tom Souville tricks in swimming. There is nothing Tom Souville can do that I cannot do."

They were silent again, staring at the distant and harmless-seeming gray thread of the mud bank.

"There's one more thing," Newton said at length. "How much can you fight?"

Marvin looked thoughtfully at his knuckles. "I don't rightly know. I never had to fight very hard. What I've had to do has come easy."

Newton felt of his upper arm and appraised him carefully.

"Well," he said slowly, "well, I'll tell you. I'll tell you just how it is. It's a hard job to escape from these hulks—a dreadful chore! 'Tisn't as if you just escaped whenever you felt like it; you've got to have money, and you've got to protect yourself from informers, and you've got to be prepared, and you've got to have the good will of the rest of the prisoners, and you've got to have the permission of the governing committee, and you've got to be relieved of your prisoner duties. Then, when all those things have been arranged, you're obliged to go to work and cut your way out. It's the hardest work in the world! If you laid out on a topgallant yard night and day for a month, trying to hand a sail that's stiff with ice, and never got it handed, it wouldn't be as hard work as getting out of these hulks, even after you've got the permission and the money."

"My money was stolen when I came aboard last night," Marvin said. "How much money does it take?"

"Wait," Newton said. "I'm coming to that. Now I'll tell you how it is: I want to get out of this place! 'Tisn't that I can't stand the bad food and the bad air and the bad clothes or the bad Frenchmen. These bad Frenchmen, they're a joke! They're so eager to take advantage of us Americans that all you got to do is to give 'em an inch of rope and they'll hang themselves. See this overcoat?"

Marvin nodded.

"That's a French coat," Newton said. "They think I'm easy because I'm little and look worried when I gamble with 'em. The Frenchmen aren't anything as long as you watch 'em—not anything! What I can't stand is wanting to get at these English and not being able to! Listen!"

He took Marvin by the upper arms and seemed to shiver in the grip of a violent emotion. "Do you know why they take so many prisoners and starve us the way they do? It's because half of England's fattening on our hunger and nakedness and cold. The more of us they capture, the fatter England grows. Seventy-five thousand of us, French and Americans together, and the contractors take money for clothes we're supposed to get, but never do, and for food that's never fed to us! The commander of this ship, the drunken hog, fought to get the job! It pays him seven shillings a day, but he'll be a rich man in three years, hunting foxes in a red coat and talking about filthy Americans! I was secretary to a captain, I tell you, and I know what I'm talking about! I've got to get out of here! I'll blow up if I can't fight 'em!"

"I don't blame you," Marvin said thoughtfully, "but if it's as hard to escape as you say, you'd be better off, wouldn't you, to stop talking about it?"

Newton gripped the high bulwarks of the prison ship and

laughed exultantly. "Stop?" he cried. "Stop? Why, no! I've just started! I've been waiting for the right men! For the right men! It's my turn to go and you're the man I want to go with. You're strong and you're big. You'll make it, and if I go with you, I'll have no trouble. This man, too"—he whirled to poke Argandeau's arched chest—"he'd get through, and the Indian you brought aboard. There's nobody else aboard this hulk I'd risk it with. I don't think the others could make it. They're weak and hungry. Most of 'em are sick. Most of 'em have been in jail too long. You're different! When I saw you come aboard, it seemed to me you must be the man I've been waiting for ever since they threw me into this"—he laughed again—"this demi-paradise; this precious stone set in the silver sea; this England!"

Marvin looked quickly over his shoulder at the four marines, lounging at the forecastle rail; then stared intently at Newton.

The small man hitched up his long overcoat around him. "I'll tell you how it is," he said, and his crinkly yellow side whiskers seemed to quiver. "If you can lick a man as big as you are, and maybe a little bigger—if you've got the heart to take a pounding and give back better than you get—I can contrive for the three of you to have a chance to go. I can do it! There's only one stipulation, and that is that you take me." He shivered. "You're the man I've been looking for' Yes, sir, you'll make it!"

He hesitated, seeming to withdraw a little into his voluminous outer garment; then added, "Or you'll probably get killed trying."

Marvin drew a deep breath, but in spite of it, his voice trembled somewhat: "That's reasonable enough. Just show me who I've got to fight to get myself out of here."

# XVIII

Two of the long wooden benches in the lower battery had been dragged into the corner where Newton's hammock hung at night, and so arranged that they protruded from the corner in a narrow V.

At the point of the V sat Newton, flanked on each side by five committeemen. Two other committeemen sat on the deck, ten feet in advance of the point of the V; and to Marvin, who waited restlessly near them, they volunteered the information that they were thus stationed as pickets to warn away such prisoners as might be tempted to intrude on the committee's deliberations.

Nor was their office an idle one; for the deck was crowded with men, arguing, yammering, whistling and singing; some of them cutting soup bones into miniature planks for the making of ship models; some weaving delicate boxes from fragments of straw, or carving dolls and chessmen from beef knuckles; others patrolling the deck ceaselessly, offering for sale a desirable sleeping location, the butt of a candle or a thimbleful of grease for use in a lamp; still others trying to sell their services for the repairing of shoes or the mending of clothes. Among them moved emaciated, half-naked Frenchmen, prowling restlessly in search of unknown matters, or soliciting patronage for the gambling tables in the upper battery.

"Sheer off!" the pickets growled to all of them. "Sheer

off! Committee's in session for the good of the deck! Sheer off!"

Marvin, allowed inside the picket line by Newton's orders, heard Newton address the ten committeemen.

"There's several things to come before this meeting," he told them. "First is, what's to be done about getting some kind of answer out of the American agent? There's fifty-seven Americans next door to naked, and sixty-six without coats of any kind. By December there'll be two hundred without any clothes except rags so rotten that thread won't hold 'em together. Twelve hundred new prisoner suits were supposed to be delivered last month, the French say, but they say we'll never see 'em. Osmore and the contractors keep the money, and the clothes never even get made. If we can't get help from Beasley, we'll freeze, all of us."

"How many times has he been written to?" asked a sour-visaged man whose mouth was puckered as if from the eating of persimmons.

"The committees on this hulk have written him eighteen times since August fifteenth, Captain Taylor."

The committeemen moved restlessly on their benches, and it was Captain Taylor who broke the silence again: "If the contractor would buy back our fish allowance next fish day, we might get enough to put an advertisement in *Bell's Weekly Messenger,* requesting that he pay some attention to his fellow countrymen."

"That's all right," complained a man whose head and chest were enveloped in a hood of flour sacking, "only it appears to me this taxation business is getting kind of over-done. I don't feel like these men ought to be asked to give up any more food, not even those smoked herrings. They're about starved already; so starved that if they got took sick, with the doctor paying no attention to sick men, they'd die in a minute!"

"There ain't anybody can eat the fish, Henry!" Taylor objected. "The French, they say they marked some of 'em, so they can be recognized, and they been in use for seven years—delivered at three pennies and bought back for a penny."

"Maybe so," Henry admitted, and Marvin saw that his face had an unearthly whiteness to it—the whiteness, almost, of the belly of a flatfish. "Maybe so; only the next time we get 'em, you watch me eat mine! I'm getting so I can eat anything—even a newspaper that's been wrapped 'round a fish!"

"Yes," Newton interrupted, "and there's another thing. Our *Statesman* subscription runs out next week, and that means twenty-eight shillings a month for the paper and sixteen shillings a month delivery charges." He laughed bitterly. "Twenty-eight shillings a month! No wonder the English don't know anything. Knowledge comes too high! Anyway, we got to sell two days' fish and one day's bread to get that renewed, provided you want it renewed."

"Want it renewed!" one of the committeemen exclaimed. "We got to have it renewed. If there ain't any news nor anything to read, there won't be anything to talk about, and we might as well be dead."

"Newton," said sour-mouthed Captain Taylor thoughtfully, "how much of that sixteen shillings goes to Osmore?"

"Probably ten," Newton said promptly. "He might get fifteen. Even so, it's no use trying to do anything about it, because the one that tried to make trouble would get the black hole for two weeks. 'Tisn't worth it! Gosh! I'd rather give up all my fish forever than get two weeks black hole!"

"I move," said Henry, from the folds of his flour sacking, "that this committee communicate with Beasley in writing for the nineteenth time, and send a letter to the President of the United States saying that the American agent for prisoners of war in England does nothing to prevent said prisoners from being treated like some sort of weasels. I also move that enough of our fish be collected and sold by the president of this lower battery to obtain the *Statesman* for another month."

"You know there's no use writing to the President of the United States," Newton objected wearily. "There's no way of getting it out except through an escaping prisoner; and if it was ever discovered on an escaping prisoner, the whole committee'd get the black hole, and all the other prisoners would have their tools and trades seized and destroyed! I'd like to hear that motion restated."

Henry jumped to his feet, pulling at the flour sacking around his throat. "'Tain't right!" he exclaimed, his voice shaking as if with cold. "My God, you can't starve men and trample on 'em and murder 'em like this, and keep 'em gagged while you do it! You can't, I tell you! You——"

"Henry!" Captain Taylor said sharply.

Henry's voice persisted, shrill and trembling, "They treat us worse than animals, the damned rotten skunks! They can't keep me quiet! There's some way to get help—there's got to be!"

"Henry!" Captain Taylor shouted. He grasped Henry by the arm and pulled him down on the bench, shaking him roughly. "You're elected committeeman to set an example to the rest of these prisoners. See that you do it!"

Henry drew a deep and quivering breath, and the committeemen stared at their travesties of shoes, a strange and silent gathering.

"Well," Newton said at length, "we don't need it put in the form of a motion. I'll get the *Statesman* and tend to writing to Beasley again."

He cleared his throat and rose to his feet, drawing his long, ragged overcoat tight around him. "There's one more thing, and that's the question of who goes next." He eyed the committeemen significantly; and they, coming suddenly to life, fixed their eyes eagerly on him.

"We're wasting time," he went on. "Everybody wants to be next and nobody's willing to recognize the claims of anybody else. Meanwhile the food and the grease has accumulated without any work being done—no work at all! First thing you know, some of the Frenchmen, they'll get through and get stuck in the mud. Then they'll double the boat patrol, and Osmore'll have the planking sounded four times a day instead of once. This business ought to be settled, and settled now. Somebody's got to get letters out of this place, so we can get some money, and I say we ought to agree on somebody that can do it."

"I was one of the first Americans aboard this hulk!" Henry exclaimed. "You know it too! I ought to have first chance!"

"Henry," Captain Taylor said kindly, "you're wrong about this! Your spell in the black hole was pretty hard on you—harder'n you thought for, I guess. I notice you going up the ladder mornings, and you blow like a porpoise when you get on deck. You haven't been getting near enough food, and you'd never even reach the mud bank."

"I tell you I would!" Henry said. "I'd rather die trying, anyway, than not try at all!"

"Yes," Newton said, "maybe you would, but we wouldn't rather have you! Now you listen to me! I say the thing to do is to turn this over to a new man, fresh aboard."

Captain Taylor shook his head, and from the look of his mouth he might have been eating chokecherries. "No," he said, "you figure he'd be successful because he'd be strong and well fed; but you don't want to forget that these men here in this lower battery have got something almost as good as strength—they're dreadful mad! They hate the British worse than anything on earth!"

"That's what I say!" Henry exclaimed. "That's what I been trying to tell you! I'm dreadful mad, and I'd be as successful as anyone!"

Newton stared thoughtfully from Henry to Captain Taylor, who quickly lowered his eyes. "No," Newton said, "that isn't the way I figure. The way I figure is that it would be easier for everyone to agree on a new man—a man they never saw before—and I figure he'd be quicker doing the work—doing the cutting. 'Twouldn't be so hard for him to drive himself as it is for us, who've been breathing poison down here every night."

"They wouldn't agree," Captain Taylor said.

"I won't agree!" Henry stubbornly insisted.

Newton crouched down between the benches and looked up into the thin and sullen faces of the committeemen. "I had word from Osmore yesterday," he whispered. "Captain Stannage and the rest of his friends are coming aboard Saturday afternoon to get drunk again, ladies and all, damn the blowsy sluts!"

"Osmore sent you word?" Captain Taylor asked. "I suppose that means——"

"Yes!" Newton exclaimed. "It means he'll bring Little White with him. It means he aims to have a couple more of us hammered to a jelly, just to keep his friends in good spirits. Osmore told me to make the usual offer."

The committeemen growled angrily, and Captain Taylor shook his head. "I don't like it!" he said. "It's a bad business, this Little White! I wouldn't mind if it was Frenchmen he jellied, but it goes against the grain to hear him howling his black laughter and see him smashing our people until they're no more than raw meat, and they submitting to it for the sake of a twenty-shilling note!"

Newton laughed confidently, and his crinkly yellow side whiskers seemed to bristle, so that he had the eager look of a small dog on the trail of game. "All right! But what if Little White got smashed himself when he set out to do the smashing? What do you suppose Osmore'd say, and Stannage, and those wenches of his that have been tittering at us and looking at us all summer as if we were foxes in a cage? How'd you like to watch their faces while their little pet gets some of his own medicine?"

The committeemen stared at him with eyes that suddenly glittered. Captain Taylor looked over his shoulder at the tall figure of Marvin, standing behind the two lookouts; then turned back to Newton with a sour smile. "So that's it!" he said. "Well, it's a thing we'd be powerful glad to see, all of us, and it might put heart into us, what's more; but it appears to me you're expecting too much."

"What if I'm not?" Newton demanded. "What if he can do it? Would you be willing he should be the next in line? Would you agree on him?"

"What you so anxious about him for?" Henry demanded.

Newton turned on him. "My land! Can't you see? He'd be fighting for the chance to get out, and for the money to take advantage of the chance!"

"Bring him over here," Captain Taylor said.

In response to Newton's call, Marvin stepped over one of the benches and stood between the two rows of committee-men. "Daniel Marvin, of Arundel," Newton said. "His barque was cut out of Morlaix by the *Sparrow* schooner."

The committeemen eyed him almost carelessly, as though their interest in him was slight. "Marvin?" Captain Taylor asked at length. "Marvin? Seems to me there used to be a Marvin out of Arundel in the *Talleyrand* brig, trading in Havana."

"The *Talleyrand* brig was my father's."

"H'm!" Captain Taylor said noncommittally. "Was your father cut out of Morlaix?"

"No, sir. I was aboard the *Olive Branch* barque. Captain Dorman was master—Captain Dorman, of Arundel. He was killed in the doldrums, trying to fight off a British gun-brig. His daughter took command of the barque and brought her into Morlaix. She's alone there now."

The committeemen, Marvin felt, had lost all interest in him, for their glances at him were few and furtive.

"Seems to me I heard tell," Captain Taylor continued finally, "that the *Talleyrand* brig was so named because your father helped Talleyrand to buy land from General Knox."

"Yes, sir."

"What reason you got for thinking you could beat this Little White if you ain't ever seen him?" Henry demanded suddenly.

Marvin stared down at his knuckles and worked his left shoulder under his jacket. "I don't know that I could. They say he's a good fighter, and heavier than I am. Well, I've thought about him, and I believe I've figured out a way to offset his extra weight. I've figured out a new way to fight. Still, I wouldn't be interested in trying unless I knew I wasn't wasting my time."

"Wasting your time!" exclaimed another committeeman harshly. "Why, there's a standing offer of twenty pounds to the man that beats Little White! Little White's boss, Stannage, who's a friend of Osmore, made that offer. Twenty pounds to any prisoner that does it—twenty shillings to him if he tries and doesn't."

Marvin nodded. "I don't take much pleasure in fighting," he said. "I wouldn't risk it if there was nothing in it but the twenty pounds."

Newton seized Marvin's wrist and raised his arm. "Look at his reach!" he told them softly. "It's the first time we've had a man aboard with a reach like that! It's nearly as good as Little White's!"

"If you knew you weren't wasting your time," Captain Taylor reminded him, "you say you'd be interested in fighting this Little White?"

"Yes," Marvin said.

"Whether you could beat him or not?" Henry asked.

Marvin nodded. "I want to escape from this hulk," he said. "I want to get back to Morlaix. If nothing stands between me and getting there except beating this Little White, he'll have to kill me to beat me."

Newton laughed, a laugh so nervous that it was almost a titter. "There it is!" he exclaimed to the committeemen. "What more do you want than that?"

"What is it you figure we ought to agree to?" Captain Taylor asked; then puckered his mouth sourly.

"Nothing unreasonable," Marvin said. "I want to be allowed to escape, and I want the right to pick the men that work with me and go out with me—if it ever comes to that. Three others I'd want to take, no more; and all for good and sufficient reasons. I'd expect all four of us to receive the usual supplies and protection while working."

"You mean nobody else would be allowed to use your cutting, provided you're successful?" Henry demanded.

"Not for three nights—not until we've had time to get clear."

"I don't agree!" Henry declared angrily.

"Oh, here, here!" Captain Taylor said. "That's fair! If they get away, we can pass men through the bulkhead to answer to roll call, so the four won't be missed; and when the three days are up, everyone can go that has enough money and food. If one of the four should be caught, nobody else would have a chance anyway."

"Well——" said Henry weakly. He looked helplessly from one committeeman to another, his face chalk-white in the flickering light that danced across the ceiling from the reflection of the sun on the crinkled water of the Medway.

"Gorry!" exclaimed a committeeman in dogskin trousers, one of the legs being made of the skin of a red setter and the other of the skin of a coach dog. "Gorry! I say yes—whether he beats him or not!"

"No!" Captain Taylor protested sternly. "Not unless he beats him! If he's willing to try under those conditions, I say yes, and so does Henry. You do, don't you, Henry?"

"Yes," Henry said reluctantly, "I guess I do."

A glance at the other committeemen seemed to satisfy

Captain Taylor, for he nodded soberly to Newton and then rose from his bench to prod inquiringly at Marvin's biceps.

"In that case," Newton said briskly, "this meeting stands adjourned and I appoint the entire committee to demand a contribution of salt from each prisoner so we can get his hands in pickle with no loss of time."

## XIX

THE barge that drew up to the landing stage of the *Crown Prince* hulk at noon on Saturday seemed to blaze with color; for the oarsmen wore uniforms of blue flannel with the arms of the Stannages on breast and back in silver, gold and red; while in the cockpit sat Stannage himself, resplendent in a hussar's uniform, all gold and scarlet. Around him clung a group of damsels in silks, furs and feathers—damsels whose conversation seemed to Marvin, as he peered over the bulwarks at them, to consist largely of shrill laughter and shriller screams.

Between Stannage's knees crouched an enormous brown dog, thin and yellow-eyed, that panted constantly despite the chill wind that blew across the Medway, and cast longing looks over one side of the barge and then over the other. Close behind him stood a towering, smiling negro, whose noisy laughter ran like an undercurrent beneath the high-pitched merriment of the captain's gentle companions, and whose Eastern splendor dimmed the finery of the others. On his head was perched a vast turban of yellow satin, decorated with a tall plume held in place by a glittering bauble seemingly made of pearls and diamonds; beneath his short jacket of crimson satin a broad sash of gold cloth shone dully against the velvety black of his skin; and crimson satin trousers, voluminous enough, Marvin was sure, to make a dozen potato sacks, hung to his ankles, where they were fastened by tight gold bands.

"There he is!" Newton said. "There's Little White! What you think of him, Dan?"

Marvin shook his head. "Why," he said, "he looks like a handy man to have around a pivot gun or a galley stove, provided he got a rap from a belaying pin every few minutes to remind him where he belongs."

Newton nodded. "That's something he hasn't had in some little time. These people over here, they're all excited over Molineaux, the American negro who fought Tom Cribb. In consequence, they can't see a black man a little bigger than usual without thinking he's a fighter, and making a pet of him."

Cackling hilariously, Little White, evidently at his master's bidding, leaned over and took one of the damsels beneath the arms as though she had been a doll, held her for a moment over the side of the barge, so that she screamed and kicked like an excited child; then deposited her on the landing stage and spanked her briskly to start her up the gangway.

Stannage, a gaudy figure in his scarlet, fur-trimmed hussar's jacket, laughed as heartily at the playfulness of his dusky favorite as did any of the jeering prisoners that peered down at him from the bulwarks.

Marvin moved uncomfortably. "Why," he said suddenly, "this Stannage ought to have his face washed and be put to bed! He's only a child! He's never a captain—not at his age!"

"Oh, isn't he?" Newton exclaimed. "Well, he is, and he's more than a child! He's an idiot—the idiot son of rich idiots; so his family bought him a captaincy to get him out of the way. It's an old English custom! There's regiments over here officered entirely by idiots and children whose places have been bought for 'em. You can do anything with money in England; there's no place that's not for sale—church, state, army or navy."

Marvin laughed. "I guess they're not so bad as that!" he said. "If you're trying to make me madder at them than I am, you don't need to—not by lying about 'em."

"Lying?" Newton cried. "Lying? Why—well, wait till you know 'em! Lying! It was only a couple of years ago that the Duke of York was helping Mary Anne Clarke to sell any job in England to the highest bidder! The King's son and a bawd! It's no use having merit in England, not unless you have money along with it; and if you have no money, you're no better than a criminal! They pressed me into their damned navy, and I know 'em, and I'm glad I do, because it isn't Nature for people like that to win wars from people like us. That's mighty small consolation to a man who's buried in the hulks! Mighty small, but better than nothing!"

The boyish Stannage, looking petulant, came slowly and awkwardly up the companionway, dragging his enormous and reluctant brown dog; while Little White, crowding close behind with baskets, boxes and cloaks, rolled his eyes defiantly at the prisoners who watched him.

Argandeau, beside Marvin, sighed heavily. "It is well that I understand which is the master and which is the man," he said, "because if I did not, I might think that the smaller one was brought here by the black one for our amusement."

He watched the two gayly caparisoned figures mounting to the quarter-deck from the throng of emaciated, tattered scarecrows that packed the waist; then tapped Marvin on the arm. "In those baskets," he reminded him, "there is wine and fine food and yet more wine that they will be two hours in consuming. Two hours is no great time, so you must come now and have your dinner—two rotten carrots and a biscuit palpitating with weevils."

Marvin, climbing the ladders from the lower battery to the upper deck, mounted two hours later into a tumult so violent that the hulk seemed to shudder, as at the roaring of a storm—seemed almost to be sinking in a sea of sound.

The deck itself had become an amphitheater, and every exposed part of it, save for the quarter-deck and a square inclosure in front of the break in the poop, was massed with ragged, excited prisoners. There were prisoners clinging like ants to the two stubby signal masts; prisoners ranged in a triple tier along the high bulwarks; prisoners hanging like swarming bees against the face of the forecastle. All of them, wedged immovably in their places though they seemed to be, had freed their arms to shake a fist at the inclosure beneath the poop, so that the whole dreary hulk had the appearance of fluttering and vibrating, while from nine hundred throats there came an angry and derisive screaming.

In the center of the inclosure, set off by ropes from the close-packed prisoners who crouched around it, strutted the towering crimson form of Little White; and from the continuous rapid movement of his grinning lips as well as from the expression of rage on the faces of the prisoners closest to him, Marvin knew he was making game of them. From time to time he turned and looked up to the baby-faced hussar captain, standing at the rail of the quarter-deck with Lieutenant Osmore, and thence to the chattering women, who now sat comfortably, wineglasses in their hands, on either side of the hulk commander and their host. There was pride and almost admiration in the smiles they gave him; and even as Marvin, preceded by Newton and followed closely by Argandeau, forced his way from the main hatch toward the ring, a woman's gayly colored silk scarf floated downward from the quarter-deck and was deftly caught by Little White—caught and flaunted proudly in the faces of the howling prisoners.

At the sight of Marvin, crawling under the ropes of the ring with the small and heavily overcoated Newton, Little White ceased his posturing and stared intently at the tall American; then, catching his eye, he thrust out his lower jaw and grimaced horribly, his mouth spreading outward so that he seemed to have the face of an ape.

Marvin stared hard at him with a horrid fascination and shivered perceptibly, whereupon the roar with which the prisoners were greeting their champion's appearance became enfeebled with misgiving and died pathetically away.

On the quarter-deck two marines thumped on the drums slung at their sides. Lieutenant Osmore placed his right hand between the first and second buttons of his coat, frowned portentously and raised his left hand in a gesture of command. Over the hulk there fell an uneasy silence.

"You know the terms of this exhibition!" Osmore said in his shrill, domineering voice. "Captain Sir Rafe Stannage has kindly consented to permit his attendant—ah—White—ah—Little White—to display once more that art unknown to more—ah—effeminate, more cruel and more cowardly peoples—ah—the art sprung from British hardihood and love of fair play—ah—the art of pugilism!" He inclined his head to Stannage, who was staring as though baffled at a leather strap in his left hand; and from the throng of prisoners there instantly rose a roar—short, sharp and profoundly ironical.

"You know the terms!" Osmore repeated. "Any fighting or opprobrious remarks among the prisoners will result in two days black hole for the offenders. The rules of the exhibition will be Broughton's rules. Each round to be considered ended on the fall of one or both contestants. After each fall, each man to be brought to scratch within thirty seconds or be deemed—ah—beaten. No falling without the striking of an honest blow. Challenger to receive one pound for his brave attempt, and if successful—ah, ha-ha!—if successful, twenty guineas!" Osmore chuckled and cleared his throat importantly.

"The challenger of—ah—White—of Little White—ah—is"—he drew a small paper from his coat and peered at it—"is one Marvin, of Arun-del." He scanned the paper again, frowning, and repeated the word "Arun-del."

Stannage stepped to his side and looked over his shoulder. "Arun-del? He's an Englishman?"

Osmore frowned severely down at Marvin, who stood patiently at one side of the ring, his ear inclined to the prolonged whisperings of Newton. "Arun-del!" Osmore exclaimed, striking the paper with his hand. "This says Arun-del! There's no Arun-del in America!"

Marvin nodded. "A-rundle, it's pronounced."

"Never heard of the place! Where is it?" Osmore asked.

"Where?" Marvin said, looking up at him thoughtfully. "It's no great distance from Bunker Hill and Saratoga."

A whisper arose from the men crouched at the ringside, a small dry titter that spread through the dense masses of prisoners as ripples spread from the dropping of a rock in a pond.

"Silence!" Osmore screamed, stamping his foot. "Silence!" He stared balefully from one side of the crowded deck to the other, until the unseemly tittering had died away. "Save your damned Yankee impertinence for another occasion or I'll clap you below hatches, all of you! You want to see this fight, and you'll behave yourselves or not see it! I'll say this, too: It's a lesson you need, all of you—you Frenchmen with your kicking and knife sticking—you Spaniards and Italians with your backhanded stilettos and daggers—you Yankees with your tomahawks and scalping tricks! This is to do you good! You people need all the lessons you can get in the cool courage, the restraint, the skill and the endurance with which the noble art of boxing has filled the breast of every true-hearted Englishman and made the British nation the mistress of the seas!"

There was a patter of applause from the young women seated at the quarter-deck rail.

Newton cleared his throat apologetically. "I'd like to ask a question, sir," he said. He stared up at Osmore from beside Marvin, as harmless as a downy chicken peering from under its mother's wing.

"Be quick about it!" Osmore ordered.

"We hope you'll not permit any of your Lancashire up-and-down fighting, sir," Newton urged. "We wouldn't like to see our man killed or disabled by kicking or gouging when on his back."

Osmore narrowed his eyes at Newton; then swept them quickly over the throng of ragged men beyond. There was a small trembling among them, and a sound like the vague shadow of stifled laughter.

Osmore's face darkened; he opened his lips as though to rebuke Newton; then seemed to cogitate. "Broughton's

Rules!" he snapped at length. "You heard me say Broughton's rules! Get your man ready! Surgeon Rockett has kindly consented to fill the difficult post of referee."

He read again from his paper. "Corporals Quigg and Spratt will act for—ah—White—for Little White. For Marvin, Newton and Argandeau."

Two red-coated marines popped into the ring beside Little White, who straightway leaped into the air, crowing like a rooster and shedding jacket, trousers, waistband and turban in a whirl of scarlet and gold. Beneath these garments he wore small clothes of the brightest green, fastened waist and knee with yellow bands. Above them his naked torso gleamed in the pale October sunlight like polished brown wood—wood in which knots and lumps swelled unexpectedly on shoulders, arms and back. His forehead sloped back abruptly from his broad flat nose, rising to a peak at the top of his head—a peak topped with a fuzzy semicircle of hair that had the look of a thick rope of crinkly black feathers extending over his skull and fastened to his ears on either side.

He continued to crow and leap as Newton helped Marvin to strip off his shirt, the huge brown hands flapping like wings against the green small clothes; and even his eyes, fastened on Marvin, were black and hard as those of a giant rooster.

Marvin, resting against the ropes between Newton and Argandeau, had the look of shrinking from his black antagonist. The pearly whiteness of his chest and arms might have been thought to be the effect of fear, and the long smooth muscles hidden beneath that gleaming skin seemed, by comparison with the knobby brown bulges of Little White, almost weak and helpless. Yet it was strange but true that whereas Little White seemed to have shrunk somewhat with the removal of his gaudy plumage, Marvin seemed to have become larger.

Down from the quarter-deck came the ship's surgeon, his chin held high by his black stock, and a huge watch clutched in his hand. He crawled beneath the ropes, poked Marvin in the chest with a finger like a marlinespike, stared curiously into the yellowish eyes of Little White; then stooped over with some difficulty and, on the deck in the middle of the ring, chalked a square with three-foot sides.

"Now," he said, "if you're ready, my lads?" He popped out under the ropes. His hand rose and fell; and with that Newton hustled Marvin to one side of the chalked square, while one of the marines ran with Little White to the opposite side, so that the four men hung in a knot at the center of the ring.

The shouting of the prisoners had fallen away to a breathless hum, and through the hum rose a hoarse voice, a voice so rough and rasping as to sound less like a voice than like the scraping of a file on the strings of some vast violin. It was the voice of Little White. "Kiss mah han'," he growled. "Ah kill Americans wiff it."

Newton and the marine ran back to their sides of the ring and dodged beneath the ropes.

Little White threw himself into fighting position. His left foot and his left arm were thrust well forward; his right arm guarded his stomach and lower chest; his upper body tipped back so far that if he had raised his eyes, they would have looked straight upward into infinity. Standing so, he laughed, a deep, roaring, hyena-like laugh; for it was plain to be seen, from Marvin's posture, that Marvin was as ignorant of fighting as he was afraid of Little White. He had cramped himself sideways, his left shoulder turned in front of his body. His right foot, instead of resting squarely and flatly on the ground as a supporting platform for a blow, was poised on its toe, as, indeed, was his left foot as well. Both his knees were weakly bent, as though it was in his mind to turn at any moment and run like a coward from his powerful black opponent.

Roaring with laughter, Little White shuffled forward toward Marvin, who slipped off to one side. Roaring still, Little White shuffled after him, only to have his opponent slip off to the other side.

Nor was Little White the only one to roar. The deck of the hulk seemed almost to erupt with angry shouts of "Fight! Fight!" while Osmore, Stannage, the six women in their glowing silks and satins, and even the drummers at each side of the quarter-deck, hung far out over the rail to shout, "Fight! Fight!"

They moved around the ring, Little White shuffling forward and Marvin slipping off to left or right before him. Little White lashed out with a left-handed blow that cut a slit in Marvin's ear, and got from Marvin in return a veritable baby's tap—a breath of a hit, that touched Little White's eye and was gone, like a vagrant butterfly. Again, with the evident intention of ending the fight before it had fairly begun, Little White sprang forward, his fists driving like battering rams for Marvin's mark—that triangular-shaped patch beneath his ribs and above his belt. There was the crack of a hit, but it was the impact of a black fist against a forearm; the mark itself had moved away.

The prisoners groaned and hissed. One of them, close to Newton's corner, aimed a jab at the elusive Marvin through the ropes. "Stand up to him!" he bellowed. "Get out o' there if you can't stand up to him!"

Newton rapped the bellower sharply on the forearm with the edge of his hand. "Close your face!" he said. "Can't you see it's a new way of fighting?"

The near-by prisoners howled their disgust. "Be damned to a new way of fighting!" "It's a new way of running, and a rotten one!" "Make him show what he's good for!" "Make him fight!"

Minutes passed. Blood trickled from Marvin's ear; there were red welts along his ribs from the glancing blows of Little White's knuckles; but still he slipped off to one side or to the other, and shrank away before the black man's advance.

Anger had replaced Little White's hoarse hilarity. "Stan' still!" he growled, following Marvin's erratic twistings and turnings. "Isn't one of you Americans got bottom enough to stan' up to a fighter? Light somewheres, you dirty Yankee yaller bird, so's I can knock you halfway up to Lunnon!"

To Little White's amazement, Marvin laughed. "You can't fight!" he told the black man. "You can't even throw a cross-buttock."

Little White lowered his head and charged. To the prisoners, raging at Marvin's tactics, it seemed, and was indeed the case, that Marvin, at this quick movement, stood his ground instead of slipping off to right or left. As Little White's head shot past his body, Marvin's fist came up against his opponent's throat with a sound like the impact of a dead codfish against a plank. In another instant the black man's arms were around him and the first fall had gone to Little White with a cross-buttock.

Their seconds were on them as they sprawled to the deck, hoisting them to their feet and hurrying them to the ropes for a rest of thirty seconds. Argandeau held Marvin on his knee while Newton, gabbling in his ear to make himself heard above the din of the prisoners, sponged the blood from his face and chest.

"A thirteen-minute round!" Newton told him excitedly. "A thirteen-minute round, and you're barely scratched! You're like a Baltimore schooner sailing rings 'round a frigate! He can't touch you! Keep it up, Dan! Your way's the best way, no matter what these fools say! Don't listen to 'em! He can't fight! He's a flipper! I told you he was a flipper! He thinks he's fighting like Molineaux, but he isn't! He's just a big black chunk of sour beef! He hits at half arm and keeps his elbows close to his body, and he'll keep doing it until he thinks he's caught you! Then he'll imitate Molineaux again and try to chop you, and you've got him! You've got him anyway! That was a beauty—a beauty! Right in the whistle! Right in the apple! He thinks he's swallowed a hen's hind foot! Oh, oh! He's fat! He's puffy! And he thinks it was an accident! He thinks he ran into it! Look at him gulp! Look at him watch you!"

Marvin glanced across at Little White, seated on the knee of a red-coated marine while another marine dabbled water on the back of his neck. There was, Marvin saw, a soft smoothness to the black skin above the green small clothes instead of the solid wall of corrugated muscle that should have been there; and the soft smooth surface rose and fell hurriedly. Conscious of Marvin's scrutiny, Little White blinked his small eyes, cautiously stretched his neck; then thrust out his mouth in an apelike grimace.

"Keep away from him!" Newton continued. "Keep out of his way until he's careless! Then you got him! Then you got him good! Remember what I told you!"

"Time!" the referee shouted.

Little White shuffled to the chalked square, falling into a fighting position so exaggerated that he seemed on the verge of tumbling backward. Marvin came less quickly to the scratch, and in the same cautious manner that had so enraged his fellow prisoners in the previous round—with his left shoulder thrust forward and his body bent as though he were torn with the simultaneous desire to advance and to run away.

Little White's hands revolved rapidly and he pawed the deck with an enormous foot. "Stan' up!" he commanded hoarsely; then coughed and cleared his throat and coughed once more. "Stan' up, you ole tabby cat!"

He lurched forward to hurl murderous blows at Marvin, who shrank before him, ducking and dodging. Again and yet again Marvin's left fist flicked out, touching Little White lightly at the corner of the eye, and so faint and ineffectual were the blows that the groans and the jeering of the prisoners changed suddenly to a burst of laughter. Even Little White laughed, though he coughed when he did so, and at the corner of his eyes a smear of blood showed bright against his brown skin.

"Jes' a moment and I gits you!" he said. His voice seemed choked and strangled, and when he had spoken, he wheezed. His shuffle became swifter; and as it did, there came a hesitation into Marvin's movements—a momentary catch, as though he had faltered in deciding how to turn.

Little White bellowed hoarsely; his right hand rose high

above his head, and like a flail his long black arm swept down toward Marvin's neck. Instead of slipping away, Marvin moved closer. His right fist flashed upward to land upon the brown V below the ribs. The breath went out of Little White with a hoarse hoot. He tilted suddenly forward, so that his chopping blow lost its force and landed uncontrolled against Marvin's shoulder. Marvin's left fist drove once more against the negro's thick throat, partially straightening the black man, and once more his right fist whipped into the unprotected stomach that still quivered and jerked from the first unexpected blow. Little White clung to him with one arm—clung and fell backward, dragging Marvin with him; and the two of them plunged to the deck amid a turmoil of frenzied shouting such as might have come from ten thousand madmen, rather than from nine hundred half-fed prisoners.

Newton, dragging Marvin back to his seat on Argandeau's knee, shook like a shivered sail; and his voice trembled even more than his hands. "You got him! You got him!" He rubbed the blood from Marvin's cheek and ribs, and laughed almost hysterically. "It worked the way you said it would, and you got him!"

"Time!" bellowed Surgeon Rockett, above the howling of the prisoners.

Argandeau pushed Marvin toward the chalked square; and as Little White, coughing and blinking, stepped warily to the other side, Marvin snapped his left fist toward the black man's face. The semblance of timidity and indecision was gone from him, and he had the look of one who has come to the end of long waiting. Yet this look went from his face quickly enough; for as he led with his left hand, Little White half turned, threw up his head and fell to the floor.

In the same moment his second leaped at him, hustled him to his feet and dragged him back to the ropes.

Marvin, staring helplessly at Little White, felt Newton take him by the arm. "Wait!" Marvin said. He turned to the surgeon, who stood pompously outside the ring, staring at his turnip-shaped watch. "Wait! He fell without a blow! That's no fall! I didn't hit him!"

The surgeon looked up at him slowly. "You didn't what?" he asked.

"You heard me!" Marvin said. "I didn't touch him! Get him back here and make him fight!"

The surgeon laughed fatly. "You're a fine one to talk about fighting—you who did nothing but run for half an hour!"

"For God's sake!" Marvin shouted. "You——"

He stopped, staring at the pompous surgeon; then hurried to where Argandeau waited for him with outthrust knee.

Argandeau patted his shoulder, soothing him. "Remember; I have told you about these people!" he said.

The surgeon had gone to contemplating the face of his watch again. "A minute and a half he's given him!" Newton said. "Well, Dan; you do your best!"

"Time!" said the surgeon.

Marvin ran to scratch. Little White, breathing more regularly, glowered malevolently at him. Marvin grinned amiably. "You're licked, black boy! You're going to get hurt for playing tricks!"

Little White coughed and growled. Marvin slapped his outstretched left arm, a slap that tilted him forward; and as he tilted, Marvin's left fist landed wetly against his eye. Little White coughed and groaned. With hamlike hands he hammered Marvin's ribs. Marvin staggered and laughed;

then rushed at Little White and drove him backward with a succession of blows to the stomach. He fell against the rope of the ring and bounced upright. When Marvin hit him in the throat and again in the stomach, he slipped to one knee and clung to the ropes.

"Foul!" he croaked hoarsely. "He bit me!"

Marvin caught him by the fringe of hair atop his head, dragged him to his feet and drove his fist against his throat. The negro fell heavily to the deck, made vague swimming motions with his hands, and then lay still.

"Foul! Foul!" shouted Osmore and Stannage.

The pompous surgeon popped through the ropes. "Foul!" he said, brandishing his watch in Marvin's face. "The man was down!"

"No foul! No foul!" screamed the prisoners.

"No!" Marvin shouted. "Both knees and at least one hand on the floor, or the man's not down, and you know it! They're your own rules! He's down now, but he wasn't when I hit him. Don't look at me! Look at your watch, you fat swab!"

He ran to Argandeau's knee. The marine came through the ropes and dragged Little White to his corner. A hundred hands fluttered over Marvin, patting his head, his back, his thighs.

A breathless silence came upon the prisoners while they waited for the passing of the thirty seconds at whose end, according to Broughton's Rules, each fighter must either toe the mark once more or acknowledge defeat. Through this silence could be clearly heard the sound of Newton's hands, slapping and kneading Marvin's arms, and of his reiterated whisper—"He'll never make it, Dan! He'll never make it! He'll never make it! He'll never make it!"

The surgeon pushed the watch in his pocket. He leaned over to look at Little White; then stared venomously at Marvin. "Time!" he said slowly. "Time!"

Marvin walked to the chalk mark in the center of the ring. He stood there alone. In the opposite corner lay Little White. Marvin, watching him, saw one black eyelid flutter. The marine pulled at the negro's arm. He just lay there.

On the quarter-deck a woman screamed; and as if the scream had been a signal, the hulk became a bedlam of cursing, uproarious prisoners.

Newton, uttering unintelligible sounds, clambered through the ropes to throw his arms around Marvin's neck. Argandeau, tears streaming down his cheeks, embraced them both. "We win!" he blubbered. "Ah, my God! My God! I am excite! I choke! I die! We win! We win!"

Above them Stannage shook his fist at the prostrate form of Little White. "I've been sold!" he cried in his girlish voice. He leaned over the rail to point an accusing finger at Marvin. "You had no right to win! There was something wrong with it, but I don't know what! You don't deserve your twenty guineas, and I've a mind not to give them to you!" He stared about him indecisively, as if to seek support. Finding none, he fumbled in his pocket, tied some coins in a handkerchief and tossed them petulantly to Marvin; then turned suddenly to Osmore.

"Here," he said. "Where's my dog? I've been wanting to ask you all through the fight. Look at that!" He held up the empty strap and dangled it in Osmore's face.

Osmore stared at it blankly. "Your dog?" he asked. "Your dog is gone? When did you see him last?"

"After dinner," Stannage said. "One of the ladies was feeding him a sweet."

"What? You were foolish enough to let that dog run loose on this ship!" Osmore cried aghast. "I told you a week ago we had more than a dozen of these men sick from eating rats!"

Captain Stannage turned pallidly toward his six fair friends, whose sympathetically dismal exclamations pierced the air, yet went all unheard, lost under the thunder of cheering from the ragged deck below.

## XX

ALTHOUGH an early afternoon sun slanted through the heavily barred ports of the lower battery, the entire deck was a turmoil of sound, and the noisiest portion of that cavernous place was the corner in which Newton's hammock hung at night. In that corner was a school of fencing in which three pairs of fencers lunged and panted, their blades rasping and their clumsy shoes a-clatter. In that corner, too, between the fencers and the ports, a dozen men from Kittery and Portsmouth worked with files and saws, fashioning tiny planks from soup bones. As they worked, they argued; and their arguments were deafening.

Behind this human screen four men were stretched upon the deck, close to the planking of the vessel's side. Sweat dripped from their foreheads and cut furrows through the grime that smeared their cheeks. Their breathing was labored and their work unceasing.

One, an Indian, drew a small bow backward and forward. The string of the bow was looped around a drill, a small drill made from a broken fencing foil.

Marvin, beside the Indian, held this rude tool tight against the side of the prison ship, pressed there by the bottom of a bottle. The bowstring, moving rapidly, turned the drill, so that it bit slowly into the oak.

Argandeau, strangely cramped, toiled with a saw made from a barrel hoop, joining the holes already drilled. The handle of the saw was a ball of rags; and the hand with which the Frenchman clutched it was bloody.

Between and beneath these three moved Newton, filling holes and cuttings with a mixture of grease and oak dust.

At two o'clock that night a bitter wind slapped the salt waves of Gillingham Reach against the bends of the *Crown Prince* hulk. The hulk strained at her moorings and rolled a little, as if uneasy with the stirrings of the miserable freight within her. A shivering sentry paced the narrow gallery three feet above the water. He came reluctantly from behind the shelter of the stern, peered with moist eyes at the distant lights of Gillingham, bawled a hoarse "All's well!"; then vanished silently, seeking the protection of the hulk's high galleries.

Out from the blackness of the misshapen vessel there sprouted a splotch of paleness—a splotch that lengthened into the naked figure of a man; a figure smeared with grease and humpbacked with a bundle lashed high on its shoulders. Almost like a wisp of wind-blown fog, it wavered outward from the hulk and disappeared. Three other figures followed, wraithlike, to plunge without a sound into the dark river. The sentry reappeared, snuffling. He peered quickly at the inky water and the bulging sides of the hulk. "All's well!" he droned, his voice trembling with the cold; then, huddled turtle-like in his greatcoat, he shuffled hastily sternward to escape the wind's shrewd blast.

The frigid chop of the Medway stung the faces of the four swimmers. The swift current wrenched at their legs and pressed like violent icy hands against their chests. Close together, they swam onward into the endless blackness that stretched before them and weighed them down. White gouts of foam rose angrily to leap at their twisted mouths.

A wave washed over Newton's head. His arms thrashed and the quick current bore him upstream. He cried a strangled cry, and choked. Marvin's voice was close beside him—a strained and harried voice: "Easy . . . almost there . . . almost. . . . Easy!" Newton groaned and moved forward slowly, half in the shelter of Marvin's great body.

The piercing wind flagged and lulled, leaped at them half-heartedly and lulled again. The angry chop lessened and slapped less fiercely at their numb lips. The water stilled; the current slackened—almost drew them shoreward. Marvin stood upright, caught at Newton and held him. He hung limp in Marvin's arms, coughed weakly and gagged. A smell of cold decay hung over them. There was a faint splashing near at hand. Half swimming and half crawling, Argandeau came up to them, with Steven close behind. In Marvin's arms, Newton groaned and coughed again. The other three stared, panting, at the dim and noisome mud.

Newton stood upright at last, swaying and shuddering in the shallows. Marvin eyed him, then turned from him abruptly and made for the shore. At the water's edge he sank knee-deep in ooze. Gripped by it, he lurched from side to side in a slow and clumsy caper. Laboriously he withdrew one foot and then the other; and with the effort there was a sound of sucking and the issuing of a stench, dank and horrible. He lost his balance, pitching forward against the foul gray slope. His arms, thrust downward for support, disappeared; and when he struggled to his feet, the arms were black with slime. His face was black, and his body as well. He threw himself flat on the bank and wallowed forward, spiderlike. Huddled on the slope, he gasped an order to Argandeau, who laid hold of Newton and hurled him roughly upward. Marvin reached backward, caught Newton by the hair and dragged him to his side. "Move!" Marvin told him hoarsely, his voice as thick as though it rose from muddy depths. "Move or you'll sink!" They squirmed and rolled on the yielding, quaking mud like two hurt animals.

Argandeau and the Indian floundered upward through the slime to lie, spent, beyond them. Marvin gained his feet, heaving at Newton's frail body. Argandeau reached back a hand, and between them they dragged and pushed their small companion over the crest of the slope and to the flat surface of the bank—a surface that shook like jelly and sucked hungrily at their naked bodies.

This trembling mass was soft as glue, seeming to have no substance. In it their feet sought vainly for a hold, and while they sought, the surface clutched their upper legs and drew them deeper.

Gripped by this noxious treacle, the four black figures reeled forward in a wavering and dreadful dance. Gasping, they wrenched themselves half free, only to sink again and on the instant strive once more for partial freedom. They groaned and sweated in the bitter wind. Mud filled their eyes and mouths, so that each one moved in blackness, seeing nothing and hearing only faintly the rattle of his labored breathing. They lurched and fell and rose; and with each move, the slime in which they groveled was vocal, seeming to smack its lips and slobber at their agony.

There was a flame in Marvin's chest—a flame that stabbed and crackled. Dark fears smoked upward from it, and the weakness of despair. Through its cracklings Newton's thin voice reached him—a voice shrill with terror. "Dan!" it called, "Dan! Wait! I can't—can't——"

Marvin floundered toward the voice and got his hands on Newton. "Stuck!" Newton gasped. "Can't make it!"

Panting, Marvin dragged at the smaller man, who retched. The mud held him. Marvin groaned and heaved, and Newton, struggling weakly, came slowly out. Marvin's legs churned in the stinking ooze. He fell backward in it, pitching Newton over him in his fall.

Here was the end, he thought. His leaden arms, reaching for support, found only slimy thickness, into which his weary legs and body settled. Cold sickness caught his throat. Small homely pictures of his youth swam slowly through his brain: Himself, a boy once more, bathing his scrawny body in a lamp-lit kitchen beneath his mother's watchful glance; a nest of helpless field mice on the hot Arundel marshes; a sweaty minister with uplifted eyes, droning hell and endless torment, and in a near-by pew Corunna Dorman, eyeing him aslant through fingers that devoutly screened her face. Up through these little pictures came the face of Slade, staring and smiling in sardonic mirth.

In desperation Marvin reared and twisted. Uncomprehendingly he heard a splashing near at hand. Fingers clawed his ear; clutched at his arm and slipped; then clutched again. Marvin wallowed forward, hung on a sloping surface and rolled heavily into the water of the lagoon that lay between the mud bank and the meadows of Gillingham.

The distant hulks bulked against the paleness of the coming dawn. In the heart of a haystack on a field in Kent lay four exhausted men, sick from their efforts, but for the moment safe.

# XXI

A BLIND Hindu, his face shadowed by a soiled and bulbous turban and his bare brown shoulders protruding from the folds of once-white cotton in which he was swathed, sat by the dusty roadside on the outskirts of the small Channel town of Ramsgate, while his ragged attendant, a sharp-nosed, tow-headed youth, directed the attention of passers-by to the brown man's peculiar ability.

"'E kin mike fire wiff nuffin but a bit o' string an' a toofpick! Couple o' coppers, friends, fer to see a sight you'll be a-tellin' your children abaht fer the next 'undred years!"

A few citizens of Ramsgate stood stolidly before the two, seemingly hopeful that the requisite pennies would be donated by others. Two sentries, evidently stationed on the edge of the town for the inspection of strangers, peered over the shoulders of the citizens.

A provision cart, laden with straw and live chickens, drew up, creaking. One of the slouching countrymen on the driver's seat tossed two pennies into the dust at the brown man's feet. The sharp-nosed youth seized them; then shook the Hindu's bare brown arm.

"'Ere!" he cried. "Git it aht!"

The brown man, fumbling in his cotton swathings, produced a small board, a pointed stick and a diminutive bow. Then, his sightless eyes staring over the heads of his audience, he looped the string of the bow around the stick and adjusted its point to a depression in the board. The

198

bow moved rapidly; the pointed stick spun round. From the depression in the board rose a faint wisp of smoke.

The audience shifted and murmured. The horse of the provision cart, panic-struck, bolted forward into Ramsgate. The driver, shouting angrily, rose to his feet and sawed at the reins; but so keen was the interest of the audience in the smoke rising from the depression in the Hindu's board that not even the two soldiers turned to watch the bolting horse.

The horse slowed to a walk and stared around reproachfully at the driver. The cart skirted the sandy beach of Ramsgate and bore off toward the sheltering chalk cliff under which twoscore cutters, luggers and other small craft lay at anchor. Somnolent men in blue jerseys reclined against ancient docks and wharf houses, seemingly oblivious to both the cart and its occupants.

The cart came at length to a decrepit house in the doorway of which sat a whiskered man with bare feet. At sight of the carters he thrust a great toe through the meshes of a seine to hold it taut, while with his teeth and his two hands he set busily to work repairing a rip.

The driver, a tall man with knuckles strangely scarred, stared down at the net mender. "How's fishing?" he asked.

The whiskered man replied cryptically that there was a hole in nearly every net.

"I was told," Marvin said, "that a net mender by the name of Clay in Ramsgate was needing some poultry."

"I'm Clay," the whiskered man said. He withdrew his great toe from the seine and came to examine the hens in the back of the cart.

"Aye," he added, "them's 'ens, them is!" Under his breath he added with an air of finality? "Cost you ten guineas heach. Ten guineas to Calais."

"No, not Calais," Marvin said. "Morlaix."

Clay shook his head. "Calais, you'll go to," he replied sourly. "Calais, and lucky to get there." He snorted. "Morlaix! What you think we're running here? Blooming hexcursion boats?"

Marvin stared hard at the net mender and drew a deep breath. Before he could speak, Argandeau murmured quickly in his ear.

Marvin laughed, glanced appraisingly at the sky and vaulted lightly from the cart. "Calais it is," he said, "at ten guineas a man. There's two more of us on the edge of town —a brown man in an old sheet, doing tricks, and a boy leading him. Bring 'em in safe and we'll show you the color of our money."

It was close on to midnight when Clay put them aboard the lugger *Hirondelle;* and the captain, a squat Frenchman with legs so bowed a full-grown pig could have run between them without touching either, welcomed them politely and locked them in the lugger's tiny cabin.

To the four men, huddled in the dark, came the rattle of the lug sail rising. The *Hirondelle's* head fell off and the little vessel pitched uneasily in the Channel chop.

Argandeau fumbled at the cabin door. "Yes," he said, "this lock has four small fastenings. You bore beside them and we wrench it off—Pouff! Like that!" He snapped his fingers.

The Indian crouched beside him, and there began a sound of gnawing—a sound so faint that it was lost in the screakings of the lugger's hull and the slap of water on her sides.

The cabin door banged open, and the four men tumbled

into the cockpit. Three of them scrambled forward. Argandeau remained behind, smiling amiably into the lugger captain's horror-stricken face.

"A friendly visit, this," he ventured. "It is too cold and lonely in that cabin, eh? So we come out to suggest that you journey more to the southward, where it is a little warmer, perhaps."

"To the southward?" the captain asked incredulously.

"Truly!" Argandeau agreed. "To Morlaix. A beautiful town, Morlaix. You know Morlaix, perhaps? The women are beautiful to a degree."

"Morlaix!" the captain cried. "Why should I venture to Morlaix? You desire that I should lose my occupation? Name of a pig, but if I risk my beautiful *Hirondelle* on the long trip to Morlaix, I shall certainly do so!"

"If you fear to lose a situation," Argandeau told him sententiously, "abandon it. Always you will find a better one."

The lugger captain laughed bitterly. "A better one! I will be forced to become a Flushing or Middelburg man, carrying brandy to Ireland. To Ireland! My God, there is a dangerous affair!"

"Listen!" Argandeau said. He reached for the tiller and pushed it over. The lugger's head fell off and the little vessel ran more easily down the Channel. "Listen. You are a man of Calais, no?"

"Sacred heart!" the lugger captain wailed. "Calais, yes!"

"Yes," Argandeau said, "and you have then heard of Tom Souville, perhaps."

The lugger captain stared at him. "Heard of Tom Souville!" he exclaimed. "What do you think? Am I a dead man? Every man who is not a dead man has heard of Tom Souville!"

"Truly!" Argandeau murmured.

"Truly and truly!" the lugger captain agreed. "Four times that fox has escaped from the hulks. Four times he has cast foreign substances in the eyes of the British. Yes, I know him! Every man knows him! The English know him well! In his *Renard,* three days since, he has captured another English brig—a strong armed brig! You know this Souville?"

"Do I know him?" Argandeau asked. "Do I know my own nose? I think yes! We are like brother and brother together; like fish and potatoes!"

"Ah!" the lugger captain exclaimed.

"But yes!" Argandeau said. "You return to Calais and say to Tom Souville that you have done this for Lucien Argandeau, and he kiss you on both cheeks, like this!" He embraced the lugger captain and kissed him. "He will make your position more secure than Mont Blanc! That is something, eh?"

"That is something!" the lugger captain agreed. He crouched behind the gunwale and lighted a short pipe that smelled like smoldering hair. "That is something. With this wind, we reach Morlaix at sixteen o'clock, I think yes."

# XXII

THE fat landlady of the *Queen of Scotland* tavern in the fish-scented town of Morlaix raised her thick shoulders and strove to widen her eyes above her fleshy cheeks. "Ah!" she exclaimed to the tall, roughly dressed man who stood before her high desk. "Ah, but I was sorry for that lady, you understand. She was desperate, poor little one! I knew; yes. Her back, it remained straight and beautiful; but me, Victorine, I knew! She was penniless and desperate! Indeed, yes! Not that I would have pressed her, ever! No! But I was sorry—yes, sorry—and then her friend arrived." The landlady sighed, and from the vicinity of her enormous bosom came faint creakings.

Marvin stared at her from under heavy brows. "A friend? She didn't have any! She didn't know anyone here!"

The landlady breathed heavily and pursed her buttonhole of a mouth. "Ah, but yes! It was a man—ah, very much! One with fascination in his face and in his movements. Oh, a very good friend of hers! He knew her well; for he had been with the poor little one on the ship before all the misfortune of that great loss. Then he had gone somewhere for a time." Her beady eyes peered out at him from rolls of fat. "To Roscoff—I do not know. It is no matter. He was a fine gentleman. His costume was rich! A fine coat! A fine hat! Ah—ah, all of the costume rich! And he paid well, that one!" Her eyes blinked eagerly at him. "He paid very well—very much!"

"You think she was glad?" Marvin whispered huskily.

The landlady's eyes flicked across Marvin's stained and wrinkled trousers and his broken shoes. "Yes," she said, "she seemed very fond of him, that poor little one. Oh, yes, very! And why not, eh? She had a figure, that one! A back so straight and flat I have never seen! No! She brought trade; I will not conceal it! There was a roundness to her that men came here to see. And this friend of hers, he had an air. It was something to be whispered to by that man, I think!" She shuddered softly. "They were a couple, that pair! Two cabbages, eh? I see them now, departing by the Paris coach. Me, Victorine, I would give one bottle of brandy to know the words he whispered as they left." Her laugh was oily and her eyes were hidden by the rolls of fat.

Marvin looked at her for one moment longer; then turned abruptly and walked to the door. He walked decisively, yet his steps were unsteady; and the landlady, watching him, ceased to laugh. Her piggish glance dwelt coldly on his back, and from her pursed lips there burst a contemptuous puff, like the breathing of a rolling porpoise.

Three men waited in the narrow street before the *Queen of Scotland* tavern. They stared silently at the grayness of Marvin's face as he came heavily toward them.

Argandeau cleared his throat. "My friend, you have learned something. You like to tell us what it is?"

Marvin nodded slowly. "Slade," he said. "It was Slade that did it—Slade that fixed us." He studied his clenched fist. "It was Slade," he repeated numbly. "He's got money —plenty of it."

The three men watched him, and when he was silent,

Newton stirred uneasily. "The lady you spoke of," he ventured—"did you learn about her?"

Marvin lifted his eyes to the dull November sky; then lowered them moodily to Newton's face and slowly shook his head. "Nothing."

"You learned nothing?" Argandeau cried. "But it would be common news in Morlaix what became of her! Come; we go again and ask!"

Marvin eyed him. "Nothing, I said!" he repeated flatly. "Nothing! Henceforth nothing!"

Argandeau drew a long breath and nodded understandingly. "I see! I see! We cannot speak of her!" He lifted an eyebrow. "We cannot speak of her, and so we will not; but we can speak of Slade, eh? We can consider Slade!"

"Yes," Marvin said. "We'll consider Slade."

"Eh? And find him first?"

"Yes. I'm going to find him."

"Ah, when you find him," Argandeau said, "that will be something to enjoy." He pirouetted on the cobbles of the narrow street. "Where do we go to find him, my friend?"

"Paris," Marvin said.

"That is a city that *is* a city," Argandeau remarked. "Where is it in Paris that we shall find him?"

"I don't know," Marvin said. "I don't know."

Argandeau snapped his fingers. "Do not despair, dear Dan! Here in France there are men whose business it is to know many things. I think I can find a man to tell us of this Slade. You have heard of this man—Tom Souville of Calais? He is like to burst with the infinity of the things he knows! Come; we go quickly to Calais!"

# XXIII

IT WAS early morning when Argandeau led his three companions between the warehouses of the Quai de Kéroualle and out onto the egg-shaped cobbles of the dock itself, slimy from the cold drizzle that turned the buildings, the shipping and the harbor of Calais into a uniform dirty gray. Two vessels lay before them—one a tall and graceful schooner, and the other a small brig that squatted behind the schooner like a drab and dumpy mallard duck paddling ignominiously after a spotless swan.

At the edge of the dock, screaming shrill orders to the sailors at work in the brig's rigging, stood a plump, helpless-looking man in whose appearance there was no evidence of wealth, seamanship or profound knowledge. Yet this helpless-looking man was of necessity Tom Souville; for it was to him that Argandeau ran, and to him he spoke, bowing as handsomely, when he did so, as though clad in the finest broadcloth and satin, instead of the miserable shag trousers and striped shirt with which Clay had supplied him in Ramsgate.

There was something of timidity to Souville when he turned, at Argandeau's first words. His lips were slack; his eyes were wide; all in all he had the air of a person about whom there was little to fear and less to remember.

In the moment of seeing Argandeau, however, his face broadened and hardened in a thin-lipped grin, and he seized Argandeau by the upper arms, seeming almost to wrestle with him. As he did so, Marvin saw, over Argandeau's shoulder, Souville's eye flicker across him and his companions with the fierce scrutiny of a stooping hawk.

When, a moment later, he came to them, his eyes were wide and gentle and his smile diffident as he complimented them on their escape from the hulks of Chatham. "I do not need to ask how are you," he said. "You are happy men, alive and free where only a short time ago you were half dead and sealed in the tomb. I myself have known this feeling more than once. This rain seems not to be rain, eh? The whole world seems bright, and nothing too much for your efforts."

"I have told them this, Captain," Argandeau assured him. "Nothing is too much, if they have the great Captain Souville to direct them."

A look so vacuous as to approach imbecility swept over Souville's face and clung there until Marvin, nodding his head at the small brig, observed calmly that she was a tidy craft. "We heard you took her," Marvin said. "How did she sail with your *Renard?*"

"Good!" Souville said quickly. "Good! Not too good, but good! You know there is nothing sails with my *Renard*—not even any French schooner, and you well know that there are no vessels so fast as our French vessels. Therefore this *Challenger* sails well, but not so well but what I could sail a circle around her in any weather." He canted his head a little backward toward the harbor, his face as fatuous as that of a father indicating an adored child. "You have had an eye for my *Renard,* no doubt?"

"Yes," Marvin said, eyeing the tall schooner tied up beyond the brig's bows, "yes, she's a fine craft! If I could take out a craft like that, I'd make five million francs for her owners if I made a sou." He stared from her to the squat and clumsy brig. "I've sometimes thought, though, that this talk of the speed of French vessels is all my eye and my elbow. It appears to me I've seen English vessels that could sail with the best of French vessels, provided the English manned their craft with seamen instead of peasants and city boys."

"No, no!" Souville said amiably. "Look here at this *Challenger* brig. Her lines are not bad, but she is too narrow, and heavy beyond all need. Her yards are thick, like an Englishwoman's leg, and her bulkheads are like making a wineglass from a block of granite!"

Marvin nodded. "Yes, but this is not the only English vessel in the world. There was an English schooner came into Morlaix a month ago and cut out our barque, the *Olive Branch*. Now, there was a schooner!"

Souville smiled pityingly. "No, no! That *Sparrow* schooner, she is not much. In light airs, now, my *Renard* would leave her so fast she would seem anchored."

Marvin turned suddenly to Souville. "Why," he said, "here's a piece of luck! You must have heard the whole tale, or you'd never know the schooner's name. That was it— the *Sparrow!* If you know it was she that cut us out, you'll know what became of an officer who left her on the day she made port."

Souville's lower lip slackened, and into his eyes there came a blankness that was almost witlessness. "An officer," he asked. "An officer left her?"

A heavy silence descended on the little group of men— a silence broken at last by Argandeau: "There is something wrong here, my old friend," he said. "For some reason you guard yourself against us, and I think you know too much or too little."

He moved closer to Souville, making him a dignified half bow. "You suspect something, Captain; but I swear to you, by the friendship of our youth, there is no reason! These men are my friends, cruelly used by England, and more than eager to further the cause of France by doing England a hurt. This young man"—he flicked his finger tips lightly against Marvin's breast—"is a seaman, cautious with the peculiar caution of his country, and capable of inflicting great damage on an enemy. I have watched him—I, Lucien Argandeau—and I tell you that in one hour's time he thinks how to do things better and more quickly than they have ever before been done."

Souville raised his hands and let them fall helplessly. "I have heard only a little; so little that it is nothing. This officer, perhaps, had an eye partly obscured." He threw back his head, drooped one eyelid and looked quickly at Marvin, so that he seemed to peer out from under the lowered lid.

Marvin nodded, and Argandeau cursed softly in a foreign tongue.

"You knew this man?" Souville asked.

"Knew him!" Marvin said grimly. "Slade set the English on us! What we wish is to know him better."

"So you had heard it?" Souville said. "How did it happen that you heard it?"

Argandeau laughed. "How does it happen you know there will be rain tomorrow? It is something you know. This Slade, he was our enemy. I, too, am sure—very sure—he sent the Griffons, the English, to cut out the *Olive Branch*. How he informed them, I do not know, but he went ashore the day we made port, and disappeared. The next thing we know, the *Sparrow* arrives, coming purposely for us. It is a strange thing, too, that the officials of Morlaix held us and held us, anchored in the estuary, refusing to let us break bulk. These Americans, they might have been enemies of France, from the way they were treated!"

Souville pinched his lower lip between his thumb and forefinger, squeezing a part of the seeming imbecility from his face. "Then you think there may have been a connection between this Slade and the behavior of the Morlaix officials? You think he might be an enemy to France as well as to yourself?"

Marvin nodded. "He was a slave captain, and slave captains cannot live except by bribery. He was an enemy to everybody and everything that would keep him from getting what he wanted; and the thing he wanted most"—Marvin hesitated momentarily—"was money."

Souville looked hard at Marvin and then at Argandeau. "All in all, then," he said, "you consider him a dangerous man?"

Argandeau laughed angrily. "Dangerous! He should have a knife in the back; or if you are too squeamish for that, he should be hustled to Verdun and placed in the dungeons for the remainder of this little war! Tell us where he is, my friend!"

Souville seemed suddenly enlightened.

"Ah, I did not understand," he said. "In wartime it is impossible to tell. It might have been that you were in sympathy with the man. Now you shall have everything from me, frankly and freely. We will remove ourselves from this wet, eh, and go aboard my *Renard,* where we can speak quietly over a bottle of the best brandy."

He turned abruptly, no longer anything of helplessness or indecision about him, swaggered to the companionway of the tall schooner, and led the way over her side and to the after hatch. Marvin, bringing up the rear of the small procession, paused for a moment at the bulwarks to study the bows of the squat brig beyond the *Renard's* stern; then continued, whistling softly, downward into Souville's quarters.

From the dark stains on the floor, as well as from the red paint on the patched sheathing, Marvin saw that the *Renard's* barren cabin had often been used as a hospital during engagements; and Souville, rummaging in a chest for a bottle, while the others settled themselves on benches, replied volubly to Marvin's unspoken thoughts.

"You think there is small comfort here, eh? Well, that is so! My *Renard,* she goes always on business; and the quicker the business is done, the quicker we return home, eh? Therefore, I want little here for the making of splinters; little that must be thrown overboard before an engagement; for any such throwing would take time. In three months I shall have a larger vessel, with more comforts, perhaps; but I am wise to keep my *Renard* clear and clean like the boudoir of a young girl, eh?" He poured brandy into small glasses, squinted through one of them, touched the glass to his lips; then rolled his eyes ecstatically. "I drink your health and good fortune, gentlemen! The Americans, they are our dear friends and brothers against a common enemy."

"We came here to speak of Slade," Marvin reminded him.

"Yes, yes," Souville said. "Now I tell you! I see how you have suffered through this Slade, so I tell you everything! When this Slade left your barque, he went to England, where he sold information to the Admiralty for a large amount of money, perhaps fifteen thousand pounds; and he went then to certain merchants of Bristol who are engaged in the slave trade contrary to law, and threatened them with exposure unless they provided him with an armed vessel—a fast armed vessel."

Argandeau bounced from his bench, stamped twice on the floor, spat violently through a stern window and threw himself heavily on the bench again.

"An armed vessel?" Marvin asked slowly. "What sort of vessel?"

Souville shrugged his shoulders. "I have not heard, but probably a brig. The fastest ones are brigs. Later I shall know surely."

Marvin sighed gently. "Then he hasn't got it yet. Thank God!"

Souville shook his head. "No, and I am told that another month must pass before he gets it, but he had money from these Englishmen—a deal of money—and when he left England to return to Roscoff, he wrangled with the—ah—with the young woman who had accompanied him on his travels—a young woman who came to me with the tale. An interesting man, this Slade. He had promised to pay this young woman fifty pounds for favors received, but on leaving he would give her no more than twenty."

"There was a traveling companion, indeed!" Argandeau remarked.

Newton wagged his head in simulated admiration. "He'll bear watching, Slade will. He'd go far in politics or finance!"

"You say Slade returned from England," Marvin reminded Souville. "What then?"

"Why," Souville said, "then he went straight to Morlaix and to Paris. As soon as we had word from England of his activities, we traced him carefully." He frowned. "If only we had known two days earlier, we would have had him and there would have been one more enemy safe in the dungeons of Verdun! He moves quickly, this Slade of yours! Three days he spends in Paris; then he is gone, like a puff of smoke, back to England—back to his dear friends in Bristol. We have lost him, I fear. I hope it is not so, but I fear it."

"Back to England!" Marvin said. "He went back to England!" He groaned, and moved to the stern windows of the *Renard,* to stand staring down at the brig whose long jib boom rose above the *Renard's* taffrail; then turned suddenly to eye the small and pompous Souville. Surprisingly, he laughed. "I'll tell you what I'll do, Captain: I'll capture Slade myself and make some money for you in the bargain, if you'll supply me with the means of doing it."

Souville looked at him blankly. "Supply you? I do not understand!"

Marvin set down his glass and tapped the table with his forefinger. "Captain," he said, "you're playing a dangerous game with your *Renard.* She's fast, I know; but what happens to her, fast as she is, if you're caught by a frigate on a lee shore some foggy morning? At the worst, she's torn to pieces and you're killed. At the best, the English take her. Then you and your men go back to the hell of an orlop deck on a British hulk, and the fevers and bloody fluxes and black pneumonias that make the hulks as rotten as the meat they give you to gag on. You know what they are better than I do."

Souville smiled comfortably. "You talk like my wife."

"I drink to her wisdom," Marvin replied. "It's the truth.

What's more, you'll catch a Tartar some day—somebody who knows how to shoot better than you do. Look at this brig you just brought in! Shot to pieces in her yards and sails and rigging, but not a shot in her hull! If you hadn't been able to take her by boarding, you wouldn't have got her at all. Isn't that so?"

"Never!" Souville declared indignantly. "It is not so."

Marvin rose again, went to the side of the cabin and rapped his knuckles against the sheathing. "An egg-shell," he said, "like so many French private vessels. Everything sacrificed to speed! A little bad luck, and she'd crumple under you. You wouldn't have got the brig if she'd shot straight and cleared your deck of boarders."

"But you would like to have this egg-shell of mine," Souville observed complacently.

"Ah," Marvin said, "but I've made a discovery that would make her safe! I've learned how to lie off at a safe distance and batter a vessel to pieces with a long gun. I've learned how to lay guns in smoke with a raw crew."

"And never miss, eh?" Souville scoffed.

"And seldom miss," Marvin said gravely. "That's the discovery."

"There is no way to do it," Souville said.

"Yes," Marvin insisted. "I've invented a way. It can be done with a pendulum—a gangway pendulum."

Souville, plucking at an end of his small mustache, seemed to mull over the word; then slapped his knee and laughed until his mirth ended in a spasm of coughing. "A gangway pendulum! A gangway pendulum, indeed! And what happens with your gangway pendulum? Perhaps your enemies mistake you for a clock, afloat on the ocean, and never beat to quarters until they are under your guns!"

"It's nothing to laugh about," Marvin assured him, "unless you're in the habit of laughing at something that will put money in your own pocket and at the same time damage England."

"A gangway pendulum!" Souville repeated, wiping the tears from his eyes. "And what do you expect me to do about this gangway pendulum?"

"I'm offering you the opportunity to benefit by it," Marvin said. "Sell me two-thirds of your *Renard* and keep one-third for yourself, and you'll have a prime investment."

Souville became instantly serious. "You have the money?"

"How much are you asking?"

"My *Renard* is a fortunate vessel," Souville said slowly. "If I sold her, I would require a good price. If it were not that I am building another, I would not consider it at all—not at any price. For selling two-thirds of my *Renard* I would require"—he contemplated the ceiling of the barren cabin—"I would require one hundred thousand francs, gold."

Argandeau whistled, a faint, long-drawn-out whistle, while Newton, clasping his brow, murmured, "She must be sheathed with silver!"

Marvin studied the knuckles of his left hand, scarred from his battle with Little White. "That would be possible, if one-half could be paid at the termination of my first cruise, and the other half——"

"No, no," Souville interrupted quickly. "I do nothing in that way! I know nothing about you or your seamanship! You pay me one hundred thousand francs in gold, and I gamble on you, because I am a friend of America and you are my brother in arms."

"But," Marvin said patiently, "I am offering you my gangway pendulum——"

Souville expelled his breath explosively and waved his hand before his face as if freeing himself of cobwebs. "It is something fantastic, this pendulum! I have heard of no such thing, ever, and to me it has no value!"

"I think you make a mistake," Argandeau protested. "My dear Marvin has said something to me of this pendulum; and if he says it has a high value, then it has a high value. I tell you he has a flair for making strange discoveries."

Souville sighed. "No, it is something I cannot consider. And now, my good friend, the morning passes and I must attend to the repairs on this small brig."

"One hundred thousand francs," Marvin said, almost to himself, "seems to me somewhat high for two-thirds of an armed schooner. I'll venture to say I could get a brig, and a good one, too, for a quarter of that sum."

"Of course," Souville agreed, "but she would not be my *Renard*."

"No," Marvin said, "but she'd be as good as this captured brig of yours—better. Yes, sir! I could buy a better brig than that captured brig for twenty thousand francs."

"It is possible," Souville admitted politely, "but the twenty thousand francs would have to be in money, and not in conversation about a gangway pendulum! And I think you will find that even though you have money, you will be obliged to pay at least twenty-five thousand francs. Certainly I would not sell this brig here for less than twenty-five thousand."

"You will insist on twenty-five thousand?" Marvin persisted.

Souville smiled. "Francs, you understand. Not pendulums."

Marvin walked again to the stern windows and studied the vessel carefully. "It's not a bad price, twenty-five thousand francs," he said. "Not bad, if you sell her as she is. Shall you sell her as she stands, long guns and all?"

Souville nodded.

Marvin drew his bench to the table, felt in an inner pocket and brought out a small heap of yellow coins. "You've sold your brig for twenty-five thousand francs," he said, "and I've bought her, and here's a little English gold to bind the bargain. I'll put Newton and Steven aboard today to take possession, and leave tonight with Argandeau to find the balance of the money. If you'll make out a bill of sale, these gentlemen can witness it."

Souville stared doubtfully at Marvin, then moved slowly to a small chest and fumbled in it for paper and quills. "You Americans!" he said. "I think you are becrazed! Can I believe it was this brig you desired from the first moment, and that you had no desire at all for my *Renard?*"

Marvin stopped in the counting of his gold pieces to look blankly into Souville's face. "You're laughing at me again!" he said. "I'm buying the brig only so you'll feel obligated to keep me informed of Slade's movements."

With the eye farthest removed from Souville he winked faintly at Newton; while Souville, frowning, pocketed the gold pieces before him and went to driving his quill with thoughtful delicacy across a flimsy sheet of pale blue paper.

When he had finished, Marvin took the paper from him and read it carefully. Then he drew Newton to the stern windows of the *Renard* and pointed to the clumsy brig.

"She's ballasted with rock," he said. "Her center of gravity's too high, and the sail she'll carry wouldn't make petticoats for my grandmother. Throw out the rock and ballast her with scrap iron. Her yards are stout enough for wharf piling. Sway 'em down and fine 'em out. Scrape 'em till they bleed. Then she'll carry royals and skysails. Knock out the sheathing inside the bulwarks; it's no good except to make a splinter bucket out of her. Spend your money and spend it fast." He picked up his hat and eyed Newton warningly. "Trust nothing to chance. Be careful. Keep an eye on everything and be sure everything is right. We may have to sail into hell after Mr. Slade, and I want this vessel fast enough to make the trip without scorching herself or anyone aboard."

# XXIV

Marvin, followed by Argandeau, came out from the avenue that tunneled through the forest of brown-leafed chestnuts, and stood staring across terraces and gardens to the gates of the Château of Valençay, and to the enormous pile of pallid stone beyond, looming against the blue November sky as dangerously as a cliff rising abruptly from a lee shore.

They studied the two round towers at either end of the château's long gray bulk—towers topped with shining rounded domes, so that there was a hint about them of gigantic warning lighthouses; then, having studied them, they fell suddenly to brushing their garments and arranging their cravats in the shelter of the lofty boxwood hedge that stood between them and the gardens of the château.

Argandeau sighed and shook his head. "It is possible that the thing may be accomplished," he said, "but not unless I tell them loudly that you are an American and therefore insane! You must remember the French do not do things in this way! They do not try to walk in to see a great man as if he were no more than a black cook in a forecastle! No! They write him a letter, and his secretary and mistress read it, and at the end of three months they may be promised an appointment which will not be kept. I tell you I think it would be well to have a letter written, in case this man is thrown into a rage because you come calling on him as if you were Metternich or Marshal Soult. I tell you he is a prince and a duke and a bishop, and nearly as great a man as Bonaparte himself."

"I'm glad to hear it," Marvin said. "He owes my father eleven dollars."

Argandeau examined Marvin carefully from head to foot. "Eleven dollars, now that we have spent everything on your clothes, is a great deal, and I wish we had it; but it is true that your clothes were worth the price. If you were older, with a red face and a puffy nose and a swollen stomach, you would look like a general or an admiral yourself, or a duke maybe. It is a pity you are not seeking help from a beautiful woman rather than from this great gentleman, who is able to talk anyone into thinking that black is white, or that it is possible to live without money. My Spanish rabbit, she had a proverb about such an affair. 'There are some men,' she said, 'who would not loan you fifty pesetas even though they were offered the Alhambra as security; but almost any woman, provided she is over ten and under ninety-eight, will lend you all she possesses on no greater security than a mouthful of lies about love.'"

Marvin rubbed the dust from his boots with a wisp of grass, carefully brushed the tight dark-blue trousers that were strapped beneath them, ran his finger around the inside of the high stock that rose above his frilled shirt, and examined his snugly fitting, long-tailed coat for blemishes. "Look here," he told Argandeau. "Look at me carefully. Be sure there is nothing about me to prevent this great man from listening attentively to what I say."

He placed his cocked hat a little on the side of his head, thumped his gold-topped cane in the dust of the road, rested one hand on his hip and stared almost defiantly at his companion.

Argandeau walked slowly around him. "It is perfect," he insisted. "Perfect! The seals of your watch, they look entirely real. There is nobody who would think the head of your cane was anything but gold. Also you carry this cane with an air, and the shoulders of your coat are narrow, so that you have a look of delicacy almost—nothing at all like a man who could put Little White under hatches in three rounds."

"Then try to find the door of this building and get me into it," Marvin told him, "so I can forget my clothes and do what I've come for."

He took off his hat, placed it, folded, under his arm, flourished his cane experimentally and glanced expectantly at Argandeau. Argandeau, however, seemed to have forgotten his existence; for he was staring, with eyes as large and round as plums, at the boxwood hedge that bordered the avenue.

Turning quickly, Marvin saw, above the clipped top of the hedge, a woman's face. In the very moment that he turned, an expression of annoyance crossed it, and it sank slowly from sight, leaving in his mind's eye a picture of black hair piled in a high knot, a pointed chin and large blue eyes beneath black brows as curved and slender as a bent hunting bow.

From beyond the hedge there came the sound of soft-voiced expostulation, followed by rapid protestations in the voice of another woman.

"Two rabbits!" Argandeau murmured. "One held up the other to look over, but let her slip."

"Sir from America!" called the soft voice from beyond the hedge. "It is the duke you visit?"

Marvin cleared his throat. "Talleyrand, ma'am."

"Yes," the soft voice continued. "You walk straight ahead through the great gates into the *cour d' honneur*. Across the court, on the right, is the *perron* of the vestibule. Do not go beneath the arch, or you will lose yourself."

"Thank you, ma'am," Marvin said. "I've been afraid I might not find him." He took Argandeau by the arm and set off up the avenue toward the imposing bulk of carved gray stone.

"Wait one moment!" the soft voice called. Then, closer to them, it added: "It may be you meet delay if you go to the vestibule. M. de Talleyrand is amused to see Americans, always; but he is here not often; and since you arrive on foot, the guards at the vestibule might neglect, you understand. The King of Spain, he is detained here, and so there are guards. Walk to the gates, therefore, and wait. I take you to another entrance, more quick."

"Thank you, ma'am," Marvin said again. He moved quickly to the opposite side of the avenue, drawing Argandeau after him. Argandeau skipped a little, and blew a kiss toward the sky. "Two rabbits!" he whispered ecstatically. "It was a proverb with my Spanish rabbit: 'Push Lucien Argandeau into a gutter and he will come out sweet with musk!' "

"You fool!" Marvin said. "You'd want to talk about women if you were caught in the breakers and next door to death! God knows what harm you've done us with your gabble! Get back to the inn and wait there for me!"

"But there are two of them!" Argandeau protested. "While you are engaged with one, it may be that I can secure the cost of our lodgings from the other. Have you forgotten that we have not one sou in the world? Not one sou among the pair of us?"

His protests, however, were vain; for Marvin, his cane swinging jauntily and his cocked hat somewhat aslant, went briskly from him toward the distant gates without a backward glance.

The two women came through an opening in the boxwood hedge, chattering to each other as if they could never find time to finish what they were saying; and to Marvin it seemed they were little more than girls, pretending, with youthful coquetry, to have forgotten he was to wait for them at the gates. Yet there was nothing of coquetry in the glance the black-haired girl turned suddenly toward him; only inquiry and something of puzzlement.

"The other," she asked. "He does not wish to visit the duke also?"

Marvin shook his head. "He came to keep me company. He went back to the inn."

"*Le Roi d'Espagne?*" she asked. "You are remaining at *Le Roi d'Espagne?* You will be uncomfortable, I think."

When he was silent, she turned from him and slipped her arm in that of her companion, saying over her shoulder: "You come with us, please. We take you to the tower, where the duke sits in the afternoon." She chattered a little to her companion, a round, brown girl whose brown hair was piled in a knot even higher and more pointed than that of the black-haired girl; then to Marvin, as if to put him at his ease, she said: "How far have you come?"

"From Calais," he told her. "From Calais since Tuesday."

"Then you have good horses," she said, "but I fear you break all your springs."

"No, ma'am. We came on foot."

The black-haired girl halted her companion and spoke rapidly to her; then stared at Marvin. "What is this you say? You walk from Calais to Valençay? And since Tuesday? Is it possible that a man can do this? I think no horse could do it!"

"No, ma'am," Marvin agreed, "but it was more important for me than it would be for any horse."

Again the black-haired girl spoke volubly to her companion, whereupon the two of them scrutinized Marvin as if in search of something about him that had hitherto escaped them. "It must be indeed important," the black-haired girl said. "Do you come direct from America to this place?"

"No, ma'am. From England."

"From England! But you are at war with—— Then I ask you, do you come direct to England from America?"

"No, ma'am. From China."

"From China? I do not know where—ah, *la Chine!* Ah-hah! Then it is important because you are *diplomatique,* eh? No! That is not so! If you were *diplomatique,* you would come here in a coach, and drive about this court with a great fracas, cracking the whip and blowing the horn and frightening the sparrows for two days! You cannot be *diplomatique!* But still the matter is important! Now I must think what it is so important as to bring a gentleman on foot from Calais to Valençay. Either it must be——" She stopped and eyed Marvin absently. At length, still silent, she drew her companion onward once more and, followed by Marvin, continued through the formal gardens that lay between the court of honor and the squat, round-topped tower in which the château ended.

At the angle between the tower and the main wall of this

vast gray building there was a small door; and at the door
the round, brown girl turned away, running lightly toward
the main entrance. The black-haired girl looked gravely at
Marvin. "Now you go in to see M. de Talleyrand. Perhaps
you like better to tell everything to me, so that I help you
with him?"

"Thank you, ma'am," Marvin said. "I wouldn't want to
trouble you."

"But it is no trouble! Come; you tell me, and I shall see
whether I have guessed correctly why your visit is important. Then I help you with the duke."

Marvin coughed. "I think, ma'am—no offense meant—
that it would be better if I told Talleyrand himself. It's he
that must help me."

She smiled faintly. "You are cautious, and it is no great
fault to be cautious at the proper time. I think it would
make a difference, perhaps, if I say to you that I am a member of the duke's household. It is possible you consider me a
servant."

"No, no!" Marvin said. "I can see you're a great lady!
But a lady can't—ah, that is to say, if I can't convince the
duke, how can a lady convince him for me?"

The black-haired girl opened her eyes wide. "How? You
do not seriously ask me how! Surely you do not think there
is any wise man but knows he can do better at anything at all
by taking the advice of a woman! Surely you know that any
wise woman can persuade a man into doing whatever she
desires!"

"That's no doubt true," Marvin admitted, "but it's my
belief that for every wise woman there are fifty foolish ones
who consider themselves wise."

He shot a quick glance at her, and found her smiling more broadly.

"And I am one of the fifty?" she asked.

"How can I tell, ma'am? You know it's important I should see Talleyrand, and still you keep me from him. Is that wisdom, ma'am?"

She shrugged, opened the door in the angle of the wall and preceded Marvin into a small vestibule, where she dropped her long brown cloak on a table. Marvin saw then that her yellow dress had next to no sleeves, and that, on one side, the skirt was slashed as high as the knee, almost as though a small staysail had been cut from it.

She arranged her hair, looking up at him from beneath her elbow. "It may be," she said, "that the King of Spain is with him also—the one who was stolen by——" She wagged her head, frowned severely, thrust one hand into the front of her gown and the other behind her back, and puffed out her cheeks, so that she had a look of Bonaparte about her. "If he is there," she added sedately, "do not be disturbed by him. He is not much of a king."

She opened another door on the far side of the vestibule and went quickly into a circular chamber so large that for a moment it seemed to Marvin an empty blur of enormous pale carpets and gilded furniture heavily garnished with lions' heads. Out of the blur came a vast hooded fireplace, and windows opening onto an ancient and heavy cloister. Near the fireplace was a table at which sat a man with a face like parchment, his chin propped so high by a thick collar that he had an air of disliking the odor of the place. Yet his features were so placid as to seem lifeless, and his eyes peered out of the blank whiteness of his face like black paper pasted behind the eyeholes of a mask. In a reclining chair on the opposite side of the fireplace lay a swarthy, sulky-seeming young man, rubbing a finger moodily over the strings of a guitar.

The black-haired girl curtsied quickly to the gentleman at the desk. "Uncle Maurice," she said, "I have found this young man from America with something important to say to you: something so important that he cannot tell it to any woman—only to M. de Talleyrand himself—so I think it must be the most important thing that ever was known."

# XXV

TALLEYRAND rose from his desk, smiling with an exquisite gentleness, but he did not move forward to greet his guest; and Marvin noticed that one of the shoes the great man wore was misshapen, as if the foot within it were crippled. The voice was rich and of a silken suavity:

"From America! I find this a great honor that a gentleman from your fine young country should come here to Valençay to see me—a great honor, and a surprise as well. Sit, please, and tell me who has sent you, and how do you learn I am here? It is almost never I come, and it is only four days since my niece and I set out to escape the turmoil of the Rue St. Florentin."

Marvin, uncomfortably erect in a small, hard chair, glanced from the smiling, mask-like face of Talleyrand to the black-haired girl, who had gone with the sulky man to stand beside a roulette wheel at a long window through which appeared the broad expanse of park, a dark belt of forest beyond, and, most distant of all, the little town of Valençay, its white roofs and Gothic church spire glistening in the afternoon sun.

"Why," he said, "nobody sent me. I came because——" He broke off and stared at the brilliant bindings of the books that encircled the room, and at the painted nymphs rioting on the ceiling. "It's a mistake, of course! We had a brig, the *Talleyrand,* named for a Frenchman who came to Arundel and was taken by my father to buy land from General Knox, years ago. I thought it was you; but surely it was never you who needed to buy lands in Maine!"

As if to himself and almost as an afterthought, he added: "And owed my father eleven dollars. It's not likely!"

Talleyrand lowered himself to a chair beside Marvin and looked intently into his eyes. "Eleven dollars?" he asked politely. "I have no recollection of——" He paused. "It is true, certainly; for no one would spuriously imagine the peculiar sum of eleven dollars; but it is strange that I—— Perhaps you remember your father telling the circumstances of those eleven dollars?"

"It was a wager," Marvin said. "You wagered that a certain Cap Huff could eat no more than twenty-four ears of corn. He ate thirty-five, my father said, and so you lost eleven dollars."

Talleyrand nodded. "It is the truth! I remember it! After he had eaten the corn, he wished your father to wager me that he could also eat two pies of squashes. It all comes back! Dear me! Dear me! And you say I did not pay this wager?"

"My father said it was because of the buttered rum," Marvin said. "You went away early the next morning; and my father said any man might be forgetful in the early morning, especially after being free with the buttered rum. He said, always, it was worth more to him to be able to say Talleyrand owed him eleven dollars than to say Talleyrand had paid him eleven dollars."

"It was wisely said," Talleyrand agreed. "I hope your father is well? He found excellent land for me—excellent land—and so it was possible for me to live, selling a little here and a little there. Yes, yes, I remember; fools and wise men in America, they bought land at any price, anywhere! Tell me, your father is happy and successful?"

"He lost the *Talleyrand,* but now he owns another. When I go back, I shall take her out."

"You mean you will be captain of the ship?"

Marvin nodded. "Yes, and that's why I've come here."

"But of course!" Talleyrand exclaimed. "It is important that you return to America! I understand your eagerness, and I tell you that it can be arranged easily. You may be perfectly sure it shall be done."

"That's not it," Marvin said. He cleared his throat. "There's not time to go home. That is, the vessel I'd have if I went to America isn't the kind I want, and I want one now. I can do twice the harm to England if I can take out a vessel from France."

"Twice the harm?" Talleyrand asked. "I do not understand. If you sailed from America you would be more likely to discover unprotected British vessels, eh?"

"No, sir!" Marvin said. "It's in their home waters that they lack protection. You waste no time hunting 'em, for they're always to be found; and if you're cautious, you can surprise 'em where they least expect it."

"Now I see," Talleyrand said. "What you desire is a fighting vessel! You may depend upon it, I will assist you to this willingly. How much shall you wish to pay for this vessel?"

"No," Marvin said, "it's not only a vessel. There's another thing." Embarrassed, he glanced at the black-haired girl, to find her staring thoughtfully at him over the shoulder of her sulky companion. "If I take out a private vessel from France, I'll need a commission, and it must be got from the American Minister—from Mr. Barlow in Paris. It's not only to get the vessel that I need your help, but to get the commission as well."

Talleyrand smiled almost sleepily. "But my interference is unnecessary, sir. You are—how shall I say?—you are perhaps overcareful in all this. Why do you not, my friend, go straight to Mr. Barlow and tell him what you wish? He is a gentleman and a poet, a trifle pompous and overcredulous, perhaps, but not at all a stickler for form. You will find him sympathetic, I am sure."

Haltingly, and with a kind of desperation, Marvin attempted to explain: "I wouldn't have come here if I could have seen any other means of getting what I needed. I must have someone to vouch for me to Mr. Barlow. I have no papers—they were taken from me by the British. I thought you might——"

"But even without papers," Talleyrand interrupted, "there were other seamen from your ship who can vouch for you—other officers? Were you the captain of the ship?"

"No, sir," Marvin said. "No, sir."

"Then who was the captain and where is he?" Talleyrand persisted.

"A lady was the captain. She thinks—she thought—it might be—that is, I can't let her——"

The black-haired girl moved to Talleyrand and leaned against his shoulder. "It was what I suspected!" she cried. "He had an air about him! I said to myself, 'This important matter has a woman in it.'"

"Well," Marvin said slowly, "I'll try to explain. You see, if I should go alone to Mr. Barlow, he'd ask about this lady, just as you have, and it might be he'd have learned from her—or from someone with her—that I'd been responsible for the loss of her ship to the British. Then he'd never issue a commission to me, and I could do nothing for her." He hesitated; then spoke haltingly: "You see—she's prejudiced against me—I think she's been told that I—that I—well, I think she was made to hate me."

The black-haired girl sank to her knees beside Talleyrand's chair. "Oh, the lady hates him!" she cried. "No wonder! Have you perhaps expressed to her your opinions concerning the wisdom of women?"

Talleyrand dropped an admonitory finger on her shoulder. "Of course," he told her, "you know everything about this affair, after hearing a few words; but I am older and duller, and there are still a few things obscured from me." To Marvin he added, "Now you begin, so that we may know about this lady you love, but who loves another gentleman who has been prejudicing her against you."

"That's not so!" Marvin added. "That's not what I said, and it couldn't be true! She's hasty in her judgments, but she couldn't—she'd never——"

"Tell from the beginning," the black-haired girl insisted, leaning comfortably against Talleyrand's knee.

Before Marvin had finished his tale, the swarthy, sulky-looking Spanish king had ceased to turn his roulette wheel and had gone gloomily from the room, evoking doleful sounds from his guitar; and a servant had come to light the tall candles around the walls. When Marvin had finished, Talleyrand fingered his high stock and stared at the ceiling with expressionless black eyes.

"It is all quite plain," he said. "Not only must I intercede for you with Mr. Barlow, but if I do what you wish, I must purchase this vessel and intrust it to an untried captain, and all with no certainty for me of receiving any return whatever. Does this seem to you fair? To me it has the air of placing money carefully"—he dropped an imaginary atom from his finger tips—"in the ocean."

Marvin sat forward, balanced on the extreme edge of his chair. "No," he said. "You can't lose—not unless they sink my ship and kill me! If we have no luck, I'll pay it back after the war, with interest. But we'll—I can feel luck when it's close; every seaman that's worth his salt can feel it— we'll have my pendulum! You'll have the use of my pendulum! They'll never catch me while I have my pendulum! You'll have your money back ten times over!"

Talleyrand waved a white hand languidly. "It means nothing to me, this pendulum. You have thought about it; it exists only in your brain, eh? It seems to me a simple thing; so simple that our great seamen would have discovered it before now if it had value."

"Yes, it seems so," Marvin admitted, "but they haven't. Not even Nelson! Nelson said guns at sea aren't any good except at point-blank range, when they can't miss. He was wrong; but he's right, too, as long as guns are fired by guesswork, as they are now. Why, at long range, both the French and the English, all of 'em, fire with the roll of the vessel—as she rolls downward or as she rolls upward—hoping that one or two shots will be lucky enough to get home. A hit at long range is an accident today, unless a gun is handled by an expert rifleman; yes, and at long range there isn't one gun crew out of a thousand that could hit a mark the size of this château! With my pendulum there'll be no guessing about it. Every time I fire a long gun, I'll fire from an even keel, and I could hull this room four times out of five at half-mile range."

To Marvin it seemed that Talleyrand and his black-haired

niece eyed him with as much of disfavor as disbelief. "I don't mean to brag," he told them mildly. "I've always looked for easier ways to do things, and almost always there's an easier way. It appears to me most people make things as hard for themselves as they can."

"Yes, I think it is so," Talleyrand said, "and I am interested in a part of what you tell me. I am interested to see how you are confident. You speak of England's great fleet as if it were nothing at all! It has destroyed our navy utterly—our fine, powerful navy—and yet it seems to be in your mind that a few men with a few small fishing boats can strike a blow at England that will be felt."

"And so they can," Marvin said. "So they can, provided their seamanship is what it should be. All that's necessary is to keep out of range of heavy war craft and sink the slow and clumsy merchantmen."

"Of course," Talleyrand admitted, "nothing else is necessary, provided, as you say, their seamanship is superior. When I was in America, I studied the inhabitants of your fishing cantons, and it was clearly to be seen that your fishermen are not to be compared with those of Europe, and that fishing in America is not a means of forming sailors and turning out strong and able seamen. It is a lazy calling in America, except in the case of the whalers of Nantucket."

"But we don't use fishermen on our merchantmen," Marvin protested. "We use seamen."

"But your seamen are fishermen first," Talleyrand said placidly. "I have been in your fishing cantons and written papers on the subject for our National Institute."

Marvin gripped his clenched hands between his knees. "Well," he said slowly, "we have many fishermen. We also have many merchantmen, and we've been forced to sail differently from the English merchantmen. They heave-to at night, most of them—send down their royal and topgallant yards and masts, even—whereas we crack on. Their ships are half manned with landsmen, because the navy steals their crews. We've had to be better seamen than the English, and so we are. You may depend upon what I tell you! If you help me with this vessel, you'll never lose by it. I'll—I'll make my father responsible in case I'm killed. I'll do anything—anything——"

Talleyrand, assisted by his black-haired niece, rose to his feet and stared with a faint, blank smile at the top of Marvin's head. "But of course I will help you!" he said. "Of course! Now I must think!" Again he scrutinized the ceiling on which half-clad nymphs cheerfully encouraged the advances of a disreputable satyr. "When is it you wish this vessel?"

"At once," Marvin said eagerly. "If I can't get to sea in two weeks, it might be—I might not be able——"

"Now let me see," Talleyrand interrupted. "I think it is best to do thus: Go now to your inn, and you will have word from me about this." The black-haired girl turned from him and went to stand by the window once more, idly turning the roulette wheel. "Yes," Talleyrand continued, "that will be best. There are things to be arranged."

Marvin hesitated. "If you could give me letters—to Mr. Barlow—to your bankers—I'd walk night and day to get to Paris with them."

Talleyrand's smile became indulgent. "No, no!" he said. "Nothing would be gained. The best thing is to wait patiently at your inn, and soon you will hear from me." He shook Marvin's hand warmly and limped with him to the door. "To have the pleasure of this visit is like a breath from

America. Soon—very soon—we shall have the pleasure again, eh?"

The outer door opened and closed, and Marvin found himself standing in the angle of the towering wall.

When, a little later, he entered the main room of the *Roi d'Espagne*, Argandeau bounced upward from the table where he sat over a brandy bottle with the inn's proprietress, a large woman with a black mustache.

"You have got it!" Argandeau exclaimed, looking into Marvin's eyes.

Marvin nodded. "I have the promise of it. He has promised everything."

"And it was all promises?" Argandeau persisted. "Surely he gave you the eleven dollars he owed your father!"

Marvin shook his head.

"Promises!" Argandeau exclaimed. "But I know these promises! Now it will be necessary for one of us to go back to see those two pretty rabbits that were behind the hedge."

## XXVI

THE note that came to Marvin on the following afternoon was brought by a serving man in a green livery, and at the sight of the man and the letter he bore, Argandeau sighed softly. "Thanks to God!" he murmured. "The woman who owns this inn has been feeding us for love of me, but when she sees you have a letter at last, it may be she will be content to continue trusting us because of our prospects."

But the note contained no news of anything so definite as prospects; it did, however, cause Marvin to return anxiously to the spot where he and Argandeau had first come out from the avenue of chestnuts to find themselves confronted by the long gray walls and the squat round towers of Valençay.

As on the preceding day, he stood staring at the enormous mass of masonry and seemed to listen; then, apparently hearing nothing, he turned from the avenue, entered the edge of the chestnut forest and emerged on the leaf-covered grass of the château gardens. Even before he had left the shelter of the chestnuts he caught sight of her, swathed in a long gray cloak and sitting on a stone bench against the boxwood hedge; and it seemed to him, as he went toward her, that she eyed him with more indulgence than pleasure.

She nodded so that her black curls bobbed when he stood before her. "So you come back," she said, and to Marvin her eyes looked as round and guileless as those of a little child. "It must be you are no longer afraid you may be helped!" She gave him her hand; and Marvin, after holding it a moment, released it and coughed.

There seemed to be something of the schoolmistress about her as she wrapped herself more snugly in her gray cloak. "In America you do not kiss the hand of a lady?"

"Well," he said apologetically, "it is not—there are times —I mean, if we thought——"

She drew her hand from beneath her cloak, stared at it critically and again extended it to Marvin; yet, when he had taken it and bent over it, she drew it away from him as suddenly as she had brought it from under her wrap. "I must tell you at once," she said. "My uncle has changed his mind. It is impossible that he help you."

"Impossible!" Marvin exclaimed. "What do you mean? He said he'd help me! He *promised* to help me!"

She shrugged her shoulders. "There are things you do not understand."

He turned slowly to look at the thick tower of the château, with its outlandish rounded top. "Yes, that must be true," he admitted. "I do not understand how any man can make a promise and then break it for no cause." He rapped with his cane on the gravel walk. "I must see him again! He cannot break his promise like this!"

"It is no use," the black-haired girl told him. "In one little hour he departs for Paris, and it is quite, quite impossible that he should see you now."

"But there is no one else I can go to!" Marvin cried. "No one! There's no one in France who would lend me the money, except this man my father helped. If I could see him for five minutes——"

"But I tell you there are things you do not understand!" she insisted.

Marvin laughed. "I understand that I've lost two days through the promises he never intended to keep."

"Now you are bitter!" she interrupted. She patted the bench; and Marvin sat beside her, dropping his hat and stick on the gravel walk. "You do not understand Frenchmen, you Americans, any more than you understand women. My uncle, M. de Talleyrand, he would have helped you, yes, and gladly, if it had not interfered with his ideas of right and wrong."

"Then why did he promise?" Marvin said harshly. "Does he manufacture new ideas of right and wrong each day?"

She bent forward to look into his face, shaking her black curls so that a faint, penetrating fragrance rose from them. "Are there no promises broken in America?" she asked. "Here it is the custom; for if our great men said 'No' to everyone's demands, they would have poniards in the backs, all of them, in one day's time; and a great man with a poniard in his back is no better than a dead carp in the moat. So they say 'Yes' when they mean 'No.' If you had been a statesman you would know the truth of this. Maybe you do not have statesmen in America."

Marvin shook his head. "This is talk that means nothing, like your uncle's talk about American seamen. A broken promise is a broken promise, and nothing can change that. As for his ideas of right and wrong, they're probably no better than the papers he wrote for your National Institute on the fishing cantons of America. Fishing cantons! Good God!"

She came closer to him, so that Marvin felt the warmth of her shoulder through the sleeve of his coat. "No, no, no!"

she said. "It is only that you do not understand, you Americans! Listen now, and I explain everything to you. My uncle, he loves France, but he does not love this small butcher"—she pretended to glower, thrusting her fingers into the front of her cloak and inflating her cheeks so that she had a look of Bonaparte about her—"this madman whose desire for power is hurrying France and all of us into one large grave!" She seemed to shiver, so that Marvin took her hand and held it in both of his.

"One month ago," she continued, smiling up at him, "this madman buried himself and his army in the depths of Russia—in Russia, and with winter moaning at his shoulder! Only this week we have had the news. He has burned Moscow! He has destroyed his shelter and his provisions, and the Russians are on every side of him: millions of them! He is audacious and imprudent and a madman; so it is inevitable that he and his army must sink, either beneath the numbers of his enemies, or beneath hunger, or beneath the snow. Already they are as good as buried. It is the beginning of the end. That is why Maurice has come to his château—to tell the Spanish king, who was stolen out of Spain and imprisoned here by the madman, that soon he can go back to his own country. Now you are able to understand it, eh? If my uncle helps you to go out on the ocean with a device that will be bad for England, then England might be longer in chopping off the madman's head and restoring peace to France."

"It's what I suspected!" Marvin said. "It's an explanation that doesn't explain. He'll help his brave allies, the Americans, if it suits his plans; and I'm his friend, unless it's inconvenient for him!"

"No," she assured him, "it is only that we, you and I, do

not have great minds, like my Uncle Maurice. He is French, and the French people have ideas. You are materialist, thinking of the cost of your ship, but Maurice thinks above such things. He thinks of nations, moving against one another like a game of chess, and what is best to be done in each small move, you comprehend?"

"No," Marvin said.

"But you must! You speak of friendship! Do you think friends are common as herring? They are not! For poor people, perhaps, they are no more scarce than blue diamonds; but for the rich and powerful they are as rare as unicorns! My Uncle Maurice has discovered that there is no man he can trust. Through one man he lost two million in the stock market; through another he lost his beautiful home, the Hôtel Monaco. Even by Bonaparte, for whom he had done everything, he was called a thief—a man without faith or honor! By Bonaparte!"

"It seems impossible!" Marvin said gravely.

"But it is true!" she insisted. "It was while that madman fought in Spain. His brother Lucien returned to France with millions and millions he had taken from the Spaniards, and Bonaparte said he had acted wisely. But when my Uncle Maurice returned with only two little millions, this madman called him names, worse than a dog; worse than a pig! No, there is no man he can trust! From one woman, two women, perhaps, he can have sympathy and friendship. From a man, no! It is the same with me. I cannot trust any woman. I take pleasure in the company of some, certainly; but all of them —all!—they will say any bad thing about me behind my back, whenever it pleases them! If I want friends, I must find them among men—Maurice and my husband and perhaps one more, or two."

"Your husband!" he exclaimed.

She twisted quickly on the bench, drawing her hand away; then leaned backward to smile up at the expression on his face. "You see, I have told you there are many things you do not understand! When you are older, and have sailed your ship to many ports, you will no longer be like a little boy. Then, it may be, I would no longer offer to help you if you came hunting for assistance from my Uncle Maurice."

She leaned toward him again; and again from her small pyramid of black curls there rose that faint and penetrating fragrance. "You see, I am telling you secrets. When you are in need of a lady's help you must appear helpless and far from home, and a little frightened, especially of her. Then she will feel at once that she must protect you, and see that you are made happy."

Marvin stared helplessly at her for a moment; then stooped for his hat and stick and rose to his feet. "I'll try to do better another time, ma'am."

"But you are obstinate!" she cried. "Never have I seen a man so obstinate! Can nothing make you believe that somewhere there is a woman wise enough to help you?"

"Why," he said, "I'm beyond help, if you've told me the truth. Your uncle won't help me, and there's no help for that, is there?"

She jumped from the bench and stamped her foot an inch from his own. "So you will walk back to Paris, because of your pride, penniless and helpless, and able to do nothing against your enemy, or for the lady he is stealing out from under your nose! Nothing, do you understand? Nothing! This Mr. Barlow, the American Envoy of whom you speak, he is not in Paris. He is not in France, even. He has been summoned to Vilna by the madman, and has gone to him. Like all the others, he has plunged himself into Russia and into his grave at a word from Bonaparte."

Marvin stared at his hand, clenching and unclenching it as though he found it painful. "Did you know yesterday that Mr. Barlow was not in France?" he asked.

She nodded. "Of course. And I knew more. I knew that a gentleman has recently come to Paris to act in place of Mr. Barlow. I myself know this gentleman."

"And so," Marvin said thoughtfully, "you let me go on thinking that Mr. Barlow was in Paris!"

She shrugged her shoulders. "It was not I who let you go on thinking. It was Maurice, who had his own reasons. Diplomats, you understand, consider it unwise to speak the truth or tell what they know. And who am I to disabuse you about anything, knowing that you believe there are fifty foolish women for every wise one?"

Marvin stared at her helplessly. "You know who it is that took Mr. Barlow's place? Who is it?"

She hesitated, her eyes on his face: then seemed to reach a sudden decision. "The gentleman's name is Barnet. He was the consul of your country in Havre. I myself know this gentleman. If I ask something of Mr. Barnet, he cannot refuse me." She came close to him and placed her hand on his shoulder. "But of course you think we women are foolish—all of us!"

He shook his head. "No: not all of you. If ever I had such thoughts about you, I made a mistake."

"Ah!" she said. "A triumph! The gentleman pays me a pretty compliment by saying he made a mistake! What, then, will the gentleman do?"

"Do?" he asked. "Do? I don't know what I'll do. I don't know. I'll try to think of something to do."

She made a sound of exasperation. "Almost I am tempted to do nothing for you, after all! If you need help so much, why is it you do not ask me for it?"

"It's not only a letter to Mr. Barnet that I need," Marvin said. "I've got to have money, and a deal of it. I'd mislike asking a lady for money, even if she could give it to me, and even if the lady had no husband or uncle to consider. It wouldn't seem—it wouldn't seem wise!"

"But I am not going to give it to you! First you must make it possible for me to get enough to lend you, and then you must repay my loan as you said you would repay my uncle—twice over—three times over!"

He was silent, studying her.

She laughed lightly. "You see, now, I am wiser than you have thought. You have thought, all this time, that I am impatient to give you what you need; but now you find you do not know, even, how you shall help me get it!"

"How I can help you get it," Marvin said slowly, "I have no idea, but you shall have a paper guaranteeing you 300 per cent profit on your venture—and I shall assume that you're as impatient for money as I am for a ship."

She sat on the bench again and looked up at him out of the corners of her eyes. "You are a nice young man—so nice that it would be easy to forget that one must be careful always about matters of business. Yesterday you told us of a pendulum. Of course, I know nothing of pendulums; but there was once an English gentleman who came here to see my uncle, and he spoke of your M. Benjamin Franklin, calling him one of those damned Yankees who could do anything." Her eyes twinkled. "It may be that he was right, and that there is something about Yankees that enables them to do more than other peoples. It might be that your pendulum is something new and wonderful. It might be, even, that you could invent other things if the need arose—that you could invent a safe manner of playing roulette. The thought came to me yesterday when I stood by the window and spun the wheel." She raised her eyebrows and sighed. "Here am I, obliged to play at roulette with my friends again and again each week, and each week the amount I owe is greater and greater."

In spite of the little smile that curled one corner of her lips, it seemed to Marvin that she was more than half serious in what she said. And after all, he thought, he *was* one of those damned Yankees.

He pondered on the structure of the gambling wheels he had seen aboard the prison ship. "I know little about gambling, ma'am," he said at last, reluctantly. "The Frenchmen on the hulks, they seemed to think a system does no good. That's what you're asking me to invent, isn't it? A system at which you can win? If that's it, ma'am, I'd better not waste my time or yours; for by the time you've won what I must have, the need for it will be over."

Again she jumped from the bench to place her hand on his arm. "But I seek only a method to keep me from losing! You said to my uncle that there is always an easier way to do things; so, if that is true, it is only necessary for you to play roulette a little, in order to find an easier way for me to play it. Then I shall quickly save enough for your ship, and I can give it to you even before I save it!"

"Play roulette a little!" Marvin exclaimed. "There are reasons why I couldn't play roulette, even though it was played with buttons!"

"I know," she added hurriedly. She drew an envelope from the front of her gown. "It is here! What Maurice owed your father, with the interest for all these years, and a little more, too, since you are doing this for me."

At the look in his face, she flirted her fingers airily. "But it is nothing to twist the nose over! Nothing! Maurice, he had intended to return this to you, you understand, but affairs were pressing, so I am doing it for him. Yes, it was his money."

She eyed him. "I truly think it was a part of the very money that he brought home from Spain, as one brings home dust on his shoes without knowing how or where it was acquired. And it is a favor for me that you are doing with it—a favor! You must take it and go quickly back to Paris. There you will visit No. 9 in the Palais Royal. There are many gambling apartments in the Palais Royal, but No. 9 is the fashionable address. At No. 9 you study the wheel, morning, noon and night, and then you make me a little system, eh? You make me a little system, and I will come there soon—soon. If the system has merit, you shall have what you need from me."

She pressed the envelope into Marvin's hand, nodding at him as at an obedient child. Then her little smile seemed to harden and her eyes to turn a paler, colder blue. "But don't forget—the money I lend you in Paris for a ship—that's business. Three hundred per cent."

She laughed and added: "It's the kind of business I like; a chance to get three for one, and the three to come suddenly! And what would you? It's the spirit of the times —everybody playing with gold and golden bubbles—and I'm a woman of the times. My husband lost sixty thousand livres last week on the advice of a ballet girl. I would like to show him how business should be done with a reliable Yankee gentleman."

She glanced suddenly at the watch that hung from her neck. "Heaven! It is already one hour, and I must depart with Maurice!" She reached up, drew down Marvin's head and kissed him abruptly; then ran lightly toward the château.

# XXVII

THE turmoil that filled the high-ceiled rooms on the second floor of No. 9 in the low, dark-gray buildings of the Palais Royal seemed to pass lightly over Marvin, who sat at an end of one of the four crowded roulette tables. On one side of him was an aged harridan, her head swathed in a green turban from which rose a single ostrich feather; her cheeks were a hectic pink and her bared shoulders protruded angularly from a gown of a sickly yellow. On the other side was a girl as young as she was scantily clad; and the two of them stared frequently and invitingly at Marvin and the pile of colored plaques that he shielded beneath his big hands.

Close behind his seat stood Argandeau, resplendent in a long-tailed coat of delicate gray and trousers of a pale but brilliant blue; and the two of them whispered together, regardless of the crowd that surged around the tables—a crowd of officers, fops and women whose dresses, slit to the knee and even to the thigh, seemed about to, and sometimes indeed did, slip from the shoulders that held them precariously suspended—a crowd that screamed and chattered so shrilly as to drown in billows of clamor the staccato rattle of the roulette balls and the croupier's monotonous: "Make your plays, gentlemen and ladies. *Rien ne va plus.*"

"There it is!" Argandeau whispered. "Thirty-three! Four times this croupier has rolled it into the last dozen. He is in a groove! I say put it on the last eighteen, before he can escape from the groove!"

"The last eighteen," Marvin agreed, "but if we lose, we may be here the rest of the afternoon and all night as well!" He pushed twenty-five white plaques to a near-by section of the diagrammed table, rested his chin on his hand and stared up at the cluster of hanging lamps that burned dimly in the hot and smoky air. The ball whirred in the wheel, slowed, bumped against the nubbins, tripped on a slot and freed itself; then darted to its final resting place like a frightened mouse.

"Nineteen, red, uneven, last half," droned the croupier. He swept plaques from the board, reached over with his rake and knocked down Marvin's pile, counted it quickly and deftly pushed him an equal number of white counters.

"There is another finished," Argandeau said gently. "The fourteenth this afternoon! It is a good time to start another, eh? He is getting away from that last dozen, and soon I think he will roll it into the first eighteen."

Marvin, his hands cupped around his pile of plaques, rose in his place and looked uneasily behind him. At Argandeau's elbow he saw a small pyramid of black curls and a pair of blue eyes that stared innocently into his.

She nodded to him. "I am here, you see."

Marvin divided his earnings and handed a part of them to Argandeau. "Play carefully," he warned him. "What you win will go into your pocket, but what you lose must come out of it, also."

With that he relinquished his seat and joined the black-haired girl, who slipped her hand eagerly beneath his arm and turned him toward the curtained booths that lined the passageway between the roulette hall and the refreshment room. When the curtain of the inclosure she selected had dropped behind them, she made a pretense of fixing her curls and, as she did so, looked up at him from under her elbow.

"Now you are a little boy again—a sulky little boy. But it is not my fault. I came here as quickly as I could; not one moment sooner could I come!"

"You have no business here at all," Marvin said. "I believe every bad woman in Paris must come to this building."

She raised her eyebrows. "I do not know how to distinguish the good from the bad, and it would be interesting if you would tell me. It is the fashion to come here. You will see Madame de Staël here, and Madame de Senlis, as well as many of the laundresses, butchers' wives and cooks' daughters that Bonaparte has honored with titles. Ladies who come to our house for dinner come here to play; and some of them, I think, are quite, quite good, though I am not sure what you mean by 'good.' You are doomed to be an unhappy young man if you think that no woman is a good woman unless she has made no mistakes and had no desires, ever; and in case you wish that sort of good woman, you must be careful to marry a plaster saint out of a church."

"Well," Marvin said uncertainly, "well——"

She dismissed the matter with a movement of her shoulder. "You tell me now about our system. I have seen enough to know that you have discovered one."

Marvin drew up a chair to the booth's table and fumbled in his pocket. "I'm sure of one thing," he said, "and that is there's no system at all by which you or anyone else can be sure of winning." He brought out a thin packet of bank notes. "Still, it's possible to be lucky for a while. I've won enough to buy food and get new clothes for Argandeau; so here's the money you loaned me, over and above my father's eleven dollars, plus 6 per cent interest for nineteen years."

"Pouf for your 6 per cent and your nineteen years!" she cried. "Tell me how it was done!"

"Why," he said, "it's simple enough. Any child must quickly learn that his money will vanish like smoke at roulette, unless he plays the even chances—the black or the red, the odd or the even, the first eighteen numbers or the last eighteen. To stake your money on a single number is like throwing it in the fire."

"Sometimes it is possible to win on a single number," she said. "It is exciting, that!"

Marvin only laughed.

"To win by the even chances is too slow!" she objected, then.

"Of course it's slow! It's slow, and hard work; and you must be tireless, and keen in your judgment."

"You make it seem like a business rather than a game."

"So it is! So is everything else, if you want to win. I've been told there are some countries, even, where people make almost a business of love."

"Very well," she said impatiently. "We play on the even chances. What then?"

"Well," Marvin said, "when I studied the game I found that people met disaster most frequently from overreaching themselves. They'd become impatient, after many small winnings; so they'd bet largely and lose everything in two turns of the wheel. Therefore, it was necessary to find a method to prevent that—a method that would aim to win a small amount of money in a short time, and to begin again whenever the small amount had been won."

He set down some marks on a sheet of paper and she came and leaned against his shoulder, watching him. "For convenience," he said, "we'll say we're playing with plaques of one franc each." On the paper were five upright marks, close together. "Each of these marks," Marvin continued, "represents one franc. It might easily represent five francs, or ten, or a hundred, but we'll call it one franc. Suppose, now, that you start to play, having in mind that you wish to win five francs, and that when five francs have been won, you must start from the beginning to win another five. You have a line of figures—five ones—five one-franc marks. You must play, always, the figures at each end of the line. That is, you play a one and a one—two francs— and you play them, say, on the red. If you win, you receive two francs from the croupier, and you cross off the two end figures. That leaves three ones. You still play the numbers on each end—both ones. If you win, you receive two more francs and cross off the end figures. That leaves a single figure, which you play—one franc on an even chance. If you win, you cross off the last number and receive one franc. Then you've won five units—in this case, francs. If each unit had been ten francs, you'd have won fifty. So your venture is finished; your numbers are entirely crossed out. Therefore you set down five more ones and start over again."

She tossed her head. "And if I lose, I double, eh? That is no system!"

Marvin ignored her words. "Again you commence by playing the end numbers—two ones. You lose. This time you cannot cross out a figure; instead you must add the Figure 2 to your row of ones—a number greater by one than the last number. Then you play the two end numbers—a one and a two—three francs. If you lose you add the Figure 3 and again play the ends—a one and a three. If again you lose, you add a four, and play a one and a four. This time you may win; if you do, you cross off the one and the four, and play the end figures of those that remain —a one and a three. If you again win, cross off the one and the three, and play a one and a two; but if you should lose, add a figure larger by one than the last number not crossed off. When finally the numbers are entirely crossed out you'll again have won five units—five francs—so once more you write down your five ones for a new venture."

"Why," she said slowly, "I think there may be something in it. It seems simple, also." Her arm, resting on his shoulder, slipped around his neck, and with the impulsiveness of a child she pressed her cheek to his.

"Yes, it's simple," Marvin admitted, "but there's danger in it, none the less, as there is in almost everything that's exciting."

She withdrew her arm and stood a little away from him, arranging her hair and glancing at him from beneath her elbow.

"The danger," Marvin continued, "will come when you've lost repeatedly. There may come a time, then, when you're setting down larger and larger figures with each loss, and must stake thirty or forty or fifty francs on each play, again and again, in order to win only five francs eventually. It's not likely to happen often, but when it happens, I advise you to go cautiously—to stop playing entirely when your wagers, on a single game, have become as large as your previous day's winnings."

"Pouf!" she cried gayly. "Go cautiously, indeed! Come, we shall play your system and I shall show you there is no need for caution!" She seized him by the arm and tugged at him.

Marvin rose slowly. "Then you think you can win with this system?"

"But of course! You have won and I shall win!" She swayed against him, her blue eyes laughing up into his and her red lips a little parted.

Marvin put his arm about her. "Then you're satisfied with what I've done?" He lifted her and kissed her, kissed her a second time, and in the small and tawdry booth there was a moment of breathless silence.

At length she laughed softly. "We play now."

"It's what you wanted?" he persisted. "What you expected?"

"Yes, it is something new, and so easy that I cannot understand why nobody has discovered it before."

"Then there's still time today for you to go with me to see Mr. Barnet at the Legation; and with good luck I can be in Calais tomorrow."

"But we must play!" she protested. "Today you remain with me; tomorrow will be time enough to see this ambassador of yours."

Marvin shook his head. "There's my brig to be got ready. I've waited and waited until I'm near bursting from doing nothing. There were two American privateer captains in here yesterday, but today they've gone to Lorient, and tomorrow they're putting to sea. How do you think I felt, sitting here and elbowing all the—all the—well, sitting here in Paris when they were starting out to comb the Channel for British ships?"

"British ships!" she exclaimed. "I think there is something in your mind besides British ships."

He nodded. "There's the loan you're making me, and the 300 per cent profit I've promised to pay you on it. I've got that to think about, and other things as well." Seemingly as an afterthought, he added, "The sooner I get to sea, the sooner I'll be back with your gold."

"And the sooner you get to sea, the sooner you'll catch up with the lady who left you for another man, eh?"

Marvin took her hands in his. "A lady who has a husband of her own, and an uncle as affectionate as one I could mention, should never bother her pretty head about a lady I haven't seen for many a long week and may never see again." He kissed her almost roughly, threw back the curtain of the booth and drew her after him into the crowd that surged and gabbled between the roulette tables. On his way to the door, he tapped Argandeau on the shoulder and motioned to him to follow.

Argandeau clasped his forehead in despair. "It is against me!" he whispered hoarsely. "I am playing forty-two francs at one throw, and these buzzards have one hundred and thirty-seven francs of my money!"

"Leave it and be ready to start for Calais," Marvin told him. "We'll be on shipboard at this time tomorrow!"

## XXVIII

THE outer room of the Legation of the United States of America was a small and dingy cubicle, presided over by a contemptuous lady with green eyes and hair the color of untended brass; and it seemed to Marvin, standing humbly before her with the black-haired girl beside him, that she was filled with the need of supplying the grandeur that her surroundings lacked, and of upholding, by means of haughtiness and pride, the dignity of the country that she thought she represented.

"Mr. Barnet is engaged," she told Marvin disdainfully. "You can sit down and wait"—she nodded her head toward an inner room—"but you should have come earlier. I think it's too late for him to see anyone else."

"But I must see him today," Marvin protested. "If you'll tell him it's important——"

The contemptuous lady eyed him coldly. "Leave your card, and it's possible you can see the secretary."

Marvin looked helplessly at his companion, who sighed gently. "I seem to recall," she said to the contemptuous lady, "that Mr. Barnet was brought here from Havre in order to act and to think on behalf of Mr. Barlow, who has gone to Russia. Perhaps I am mistaken."

The voice of the contemptuous lady was hard. "No, you're not mistaken."

"In that case," the black-haired girl said softly, "it will be interesting to the Minister of Foreign Affairs to learn that there is yet another who is thinking and acting on behalf of Mr. Barlow. He will be pained, I have no doubt, to know that the thinking for your great country is done in a room"—she touched a finger tip to the windowpane that overlooked the flickering street lights of the Rue St. Honoré —"where the outlook is so obscured."

"Obscured!" the green-eyed lady cried indignantly. "Obscured! I'll have you know that window was washed last week, ma'am!"

"In that case," the black-haired girl said, "you can doubtless see the advisability of going at once to Mr. Barnet, regardless of who is with him, and telling him that Comtesse Edmond de Périgord, Duchesse de Courland, must see him at once. At once, you understand!"

The green-eyed lady stared at her unbelievingly; then rose suddenly to her feet and hurried from the room. As for the black-haired girl, she made adjustments in the curls under her bonnet of yellow silk, glancing quickly at Marvin beneath her elbow as she did so—a way she had, and not an unpleasant one either, he thought. "You see," she said, "how often it is that even a woman may help a man."

The green-eyed lady returned breathless. "Please come in!" she gasped. "I wouldn't have—I didn't know——"

The black-haired girl stopped her with a gesture. "It is forgotten; but hereafter, for the sake of your countrymen, for whom I have great sympathy, I hope that the outlook from this room will be somewhat clearer."

The three of them passed through a large waiting room in which sat a strange figure of a woman—an angular, broad-shouldered woman who seemed to have no feet or legs, and whose face, bent over huge knitting needles that clacked and clittered, was screened from them by an enormous white headgear so constructed that sharp white wings protruded beyond her broad shoulders and shook with the violence of her knitting. Before her, on the floor, rested two empty boat-shaped shoes of felt, each shoe large enough to hold a healthy infant. At the sound of footsteps she looked up. Her face was long and brown; her eyebrows as bushy as newborn black ducklings; and from under them her beady eyes stared with a suspicion made more piercing by the sudden silence of her knitting needles.

Madame de Périgord tapped Marvin's arm. "See there!" she said. "A wounded grenadier, no doubt! It would be like this little butcher of ours"—she made a Napoleonic gesture—"to seize even the women to throw against the guns!"

The angular woman rocked mightily in her chair, and from under her black skirt two ham-like feet, covered with wrinkled white stockings, thumped to the floor and groped for the felt shoes.

Marvin and his companion left her groping, and entered a smaller anteroom, the anteroom of the Minister's office. The door into the office was open; and in the doorway, looking up into the face of a tall gray-haired man who was bidding her farewell, stood a bonneted girl whose dress of gray satin clung with unwrinkled smoothness to her flat back and slender figure. She turned, and as her eyes fell on Marvin, she seemed for a moment to flame into sudden radiance. Her eyes, deep in the shadow of her bonnet's brim, held sparks of light.

"Why, Dan!" she exclaimed. "You're—I'm——"

The tall man smiled. "You know this lady? You're just in time to wish her luck. A brave young lady, I tell her, to take out a letter-of-marque at such a time."

Marvin breathed heavily, as if incapable of thought or motion. "A letter-of-marque?" he mumbled. "A letter-of-marque?"

Corunna Dorman glanced from Marvin to the black-haired girl and back to Marvin again; and her face grew blank. "Why, yes," she said, "a letter-of-marque." She smiled gravely at the tall American beside her, bowed slightly to Marvin, and made as though to pass.

"Wait!" Marvin said. "A letter-of-marque. That means you're getting a ship for ——" He stopped, seeming to swallow the word he had meant to speak.

"It means," Corunna said, "that Captain Slade helped me when I was deserted by everyone else."

"Slade," Marvin said thickly. "Slade."

"Captain Slade," Corunna said gently, "has been the soul of energy and generosity."

Marvin looked at her and said nothing.

"You must excuse me," the black-haired girl said suddenly. "I must not keep Mr. Barnet waiting." She smiled sweetly at Marvin. "When you have finished talking with this lady, you must join us quickly if you are to have your commission today." She went to Barnet and gave him her hand; then, as she passed through the doorway, she added over her shoulder, "Do not be long—Dan!"

"Wait!" Marvin said. "Wait!" But Barnet, bewildered, followed the black-haired girl into his office and closed the door behind him.

"So you're to have a commission!" Corunna said. "How strange! Are you getting one from America because the English wouldn't give you one?"

Marvin stared at her. "The English? What do you mean?"

Corunna returned his gaze steadily. "Oh, you can set your mind at rest! I haven't told anybody."

"Told anybody what?"

"How you brought down the English on the *Olive Branch*. I'll do nothing to stop you here." She made a faint movement of her hand toward Barnet's office. "I thought— I thought your own conscience would be punishment enough." She lowered her eyes.

"Brought down the English?" Marvin repeated stupidly. "How I brought down the English? I?"

She looked up at him. "You thought I'd never know, I suppose. You've forgotten how news spreads among sailors."

"News!" Marvin said. "Why, there never was a sailor's tale that wasn't a damned lie! Like barbers, they never get things right, and you know it! What is it you're trying to say? What is it Slade said, damn him! You couldn't truly think it was I——" He stopped, staring at her. "You do! By God, you do! You little fool! Slade told you, and you believed him! You little fool! You little fool!"

He checked himself suddenly, turned away from her; then turned back to face her and spoke more quietly: "I take it you're now Mrs. Slade," he said.

She looked at him with a steady eye. "Do you?" she asked.

"I wouldn't ask you the question, whether you are or not," he said.

"Wouldn't you?"

"Do you think I care?" he burst out. "Do you think I care on my own account any more? Well, I don't! I'll tell you what I care about: Your father was my friend, and that means I care about his daughter's safety. Yes, and that she isn't fooled by a pack of lies; so, husband or no husband,

I'll speak out! Husband or no husband, you've believed a rat out of the swamps of Africa, and that's what he is!"

"He's kind and generous!" Corunna cried. "You can't say these things!" She knotted her bonnet strings. "Let me pass, please!"

"Then it's true!" Marvin whispered. "You're sailing with Slade!"

"No!" she said. "He's sailing with me! With me! He's a brave officer and a resourceful man, and as captain I'm glad to have him for a first officer! Let me pass!"

"I've got a vessel, Corunna," Marvin said. "You don't know what you're doing! There's a cabin for you on our brig, Corunna."

"A cabin! What for? For me to do needlework in?"

He was silent, gnawing at his lip and staring at her.

"That's your opinion still, I suppose?" she persisted. "A woman's judgment is too uncertain to let her handle a ship?"

"Why, yes! That's my opinion! It's my opinion that most women take chances at the wrong time and for the wrong reasons."

"Oh, dear me!"

"What's more," Marvin continued, "it's my opinion that most women don't believe what's told them unless it's as unreliable as their own desires. If I told you as much truth about him as he's told you lies about me——"

"What?" she cried. "You'd slander him?"

"Slander! Do you think it's never going to be proved how he sold the *Olive Branch* to the English?"

Corunna looked at him with the bitterest scorn. "He? Ah, that's your way out of it, is it? To try to put it upon him! Wasn't it Captain Slade who led the men when they retook the *Beetle?* And where were you when it happened?

The last man out of the hold! And weren't you in charge of the *Olive Branch* when the British cut her out? Don't you suppose everybody knew you could have run her ashore and saved her for me?"

Marvin's face was white. "Slade sold you out! He went to England and traveled the country with a common trull. He sold you out, I tell you, and divided the sale money of the *Olive Branch* with the English; then blackmailed merchants into giving him a ship!"

"Indeed! And how would it be possible for you to learn any such cock-and-bull story as this unless you'd had it from the English themselves? And why do you stop with blackmail? Why don't you tell me the poor man murdered little children?"

Marvin tugged at his neckcloth as though it oppressed him. "You've got to listen to reason! What chance do you think you'll have with a man like Slade?"

She laughed contemptuously. "You're all alike, you men! Each one of you pretends he's perfect, and that every other man is a monster! You slander Captain Slade, and at the very moment you do it there's a woman waiting for you! Who is she? And haven't I as much chance with Captain Slade as she has with you? I think I have! Oh, yes, I think I have!"

"Corunna," Marvin said slowly, "there's nothing I could do or say, ever, that would influence you. There never has been. Sometimes it seems to me you've always done and said the things that would make me feel most miserable. A thousand times I've wanted to take you by the shoulders and shake you for being so contrary, but I know now there's no use trying to make you do something you don't choose to do. When they put us in the hulks, Corunna, it seemed to me I'd have to pull up the decks with my bare hands to get back to you. Well, I've lost you. I could go to the Minister now with what I know about Slade, but I won't do it, any more than you'd go to him with what you think you know about me. I want to protect you, but I won't do it by force."

He waited vainly for her to speak. Then he said: "If you feel you've got to go on with Slade, go ahead. I've got one thing to ask—that you think it over for a few minutes right now. Either he's a traitor and a liar, or I am. Well, you've known me a long while, and him a short while, but he's fascinated you. I'll ask you to think it over and decide which you'll believe—him or me. That's all. I'm going into that room for the commission this lady's helping me to get. If you're here when I come out, I'll know you've changed your mind about Slade."

He looked at her expectantly, but since she made no answer, he walked past her, tapped lightly on the Minister's door and went in without a backward glance.

It was only a short time later that he came out with the black-haired girl, carrying with him a commission authorizing Capt. Daniel Marvin of the private armed brig *True-Hearted Yankee* to take, burn, sink and destroy all enemy vessels.

There was no one anywhere in the two outer offices except the green-eyed young woman, who was staring at the dirty windows.

# XXIX

Tom souville, hunched over the table in the barren cabin of the *Renard,* counted a sheaf of bank notes; then looked up at Marvin and Argandeau and moved his small, pointed mustache so that he had the appearance of an astounded squirrel. "It is correct!" he exclaimed. "Correct! You have done it! It is bizarre—a *coup de théâtre!* You Americans! I have heard of nothing like it, ever! You say you will do a thing, and almost immediately it is as good as done!"

"Not always," Marvin said.

"But I say yes!" Souville exclaimed, jumping up and clasping his hands beneath his coat tails. "We have received, just now, an account of the privateering success of the Americans. It is something exotic! Something fantastic! The *Rossie* privateer took and destroyed fifteen British merchantmen in forty-five days; the *Decatur* took eleven in the same time; the *Saratoga* has taken eight; the *Comet* twelve; the *Paul Jones* eighteen; the *Mars* nine; the *Benjamin Franklin* six. The English, they are having a crisis of nerves!"

"My friend," Marvin said, "tell us the one thing we want to know."

Souville nodded. "I have found him. He is where you cannot get at him. He is in Dublin."

"Where I cannot get at him?" Marvin asked. "That depends! That depends! He hasn't bought a house there, has he? He isn't going to settle down, I take it." Thoughtfully

264

he studied Souville's eager face. "If you should keep company with me in your *Renard,* don't you think it probable that in time we might find some rich prizes in unexpected places?"

"And I can have the use of your pendulum?" Souville asked.

"You're laughing at me!" Marvin said gravely. "You don't want my pendulum. Your *Renard* might be mistaken for a clock!"

"No, no!" Souville exclaimed. "I want it! I will try, once, doing things in the American manner. You let me use your pendulum, and I will keep company with you. I will do more; I will find you a crew of Americans, very fine; not drunkards or vagabonds, but strong men from jails, captured in prizes. In four days I find them, and that is none too soon; for this man you want to see, who is now in Dublin, I hear he will sail in eight days."

"Eight days!" Marvin breathed.

"Eight days," Souville repeated. "Look, you let me use that pendulum and I cancel your dock charges—one thousand francs."

"What else?" Marvin whispered.

"What else?" Souville demanded. "What else? Nothing else should be needed between two brothers in arms. It is for the glory of France, and so it should be given freely, eh? Ah, well; I will act as your agent here, free of charge, making sure that our thieves of officials do not strip you to the bone when you send in a prize."

"No, no!" Marvin said. "What else about Slade? Where is he going and what will he do?"

"What is it that you decide about the pendulum?" Souville persisted.

Marvin nodded. "I'll rig one for you. We'll sail together."

Souville sighed comfortably, seated himself on his chest and folded his plump hands across his melon-like stomach. "What else about Slade? Well, there is this about Slade: In Bristol he got the *Blue Swan* brig, an old slaver, very fast. Four long nines she carries, and eight twelve-pound carronades. She went out from Bristol at night, showing no papers before she left; and as she went, she collided with two merchantmen at anchor. Yet the whole affair was hushed at once, and the port authorities were like little children about it, wholly innocent and undisturbed." He raised his eyebrows. "That can have only one meaning, my friend. There is British official connivance in whatever this *Blue Swan* brig is doing." He nodded wisely, and Marvin stared bleakly from the stern windows.

"On the following day," Souville continued, "the *Blue Swan* appears in Dublin. There is scarcely one of these Irish ports where American privateers are not welcome. It is widely known, and with some reason, that so far as England is concerned, they are foreign ports; that if opportunity is given to their citizens, they would take joy in burning any English frigate and crucifying her crew. I think your Slade has gone to Dublin, therefore, to be joined by a friend to whom he does not wish to appear an English sympathizer." He twisted the points of his small mustache and stared at Marvin, who returned his stare with expressionless eyes.

"In fact," Souville went on, "I have heard from Middleburg, the port from which smugglers run to Dublin. Yesterday a diligence arrived in Middleburg from Paris, and the passengers embarked in a Dublin cutter—two females, one of them a——"

Sheerness to Dublin, also for Fayal and Havana. There is no reason at all for these vessels to proceed to Dublin—no reason except to make the acquaintance of your Slade and his *Blue Swan*. Therefore, I say that he goes with the squadron to assist in the control of your privateers. I say that, in addition to some of the things we already know about him, he is a traitor! That, gentlemen, is the picture we have pieced together."

Marvin wet his lips and clenched and unclenched his hands as though he felt a numbness in his fingers. "Fayal!" he murmured. "Fayal! A neutral port!"

He got to his feet and looked from the stern windows at his narrow brig.

She was emerging, amid hoarse shouting, from a confused tangle of men, gear and guns. New, slender and taunt royal and skysail masts had been swayed up, fidded and stayed; and garrulous Frenchmen clung to ratlines, crosstrees and yardarms, reeving new rigging and seizing on chafing gear under Newton's quick eye.

The prolongation of her masts had given her a new look —a look of alertness. She was narrow still, and seemed, because of the absence of spring or rise in her deck, to lie as flat as a log in the water; but she was clumsy no longer, for she rode with a new balance, having the look of being caught in a swift current and of straining at the hawsers that held her to the slimy dock. Yet there was something innocent about her—a look of helpless smallness—and although Marvin knew her to be three hundred tons and more, she seemed less than a hundred.

Content at what he saw, he turned to Souville. "Find me the men you spoke of," he said. "We've got to get to sea."

Souville stepped to the cabin door and shouted shrill

orders into the companionway; then turned questioningly to Marvin. "And when we are at sea," he asked, "what then? For where?"

"Why," Marvin said, "we're for Fayal; but as a matter of precaution, we'll look in first at Dublin."

# XXX

A SMART breeze from the northwest whipped the *True-Hearted Yankee* fast through a warm ocean in which floated clots of yellow weed, and from which skittered shimmering fish that curved to left and right as if the threatening rush of her passing had given them wings.

Wedge-like, she sliced through the watery hillocks, urged onward by a press of canvas that towered upward into royals and distant skysails and spread outward into studding sails, so that the hull beneath seemed ludicrously small and helpless.

Yet there was no helplessness on her narrow deck; for the tall Indian, Steven, resplendent in the blue jacket and the crossed yellow belts of an officer of marines, drove two sweating gun crews at the laborious task of exercising long eighteen-pound traversing pieces. With the precision of machines the heavy cannon rumbled forward to the weather bow ports, the crews as silent at their hauling as the men of any king's cruiser. Boys ran beside them to place sponges, rammers and water buckets in neat piles abreast the trunnions. The two knots of men boiled around the carriages; to the eyes of the officers on the quarter-deck, they seemed to scramble like ants on sugar. Tackles were made fast to eyebolts; breechings were adjusted. With a rattle of chains the ports were triced up; the two long toms lurched forward, their muzzles disappearing through the bulwarks; quoins were rapped sharply into place. Smoothly the crews reformed in orderly alignment beside the guns.

The Indian struck an iron triangle. At the clang the gunners, squinting at their sights, shouted, "One! Two!" There was no count of "Three!" but in its place the linstocks of the gunners' mates slapped hard against the touchholes of the guns. "Boom!" bawled the gunners' mates. The gun crews made swift movements with rammers and imaginary shot; then snapped to attention. The Indian walked around the rigid crews, staring hard at them. Then he nodded. "Good!" he said. "You'll draw a gill extra, next mess. Count two after the pendulum strikes; then let 'em have it; and there ain't anything in reason between here and Fayal that we can't blow out of water!"

On the quarter-deck, Newton, scratching busily on a scrap of paper held against the triangular cover of a sextant box, whistled softly; then looked up at Argandeau, who leaned against the weather rail, scanning his features in a pocket mirror. "Twelve knots!" he exclaimed. "Twelve knots for twenty-four hours! Two hundred and eighty-eight miles in one day! That's sailing, mister! Two more days of that, mister, and we'll raise Fayal!"

Argandeau smoothed an eyebrow and returned his mirror to his pocket. "We will raise what?" he asked politely. "This place you mention—what was the name again?"

Newton looked at him coldly. "Fayal was what I said. You may have heard us speak of Fayal."

"Have I ever heard you speak of anything else!" Argandeau cried. "Fayal! Fayal! Fayal! Fayal might be heaven, it is so much in your hearts and on your tongues to be there! I have had Fayal with breakfast, dinner and supper since God knows when! I would like to think a little of the two well-laden Britishers that we took in the Channel, thanks to our pendulum, and sent back to Calais by Tom

Souville, to add to our fortunes and the coffers of that beautiful rabbit, Madame de Périgord, but I cannot, no! I cannot hear myself think because of your clack, clack, clack about Fayal! I would like to meditate on the way this cautious Old Man of ours, this Captain Caution, of Arundel, took us into the very harbor of Dublin and removed an Indiaman from under the guns of the fort itself. Hah! There is something to think about, that, as well as how my dear Marvin ever earned the name of Captain Caution! But to you and the rest of you, all these things are nothing. 'Fayal!' you scream. 'Fayal! Fayal! Fayal!' You are like uncivilized people, or infants, taking pleasure only in anticipation." He sighed heavily, as if in despair.

The door of the companionway slammed shut behind them. The two men turned to see Marvin staring upward with a frown at the brig's upper sails. Argandeau lifted an eyebrow and softly withdrew to the lee rail.

"Two hundred and eighty-eight miles, Dan," Newton said. "That means Fayal day after tomorrow!"

Marvin rapped the bulwark with his knuckles. "And so to get us there," he said, and his accusing glance included Argandeau, "you pile muslin on her till she looks like a feather bed! Get in those studding sails and skysails! Can't you feel her dragging?"

Newton ran forward, shouting orders. Seamen swarmed from nowhere, as if by magic, and scuttled up the shrouds. The studding-sail booms came in; the skysail yards were lowered and their sails close-furled by men who seemed, like insects crawling on a ceiling, to defy the laws of gravity. The brig's deck took on less of a cant: the waves through which she sliced seemed suddenly to lift her and press her on.

"Just remember that," Marvin said severely, as Newton

returned to the quarter-deck. "Any fool or Englishman can crowd on canvas, so that a vessel looks fast. What we aim to do is keep our lee rails out of water and go faster. Give her all she needs; not all she'll stand."

He took two turns at the weather rail, watching the gun crews housing the long guns amidships. "I've said it fifty times, but it'll bear repeating: This is a war we're in, and risks are the last things we want to take."

Argandeau laughed, and Marvin halted in his pacing to fix him with a questioning glance.

"Yes," Argandeau said. "Certainly yes! There were some of us who had that in mind, Captain Caution, when you ran into Dublin Harbor in daylight, and then snatched away that merchantman in the dark. There was no risk to that, of course; no more than picking up an alligator by the hind foot."

"I tell you there was no risk," Marvin said calmly. "We ran in and anchored with the British ensign set over our American ensign. There was nothing for the British to think except that we were a captured American vessel, running for safety from the French privateer that pursued us to the very mouth of the harbor. Every man in the fort could see Souville's vessel, and not one of them would ever think to look at us. You know yourself that if you do something openly with one hand, you can do anything you like with the other and never be caught at it, provided you do it quietly. To anchor under the guns of the fort was an extra bit of caution."

"Caution!" Argandeau whispered, raising his eyes to the sky.

"Yes, caution," Marvin repeated. "When they saw us do it, they knew beyond any doubt that there was no harm in us, and so gave us no thought whatever. There is no surprise so great as to do something you could not do if you tried to do it in the way you were expected to do it."

Argandeau moved his lips helplessly and shook his head.

"But Fayal," Marvin continued, looking at him thoughtfully; "Fayal is another matter. In Fayal we must be doubly cautious."

Argandeau raised an eyebrow and nodded understandingly. "Now you speak a language that has a meaning. You mean that in Fayal we must pick up *two* alligators by the hind foot."

# XXXI

A NORTHWEST wind piled dingy clouds against the cone-shaped hills that rimmed the roadstead of Fayal with an amphitheater of green; and from the top hamper of the *Blue Swan* brig, riding at anchor in the lee of Espalamaca Point, there came an uneasy moaning that seemed, to the girl who stood at the shoreward rail of the quarter-deck, too dreary and too shrill to be evoked by wind alone.

Despite her many days at sea, she had no eyes for the white houses nestling on the slopes behind her, half hidden in their vines and fruit trees; and she stared with a sort of fascination at the three war vessels that lay to westward, slowly swaying in the long swell from the tumbling waters beyond. Even though her hands were buried in the loose and heavy sleeves of a quilted Chinese jacket, not long out of a shop in the Palais Royal, she seemed to hug herself and shiver at the sight.

On the deck in the lee of the sternmost carronade sat an angular woman, her scow-like feet thrust out before her and her huge brown hands busily wielding knitting needles that seemed the size of boat hooks. As she knitted, she cast quick glances at the restless girl. "You get yourself sick with this worry," she told her at length. "Then you be no good when there is need to worry. What you worry over? Is it the shark that follows us about, looking up at us with one eye, like someone I know? He is like a kitten, merely playing. You are safe here, and soon you will be safe away—away from those damned *Anglais* with their goat whiskers. Brr!" She muttered to herself, and her mutterings were unpleasant.

"Yes, but we ought to be away now!" Corunna said, as if to herself. "Right now! If he hadn't been so kind—if he hadn't got this brig for me—I think I'd—I'd never stay here for such a——"

She fell silent, watching the distant group of officers on the high poop of the ship-of-the-line, and into her mind there came again, as there had come a thousand times before, the constant tenderness of Lurman Slade and his forethought in her behalf. It went back, this forethought, to the very day when she had arrived with Victorine in Dublin and had been installed by Slade in the captain's cabin of the *Blue Swan* brig. Victorine, grumbling in her suspicious Breton fashion at the manner in which Slade had eyed her, was stowing her mistress's Paris purchases in the lockers beneath the standing bedplace, when Slade had entered the cabin with a look of mock seriousness on his face to say that he had news—doubtful news—for her. A British frigate, he said, had just dropped anchor alongside.

She had sprung up in consternation; but when Slade, on that, had smiled, she sat down mystified. "You don't think, my dear," he had said, "that I'd have let you take the risk of coming to Dublin without guarding you against any possibility of harm! While we're on this side of the Atlantic, you're always in danger of capture and imprisonment unless we play a game with the English—unless we spoil the Egyptians. That's what we've done, my dear! I've hoodwinked them, gammoned them, told them this and told them that; and the upshot is they've given me a letter-of-marque, the poor fools! A British letter-of-marque, so that they're bound to protect us until we're ready to bid them good day! Let their frigates anchor where they will; they can't harm *you*, my dear! You'll only need to let me act as captain when they're about." He had laughed and patted her hand, and added, "I'd like to see their faces when we take French leave!"

It had disturbed her; yet she would have been ungrateful, she knew, to protest an act intended only for her safety; and so she had admired him for his resourcefulness and cunning. She had admired him still when, later, he returned to say that he had made a master stroke—arranged, even, to sail as far as Fayal with a British squadron. "With half the distance covered," he had chuckled, throwing back his head to see her more clearly from beneath his drooping eyelid, "we're as good as home! I'll claim a reward some day"— his eyes gleamed hotly—"for the way I've taken care of you! Some day, and soon!"

At the sound of a barking cough from Victorine, he had turned and left her, and Corunna had heard him shouting at the crew in sudden anger; but she told herself that what he said was true: He had taken care of her, and for what he had done she must be truly grateful. Yet beneath her gratitude had stirred a vague disquiet—a disquiet that had persisted during the long voyage to Fayal in the company of the hated Britishers, and that had grown even stronger when Fayal was reached at last, and the *Blue Swan,* despite a favoring wind, still lay at anchor within pistol shot of the squadron leader.

Ill at ease, she stared around her at the towering hills of Fayal—hills that seemed, for all their soft greenness, to threaten and imprison her.

Only half conscious of the hoarse gabble of the woman

Victorine, she stood on tiptoe to peer for the hundredth time at the quarter-deck of the ship-of-the-line, to which Slade had been rowed an hour since. "It's part of the game," he had told her, laughing softly at her protests, "part of the game. For your sake, I've got to do what I can."

Victorine emphasized her words with agitated jerkings of her knitting needles. "Who but Victorine should know the ways of men—little Victorine, yes, who has married five of them—five! One I lost at Trafalgar, and six would have married me the next day. Six out of the forecastle of the *Glorieuse,* where I had resided for nine months! Name of a name of a name, but I know them! Here and there you find good ones, perhaps—I think so—but never among the smooth ones—the ones who softly say soft things. They are like soap, the soft ones, slipping out from under the hand and vanishing for a moment; and the first thing you know, another has picked them up to use. Hah, yes! I know them, those smooth ones; fragrant and firm, at one moment, but always softening and changing when exposed to the water of flattery. Soap, they are! This gentleman of yours, he is soft and smooth. I have watched him with you. He is gentle, yes. Ah, well; I know him! It is with *you* he is gentle. With me he would not be so gentle! I have seen him look at me. When he has the chance, he thinks to himself, he will give me a kick—Poom!—and little Victorine will pop through the hull of this vessel like an eighteen-pound shot. That is what he thinks. He has no love for me, that one! I am in his way! If it were not for little Victorine, says that piece of soap to himself, he would be alone with you when he is with you, and much happier for the freedom to try to make free with you. Hah! Hah!" She laughed darkly. "Ah, well! I have no fear! Better men than he have thought to kick

Victorine through a bulkhead, but you can tell by looking at me that I have never even dented one." She rubbed the instep of one vast felt shoe with the toe of the other.

"Hold your tongue!" Corunna said absently. Her glance shot suddenly seaward, caught by a movement at the edge of the perpendicular cliff of Espalamaca Point. From behind the cliff moved the staysails and jibs of a high-bowed vessel. Even before her foremast hove in sight, Corunna knew from her slowness and clumsiness that she was a merchant craft; while from the tauntness of her rig, when her fore and main masts came into view, Corunna said to herself that the vessel was a brig, and American. Yet the girl was only partly right, for a stubby mizzenmast followed the main from behind the steep headland; the vessel was a barque, not a brig, but undoubtedly American; for at her mizzen truck an American ensign whipped smartly in the breeze.

Corunna stared blankly at the flag; then made a sound of distress with her tongue against the roof of her mouth. A cloudiness filled her eyes, as if the far-off scrap of bunting had put it there. "Well, I declare!" she cried. "I'll be switched! The poor fools ought to know better!" She stamped her foot angrily and pressed white knuckles to her lips, seeming to hold her breath.

As if in answer to her thoughts, the barque appeared to hesitate at sight of the four war craft lying close inshore. A small and clumsy crew shook out and sheeted home the topgallant sails that had been handed preparatory to anchoring, and at the same moment the barque hauled her wind and stood off, running to the southward across the harbor mouth. The American flag dropped from the mizzen, and in its place rose the British flag.

Again Corunna stamped her Chinese slipper on the deck.

"Oh," she cried, "what's the man thinking of? He's lost his mind!"

She crossed to the other rail to watch the attempt of her clumsy and guileless countryman to escape the trap of his own making; and she knew at once, from the heaviness of the strange barque's movements, that she must be an easy prey to any who pursued her.

A boat, she saw, had pushed eagerly off from the hulking ship-of-the-line to windward. It bobbed toward the *Blue Swan,* and Corunna recognized her own jolly-boat, with Slade in the stern sheets.

Victorine scrambled to her feet. "Soap!" she grumbled. "Here comes your Mr. Soap! Me, just now I prefer the company of the octopus I have saved for your dinner!" She padded to the cabin hatch, her huge felt shoes slapping the deck with something like disgust.

Slade waved gayly to Corunna, his head tilted far back to let him see clearly with both eyes. "Call all hands!" he shouted down the wind. "All hands to make sail!"

Without any word from her, a boatswain in the bows set up a piping, and by the time Slade had rounded into the lee of the stern and come aboard, a part of the crew were casting loose the topsails; while others, at the capstan, were heaving the brig short.

"What's this?" she asked sharply.

Slade chuckled and turned to look at the slow barque, forging steadily southward toward the steep slope of Guia Head. "Why," he said, "we're ordered in chase. You saw him, the poor fool! Running in with his colors set, and losing his courage when he saw us lying here! Such stupidity I never saw! He could have come in and been safe, but he lost his head and ran, the poor fool! Gave himself away into the bargain; and then thought to deceive us, like an ostrich!" There was a furtiveness to his laughter, like quick movements among dry leaves.

She stared at him; then a slow comprehension dawned on her face and she laughed delightedly. "And because we're fastest, you persuaded them to send us out alone! Well, it was worth waiting for, to go like this!"

She looked once more for the strange barque; and as she looked, its topgallant sails merged with Guia Head's sharp outline and vanished.

The topsails of the *Blue Swan* were sheeted home; the topgallant sails set over them. Amid a shouting and a clattering, the anchor was catted. The brig's head fell off to the southward and she slipped rapidly toward the troubled steel-gray expanse of open sea.

It was only ten minutes later when she rounded the headland behind which the barque had disappeared, and hauled to the westward, but in that short time the barque had set her royals and put an unexpected stretch of tumbling water between herself and her pursuer.

Corunna laughed again. "She's faster than we thought! Trust an American to be faster than she looks!" She wrapped herself more snugly in the folds of her quilted jacket and looked uneasily at Slade. "By nightfall she'll be as safe as we."

Slade, watching the distant barque from a carronade slide, muttered beneath his breath, jumped to the deck, walked quickly forward and snapped an order to the gun crews by the foremast. A whistle blew long and shrilly, and at the sound the men scattered, running to their stations.

White-faced, Corunna caught at the arm of a running

boatswain's mate. "Here!" she said. "Tell Mr. Slade I want him!"

The boatswain's mate stared at her. "Quarters!" he said, and ran on to the cabin hatch.

Slade came slowly back, stepping from side to side to give free passage to heavily laden powder boys, and Corunna went to meet him.

"What are you doing?" she demanded. "I'm in command of this vessel, and I'll have no orders given from my quarter-deck without my sanction! By what right did you order these people piped to quarters?"

He laughed gently through tightly clenched teeth. "Why," he said, "you know as well as I that we're bound to play a part—to play a part."

"To play a part!" she cried. "What part is there that we need to play when we're free from the British? What have you manned those guns for?"

He tipped back his head and looked at her along his nose. "You're excited," he said. "You forget that barque yonder doesn't know what we are. She might take it into her head to let fly at us. Surely there's no harm in self-protection." He took her arm and pressed it.

She wrenched herself free. "Self-protection! Do you think I'm blind? We'll alter our course two points, and then she'll know we're peaceable!"

His voice was low and husky: "Don't be impractical, my dear. This crew of ours—they think they're on an English vessel; and why shouldn't they? Just bear in mind they're English themselves. We'll have to handle them carefully, Corunna, or they might turn against us. In time we can swing them to our side; until then, it's best to let me handle things in the way that'll benefit us both. We'll have to show 'em it's to their advantage to follow our judgment."

"They're not English!" she said. "They're Irish! There's Americans among 'em, too, of a sort! What do you mean —in time we can swing them to our side? You're lying to me! You're trying to squirm out of something! I'll—I'll put you under arrest in your cabin!" She drew a deep, quivering breath and shivered, as if with cold.

He shook his head sorrowfully. "I was afraid of this," he said kindly. "I owe it to you and to the men themselves to do what I'm doing. Why, here's what seems to be a division of authority, my dear—you with your papers that they've never seen—papers that might be forgeries, for all they know—and me with what they take to be an honest letter-of-marque from the British Government. You can see yourself that it's a dangerous situation unless it's handled properly." He turned from her suddenly and swung himself into the ratlines to look forward at the fleeing barque; then nodded his head at the helmsman and motioned a little with his hand. The brig yawed to larboard.

"Give 'em a gun!" he shouted.

"No!" Corunna screamed. "No!"

The brig lurched. Her bow seemed to rear. The starboard bow gun crashed ponderously. A billowing cloud of white smoke hid the *Blue Swan's* bowsprit, then eddied down wind as the brig came back on her course. Slade, peering through the smoke, snarled at what he saw.

Corunna reached through the ratlines to clutch him by the ankle. "My God!" she cried. "You're not firing on them! They're Americans!"

He looked down at her through the shrouds, and his expression was one she had never seen. "This is a man's business!" he told her harshly. "There's a fortune in it for us! A fortune! I'll ask you to go below if you're afraid of seeing something that might disturb you."

Again he motioned to the helmsman. Again the brig yawed, and again the bow gun thundered. From the foretop there came a thin shouting—a shouting that spread to the *Blue Swan's* decks. The gun crews capered joyously among the guns, and powder boys leaped with excitement.

"By God!" Slade shouted. "Her mizzenmast! It's down! We got her! We got her!"

It was as Slade said, although such gunnery seemed a miracle. The distant barque had fallen off her course, and over her counter trailed her stubby mizzenmast.

"You rat!" Corunna said. "You rat!" She tugged at Slade's ankle. He laughed and stepped to the bulwark, but she caught at him again, so that he lost his balance and sprawled to the deck.

He scrambled to his feet, his face yellow. "Here!" he said. "What the hell you think you're doing?"

"You skunk," Corunna whispered. She seemed, in her rage, to have grown near to the height of Slade himself. "You damned skunk! You damned dirty slave-driving skunk! You damned——" Her breath failed her. She struck at him with her clenched fist.

Slade laughed his rasping laugh. He turned to the third officer, who watched them curiously. "The lady's excited," Slade said. "The firing's unbalanced her. We'll put her below!"

She fought silently, but Slade and his man had her. They dragged her to the cabin ladder. "Get down there!" Slade said. They lifted her from her feet and swung her through the hatch. Slade scrambled down the ladder after her and jerked her to her feet in the dimness of the companionway.

"It's a good time to have it out with you, Corunna," he said, "just because there isn't any time for it. I've coddled you along to keep you with me, because up to now you could have got away, if you tried. But now you can't! This brig's mine, not yours; and I do what I want to with it and with everything on it! I'll drop the play-acting, but I'll treat you well if you'll be sweet."

She struck at him.

The door of the captain's cabin swung open. In the doorway stood the woman Victorine, tall and angular against the stern-windows behind her.

She looked at Corunna's face and instantly stabbed at Slade with the two long knitting needles in her left hand. He gasped and clutched at his thigh. Then Victorine dragged Corunna across the threshold into the bright cabin. The door slammed in his face and the bolt shot home.

The two women heard his fist crash against a panel of the door, and after that they thought he laughed. "To hell with you this little while!" he said, and scrambled up the ladder to the deck.

# XXXII

IT WAS a brig, and American, Corunna had thought at first, that she had seen creeping around Espalamaca Point into Fayal Roads; and a brig was what it had been, an hour earlier, when it lay hove-to so far at sea that the lesser peaks below Fayal's high cone were misty nubbins on the water's edge.

"We'll take no chances," Marvin had said to Argandeau and Newton. "Rig the false mizzenmast, and stretch canvas over the ports and hammock nettings. Then we can round the point with a cable dragging and see what's before us with no danger to ourselves. One of them might come out in chase if we're cautious about it. With us as slow and harmless as we'll seem to be, it won't be the big ones that come out, either. It might be the sloop-of-war, and it might even be——"

"Stop!" Argandeau shouted. He clenched his fist, extended his first and little fingers, and with their tips touched the nearest carronade. "Be cautious! You must touch metal —so—when you give tongue to your desires, lest they turn sour!"

Marvin stared at him. "Metal?" he asked. "Wood's better. It's handier." He turned to look at the island, coldly blue against the gray sky. "If nobody comes out," he added, "we'll take our bearings and come back at dusk." He drew a deep breath. "We'll come back at dusk and see what's to be done." He struck his hand against the taffrail. "Rig the mizzenmast! Run the long guns to the stern-chase ports. Cover the ports with the jolly-boat and get a screen around the guns. I want her high in the bow, and clumsy-looking!"

So the *True-Hearted Yankee* brig had become a barque, high-sided and cumbersome; and thus disguised she had labored in from the sea, a weary traveler seeking peace and rest in Fayal Roads.

As she passed the point and opened the broad bay rimmed with white houses set on slopes of dusty green, Marvin cast a quick glance aloft and then along the vessel's narrow deck. Above him, a handful of sailors crawled lazily about, handing the topgallant sails. Before him, from quarter-deck to bow, a double row of men were ranged inside the bulwarks, wedged tight between the carronades. It was no scurvy crew that Marvin eyed, but quiet men, neat in brown uniforms from France. Satisfied, he turned to the harbor.

"There they are, Dan!" Newton said; and his voice, like his pale whiskers, seemed to tremble. "There they are! Four of 'em, and one of 'em the *Blue Swan!*"

Argandeau drew his small mirror from his pocket and examined his face anxiously. "That brig," he said, "she would be easy to approach in the dusk, eh, Captain Caution? I think we make a pleasant call tonight, and so I must shave, perhaps."

Marvin walked to the wheel. "That brig," he said to the helmsman. "That brig——" He coughed and cleared his throat. "The brig beyond the three war craft! Get her in your mind."

The helmsman stared straight ahead. "I got her."

"Get her so you can find her in the dark," Marvin told him.

"I got her," the helmsman assured him.

"All right," Marvin said. "Bear off and on and off again; then point for Guia Head. It's steep-to. Allow for a two-knot on-shore current and don't waste any time getting around the head. Straighten her out when she points due west, and hold her parallel to the coast."

"Due west," the helmsman dutifully repeated.

Marvin turned to Newton. "Haul down the colors and run up the British ensign. Shake out the topgallant sails. Remind 'em not to hurry." Newton ran forward.

"Take in the cable?" Argandeau asked. He kissed his hand to the war vessels close inshore.

Marvin shook his head. "Let the cable alone. Let it alone." Into his mind there came the face of Captain Dorman. " 'They cry unto the Lord in their trouble,' " Marvin murmured. " 'They cry unto the Lord in their trouble, and he bringeth them out of their distresses . . . he bringeth them unto their desired haven.' " He looked quickly over his shoulder, as if he thought to find an old friend near at hand.

Overhead, the topgallant sails dropped from the yards and were sheeted home. The vessel wallowed uncertainly in the heavy swells that thrust themselves beneath her and passed onward to the accompaniment of complaining gurglings from her bows—of gurglings and angry hissings, as though she protested at the trailing cable that restrained her.

A head came over the edge of the maintop and stared, open-mouthed, at the quarter-deck. "They're going aloft!" it cried. "They're going aloft on the brig!"

Marvin seemed not to hear. His eyes were fastened on the little spouts of foam that rose slowly from the foot of Guia Head and seemed to cling for a time against its rocky sides.

"We take in the cable?" Argandeau asked softly.

"Take in three fathoms," Marvin said. "No, take in two fathoms."

"It's the brig," Newton told him. "She's coming out alone."

Marvin nodded.

Argandeau passed his hand caressingly over his chin. "So it is the *Blue Swan* after all! Better I go now and shave."

Marvin looked at him.

"You think I don't need it," Argandeau said hastily. "Ah, well, I remain here where all can see how I am gay! They will speak of it in later years. 'Lucien Argandeau,' they will say, 'he stood there in the shadow of that great rock, but more magnificent than the rock itself, because he was gay in the face of danger.'" He scanned the bulging slope of Guia Head that towered above them; then cast a quick glance over his shoulder. "Now she comes," he told Marvin. "She is a brig indeed, that *Blue Swan!* She moves fast! What you think—we take in that cable?"

"Take it in and coil it down," Marvin said. "Don't hurry, but when it's done, crowd on the royals and call the men aft. I've got a word to say to them."

Released from the drag of the heavy cable, the vessel seemed to hasten forward with the surges as if impatient to reach the calmer water beyond the head. She rounded steadily beneath the dark bulk of the overhanging cliff; and as she rounded, the cliff edge, like a drawn curtain, abruptly cut off from Marvin's gaze the white houses of the town and the tall brig that followed.

With the setting of the royals, she seemed to slice knife-like through the waves, in no respect different from the fast brig that had accompanied Tom Souville's *Renard* to sea, save that her false mizzenmast swayed precariously in its fastenings forward of the wheel; while strips of canvas, stretched around the bulwarks, added to her apparent height.

Marvin stood silently before the false mast while the crew, herded by Newton and the Indian, Steven, pressed aft to crouch amidships. He looked over his shoulder at Guia Head, falling fast astern. There was no vessel in sight.

Marvin stared down at the brown-clad men before him. "You know what we're up to," he said. "We're probably going to fight the brig that's in chase of us. It may be some of you don't like the idea of standing up to a vessel that isn't a cargo vessel. If that's the case, it may make you more peaceable in your minds to know she's got specie aboard. To the best of my knowledge, she's carrying fifteen thousand English pounds. That's seventy-five thousand dollars. What's more, I propose to divide one-half of that fifteen thousand pounds among the crew of this vessel, provided the proper discipline's observed and she's taken as I want her taken. That'll mean over four hundred dollars apiece to each one of you, just for this one engagement."

"Yow!" screamed a seaman in the rear of the throng. A pleased rustling and whispering swept over the remainder of the crew.

"The commander of that brig," Marvin went on, "is an American, and as bad as they come. I think he's a traitor, bent on mischief to all true-hearted Americans. We'll soon know. If he fires on us, there's no doubt about it. Anyway, he's the man I'm after. I don't want him hurt. I want all gun pointers to keep their fire away from the cabin and quarter-deck of that brig. Restrict yourself to her rigging, so far as possible. That's why you've been told to load with chain and bar shot. Keep your sights on her bow and foremast. There'll be a penalty for each time she's hulled aft of the mainmast—a penalty of one thousand dollars deducted from the amount to be distributed among you. So you'll do well not to fire until your sights are free of smoke and you can see what you're aiming at. You've got the pendulum, and there'll be no excuse for hitting her too far aft. Make sure you hit her, too, unless you want to spend the rest of this war starving and freezing on a British hulk! That's all. Get forward and keep yourselves below the bulwarks, where you won't be seen by those in the tops of the vessel in chase."

He turned again to look back at Guia Head. As he looked, the *Blue Swan's* jibs and squaresails popped suddenly into view from behind it, almost as though a puff of smoke had shot from its foot.

"Pooi!" Argandeau exclaimed. "Here am I, ready to be gay, and I find nothing to be gay about!"

"You'll scarcely have time," Marvin told him. "On the chart there's three small islands close inshore, halfway between Guia Head and the western point. We're nearly there. I don't want to pass 'em. Drag the cable again, and keep the islands on our beam. If necessary, drop a staysail under the bow."

"Good!" Argandeau cried. "We set the stage, eh? Ah well: you can count on Argandeau to push over the scenery on him!"

A dozen men payed out the cable, and once more the vessel labored slowly in the choppy seas.

"Look! Look!" Argandeau said. "She blows out a bean, I think!"

Astern, the *Blue Swan* yawed; a fleecy ball of white burst from her bow. The distant explosion jarred the false mizzenmast in its lashings.

Argandeau opened his mouth wide in a soundless laugh. "Close!" he said, jerking his thumb contemptuously to larboard. "Close as last Friday!"

The *True-Hearted Yankee* creaked and labored onward, her officers and crew caught in a frozen silence. Under the bulwarks the men stared white-eyed at Marvin, who in turn stood staring patiently at three small islands close against the low and rocky coast.

Closer now, the *Blue Swan* yawed again and fired a gun. The ball skipped past them to windward, whacking against the swells.

Marvin came suddenly to life and clapped his hands together. "Cut the mizzen!" he said. "Cut it on the larboard side and pitch it over the starboard counter, where it'll drag and be seen from the brig! Down with the helm and point for the islands! Keep the cable dragging! Rig the pendulum! Take in the royals!"

Men scuttled crab-like over the decks, keeping their heads below the level of the false bulwarks. They slashed at the preventer stays of the stubby mizzenmast and tumbled it over the taffrail. The crews of the long guns crouched beside their pieces, growling among themselves and freeing the falls of the jolly-boat, which hung low from the stern-davits, screening the stern-chase ports.

Forward of the mainmast, at its foot, three men set up a padded iron tripod from the apex of which hung a bar tipped with an inverted gong of polished brass. At the level of the gong, and straight beneath the apex of the tripod, they made fast a small steel ring. This done, they stepped back, letting the iron bar swing free. It oscillated. The vessel rolled, and the bar, swinging off to one side, caught for a moment against a leg of the tripod; then swung downward.

The brass gong touched the small steel ring, and the vessel echoed to its clang. The men under the bulwarks made motions of sponging and ramming. The tall Indian caught the pendulum and held it still.

"Set all guns at point-blank range," he shouted, "and keep your ears open for changes!"

The *Blue Swan* was close at hand; as close, almost, as the small islands near the shore; so close that the white foam beneath her bows was reflected in her bright copper as her forefoot lifted, giving her the look of being sheathed with gleaming ice.

Marvin, staring at her with such fierce intensity that the northwest wind whirled moisture from his eyes, felt Argandeau take him by the arm.

"You see who I see, standing on a carronade?" Argandeau asked him softly. "Look how he tips back his head! And his long hair; I can see it blowing!"

"Yes," Marvin said. "Yes. They can't get inshore of us now. They wouldn't dare. They'd strike the rocks. They'll have to run past our guns!"

From the small figure on the *Blue Swan's* quarter-deck there came a hoarse shouting, indistinguishable above the wailing of the breeze in the top-hamper. Marvin, sighting at the onrushing brig along his own starboard taffrail, shouted, "Pendulum!"

Behind him the gong clanged and quickly clanged again.

"Now!" Marvin shouted. "Let go! Cut away the mizzen! Cut the cable! Strip off the false canvas! Drop the jolly-boat! Fire when the pendulum strikes! Brace around the yards!" He went to the wheel and seized it.

The deck of the *True-Hearted Yankee* boiled with men. The bow of the *Blue Swan* lay dead astern. The jolly-boat pitched downward with a whirring of falls. The pendulum clanged. With the clang, the guns at the stern ports bellowed, and the brig seemed to leap ahead, forced forward by the recoil of the guns. A thick cloud of white smoke enveloped her stern and her lower sails.

Marvin spun the wheel. "Long guns to the larboard bow ports!" he said.

Coughing and cursing, the men wrestled with the long guns, hustling them from the smoky quarter-deck and running them forward through the clumps of seamen who hauled at tacks and sheets.

A gun roared from the *Blue Swan,* lying hid beyond the smoke cloud; and another followed. Grapeshot screamed and rattled high in the rigging of the *True-Hearted Yankee.* A severed rope plumped down at Marvin's feet.

The *True-Hearted Yankee* shot ahead, clear of the smoke. On her larboard beam, the *Blue Swan* yawed from side to side, her bowsprit dangling from a snarl of ropes and splinters, and her long jib boom dragging beneath her bows.

The pendulum clanged; two carronades roared flatly from the *True-Hearted Yankee.* The *Blue Swan's* main course split apart and flapped raggedly in the wind.

The pendulum clanged again. Three more carronades flung jets of smoke toward the damaged brig. The *Blue Swan's* bulwarks, near her foremast, crumpled into splinters. Her shrouds and backstays parted and curled upward like scorched string. The foremast itself swayed forward; then, with a crackling that came faintly to the shouting gunners on the *True-Hearted Yankee,* fell slowly backward, the yards and sails stabbing and tearing at the slender spars and straining canvas of the raking mainmast.

In the time it takes a small white cloud to pass across the

face of the sun, the *Blue Swan* had become a shattered and unmanageable hulk.

Newton looked across the rail. " 'Captain Caution!' " he said, and laughed. "He waltzes across a harbor mouth filled with British guns—enough guns to blow him and his ship and all of us to China! And right on top of that he takes this brig just like machinery, and not a hair of our heads is hurt—and not many of theirs, either, for that matter. Yet there's Slade and his brig and his men at our mercy, on account of Captain Caution!"

## XXXIII

THE *True-Hearted Yankee,* her topsails thrown aback and her pendulum clanging slowly in the long swells, lay under the lee of the shattered brig; and Marvin, boarding the *Blue Swan* with the tall Indian at the head of a dozen brown-clad seamen, armed with pistols and boarding axes, found her decks thronged with a crew already beginning to be drunk and hilarious from the contents of a looted spirit locker.

On the quarter-deck, Slade, four officers about him, laughed hoarsely at the sight of Marvin and drank from the pannikin in his hand. He threw back his lank hair with a sweep of his head and spoke from the side of his mouth to his officers, who moved uncomfortably.

Marvin stationed six men at the break of the deck and motioned Steven to the cabin with the others; then spoke quietly to the group of men around the binnacle: "Where's your captain?"

Slade stepped forward. "There's no need of all this rigmarole," he said. "Go ahead and get it over with."

Marvin's reply was almost pleasant. "You're captain, are you?" He glanced at the other officers and spoke more to them than to Slade. "Properly handled, you should have had good cruising in this brig." He looked placidly at the *True-Hearted Yankee,* where round-mouthed guns seemed to stare in amazement at what they saw.

"Properly handled?" Slade asked. He drank again from his pannikin. "Handled with damned Yankee trickery, do you mean?" He laughed and turned, as if for admiration, to his officers.

Marvin stood silent, watching the drunken crew that cursed and stumbled amid the wreckage in the *Blue Swan's* bows.

"Well," Slade said in a voice suddenly quiet, "what about it?"

There was no sign that Marvin heard the words. He stood motionless with head a little bent, and seemed to listen.

Steven's head and shoulders appeared above the cabin hatch. "We can't find the specie," he said. He pitched a bundle of clothes to the deck, scrambled after it and turned to help Corunna through the hatch. Behind Corunna crawled Victorine, an angular figure, a cord made fast across one shoulder and between her knees, so that her voluminous skirts were drawn upward into bunchy pantaloons, beneath which her vast felt shoes fumbled for a foothold.

Marvin seemed not to see the two women. "You can't find the specie?" he asked the Indian thoughtfully. "That makes it awkward! Awkward!" He clasped his hands behind him and moved closer to Slade's officers.

"Ordinarily," he said pleasantly, "I'd take you gentlemen aboard and give you fair treatment, but under the circumstances it wouldn't be safe. You see, the people aboard my brig know about this man who calls himself your commander. They know what he is. They know he's a thief, a black-mailer, a liar, a turncoat."

Marvin's face grew sterner. "They'd be bound to hang him without a trial," he told the silent officers. "It might even be they'd get out of control some night and do it. If they did, they might take you as well, knowing you'd carried out his orders, and I can't have that. I can't have that!"

Slade threw back his head and folded his arms; there was a kind of pride, not braggadocio, in his attitude. "Go ahead," he said quietly. "Go ahead and get it done."

There was no flaw in his gameness; he expected no mercy and asked for none; but there was a barely perceptible quiver to Slade's mouth, and beneath the tranquillity of his voice something like a broken breath of sound, a tremor more felt than heard; and it disturbed Marvin. He looked at Slade again gravely; then turned to the officers.

"In spite of what I've been saying, I did mean to take this man home for trial, and I hoped to see him hanged, as did three of my friends here. I think they'll back me up in what I'm going to do about it now."

He cleared his throat, then went on: "Well, we've got him down, and we aren't going to do what we intended. He's lost his ship and everything else, thank God; and I guess it'll be enough for us if he goes back to England with you. If any of you like him, I guess you'd better keep him there, because if he's ever taken by any American ship, or sets foot on American soil again, it won't be good for him. I guess it's enough for us, if we ever think of him again, to know he's in England with nothing but his reputation as a traitor to make a living out of."

Slade looked at him incredulously. "You mean you're letting me go?"

Marvin laughed. "If that's what you call it," he said, then spoke once more to the officers. "Now you can see why it's awkward. For the reason I've told you, I can't take you as prisoners, nor do I propose to leave this vessel while it hides the specie of this man you call captain. It's hidden somewhere in his cabin, for there's nowhere else he'd dare to hide it. Therefore, gentlemen, I'll have to ask you to get yourself as far into the bows of this vessel as you can get. I'm going to put a match to your magazine and blow up the cabin and the specie with it." He turned to Steven. "Break open a powder keg and lay a train to it."

A stocky, red-faced officer coughed nervously and addressed him in the thick speech of Devon. "The specie kegs," he said, "are stacked in the rudder case, high up."

Slade laughed and tossed his empty pannikin over the side.

Marvin nodded to Steven, who turned and hurried below. He considered Corunna then. "I think," he said, "it's safe enough in case you wish to remain aboard this vessel. I'll have to set her afire, to make sure she's destroyed, but the guns you've heard will bring out the sloop-of-war to see what's happened. She'll be out pretty soon. But even if she doesn't come out, you're close enough to shore to get there with no trouble."

She looked at him, her knuckles pressed against her lips.

He hesitated. "In case you wish to be taken off——"

She only continued to look at him, but he thought her eyes were fierce with disdain.

"She will go," Victorine said. "Put her in your boat and take her to your ship."

"But if she doesn't want to——" he began.

Victorine pushed her red and furious face almost against his. "She will go!" she screamed. "Put her in the boat and take her to your ship!"

Steven came through the hatch with a specie keg in his arms. "Seventeen of 'em!" he said. He thumped it down on the deck.

Marvin smiled and looked back toward Guia Head.

"Put 'em in the boat," he said. "The sloop-of-war's coming down on us. Throw over the guns and set this vessel afire in the bows."

But it was the Indian who came to Corunna and Victorine. "Now, ladies," he said, "we're going home."

The *True-Hearted Yankee,* under a cloud of sail, bore to the northwestward past the rounded peak of Castello Branco Point. Marvin, at her taffrail, watched the sloop-of-war haul her wind toward the burning brig; then spoke to Newton, who stood beside him, eyeing him with proud affection. "I want Argandeau!" he said. "I saw him run forward, when we came aboard, and jump down the fore hatch. He's got no business going below at a time like this. Send for him. Tell him I want him."

It was a full five minutes later when Newton returned, pushing Argandeau before him. At the mainmast Argandeau balked and crouched, like a startled fawn, casting timid glances at the cabin hatch. Marvin stared at him, puzzled. "Where've you been?" he demanded. "What ails you?"

Argandeau wiped his forehead with his sleeve and spoke humbly in a thick voice:

"Captain, I am not gay!"

"Aren't you? What of it?"

"Captain, I ask permission to spend all daylight hours for the length of this voyage in the hold."

"What?"

Argandeau shivered. "Captain, you have heard me speak of rabbits, perhaps too much and too lightly. The one called Victorine was formerly pleasanter to the eye, as you will believe, since it could not be otherwise. At the time I speak of she was—an acquaintance of mine."

"Was she?" Marvin said calmly. "Well, I can't have women interfering with work aboard this vessel. House the long guns and make all snug. A little ordinary caution, now, will get all of us safely back to France and fortune."

"All of us?" Argandeau turned a tragic face upon him. "A little ordinary caution? It is in that manner that one speaks when it is not himself who is in danger, but only a friend! My captain, you would not be so philosophic if you had ever been loved by a volcano, and even made the miscalculation of being wedded to one! I would not admit it publicly, but it appears that one of my marriages was with this artillerist! This great grenadier! This Stromboli of a Victorine! It is my simple confession—I am not perfect—and I am at your mercy."

"How is it possible for Argandeau to fear a woman?" Marvin asked. Then he quoted almost the selfsame words that Argandeau had once said to him on the deck of the *Olive Branch*. "You in France, you are subtle! You hunt always for the heartstrings of a woman, and you play softly on them, so that she is moved to do your will."

"Ah, my God! My God!" Argandeau whispered. "I spoke as a Frenchman! I am an American now—a true-hearted Yankee. I know nothing of women, and wish to know less!"

Marvin stared hard at him. "All right, stay below during daylight unless you're needed," he said, and went below himself.

Marvin rapped on the door of the captain's cabin. Victorine opened it, knitting needles in her hand; and Marvin, looking beyond her, saw Corunna rise to stand with her back against the table, facing him.

"Well," he said gravely, "we're glad to have you aboard,

you and your friend." He glanced at Victorine. "I think I've seen you before. The knitting looks familiar."

"And why not?" Victorine demanded. "I have carried these needles for protection since the good God knows when, knitting all day, and at night pulling out what I have knitted."

"For protection?" Marvin asked.

Victorine wagged her head. "Hah, but you were right! I knew you were right when you spoke rudely to this cabbage here"—she stabbed a needle toward Corunna—"in Paris."

"Yes," he said, "it was in Paris that I saw you."

"As I say," Victorine continued placidly, "I know! Me, I know! What we females need is not compliments, but truth. Of my husbands, the most successful with me spoke truthfully to me; and I, to keep him quiet, pretended to an adoration for him that was somewhat more than I felt. Thus we adored each other! Ah, yes, he was the best of them all!"

Marvin glanced quickly at Corunna, but she was staring through the stern windows with hard, uninterested eyes at the towering blue cone of Fayal.

"Well," he said awkwardly, "if there's anything you need, either of you, you'll let us know. I thought you might like —I just thought I'd say that Steven found your sea trunk aboard the *Blue Swan*. It's here. I'll send it down to you. This is the captain's cabin you're in, but you won't need to think of that—I mean, I'll steer clear of enemy vessels while you're—well, I only mean you're welcome to the cabin."

She looked at him, and in her look there was disdain and anger still. It seemed that somehow he had been guilty of something, or that Corunna thought so; and he felt, as he had felt before, that he could never please her.

He moved to the door, then, and fumbled with the latch. "Well," he said, "it may be a month before we can set you ashore. We can't control these winter winds. You may find it hard—that is, if you'd rather not have me—if you'd rather not speak to me, Corunna, your—your lady here could bring me messages about anything you'd like us to do—like us to do for your comfort." He pressed the latch and hesitated, looking across the cabin at them. Victorine slid a sidelong glance at him above her knitting, but Corunna, examining the elbow of her Chinese jacket, might already have forgotten his existence. So he went out.

From Fayal the *True-Hearted Yankee* bore up to the northeastward. For two days Marvin, busy with the discipline and welfare of his crew, caught only fleeting glimpses of his passengers; for they, it seemed, came to the deck when he was in his own small berth, or working with his charts.

He had the thought, late on the second day, that they might find it easier if he should let them hear, as if by accident, that he would keep the deck at night, leaving it free for them at earlier hours. With the thought, he went on deck to find the brig rushing along a plain of black and silver beneath a moon so brilliant that it had the look of being closer than the distant mastheads. By its light he saw that his thought to remain in his cabin by day and to emerge only when darkness fell would not please Corunna; that here, once more, he could not please her.

In the moonlight he saw three figures leaning against the rail under the swelling main course. Two were women; and to his astonishment the third was Argandeau—an Argandeau who gestured with fearless grace toward the far horizon, and murmured with such fervor that his words poured from him with the sweet cadence of an endless lullaby.

"They must have seen me," Marvin sighed; for Argandeau's murmurings were suddenly silent; and after that the female figures, moving to the clack of knitting needles, left Argandeau and vanished down the hatch. Argandeau came to him, then, to stare with painful innocence at the moon.

"Wasn't it you," Marvin asked him, "who begged permission to stay in the hold?"

"Not forever!" Argandeau said reproachfully. "Did you hear me use the word 'forever'? Is it not necessary for a human being to come up at night?"

He moved closer to Marvin. "I must tell you! A strange thing happened! Strange, yet freighted with relief and consolation. Last night I was yonder, and suddenly she was behind me, full of recognition. Well, I took upon myself the calm of Socrates before the hemlock! A ship is a place where a man cannot run limitlessly with Stromboli in eruption pursuing on felt slippers at his heels! My friend, you await my narrative of the crisis! I will not keep you in suspense! My poor captain, Stromboli is extinct!"

Marvin looked at him. "Extinct?"

"Extinct! My once volcano! Flat as a dead fish! It can scarcely be credited, but when she saw me, she laughed; and what do you think she said to your pigeon? She said, 'It's that old Argandeau, an old rascal I used to know!' That was all she said of me; and we had a nice conversation, the three of us. You heard me, no? We spoke of the ocean and the moon and where is the best cooking in Paris. It's incredible! Even as I talk I must pinch myself and pinch myself!"

He took his cheek between his thumb and forefinger, and wrenched it. When he had released himself, he said carelessly, "Your pigeon does not talk much any more. I think she is sad."

"My pigeon!" Marvin exclaimed. "Don't call her that again! She's hated me a long while."

Argandeau rested his cheek on his hand and stared at the moon. "M'm! I think you have something on your mind. I think so. I think I have had the same thought. In the hold these past two days, sitting in a corner of the carpenter shop and also concealed in the bread locker, I have been able to give more than a little thought to the matter. I have wondered whether that rabbit is Mrs. Slade. I have had the thought also that it is something she will never freely tell you; also that a sure way to find out nothing at all about it is to ask her. The temptation to ask will return and return, stronger one year than another, no doubt; but I would not ask. No, I would not ask."

"No," Marvin said uncertainly. "Well, I won't have——"

"No," Argandeau repeated. "No! As for hating you, I think so. Yes indeed, I think she hates you; and why not? I ask you why not? For one thing, you have proved yourself right and her to be wrong; but that would not be the chief reason for her hate. No. The chief reason would be that it was not you who took her from the *Blue Swan*. I tell you there will be times when that hatred will be remembered at moments that will make you leap with surprise, like a fish."

"I *did* take her from the *Blue Swan*."

"No, that is not correct. That volcano—that extinct volcano—she *made* you take her."

Marvin struck the bulwark with the flat of his hand. "How the devil did I know? How should I have known what she wanted?"

"And there you are!" Argandeau cried. "That is what she hates you most for! For not knowing! For not knowing she wasn't Mrs. Slade! For that, and because she had found out she was wrong about everything!"

Argandeau looked at him pityingly. "You think, perhaps,

a woman will run to a man and tell him she has been wrong? That would be a fine beginning, eh?—for a woman to say she has been wrong, so that forever after he would be able to say to her, 'Hah! You were wrong about that thing, back there fifty years ago; therefore you are wrong about this matter here and now!' A wonderful affair, that, since it would reappear all the rest of your lives, causing bitter words and bitterer thoughts! No, no! It is too much to expect a woman to admit being wrong at the start, when all women know that to make such an admission is like placing a club in the man's hands—a club with which he will surely thump her—Piff—like that, when he is at a loss what else to do! Yes, yes, my good friend; you must expect her to hate you—yes, and bitterly! You must understand this! It's never the pigeon that is wrong; it's you—you entirely!"

Marvin shook his head, puzzled. "If she hates me, she hates me. How can I help it if she hates me? You don't think, do you, that I want her to hate me? I'm not anxious to have anyone hate me, least of all that—least of all—well, I don't like to have her hate me. I never hated her. The fact is—well, the fact is I never could help liking her. Even when we were children in Arundel."

He looked astern, over the dark waters, as though he hoped to see, far off, the little town beside the narrow river.

"I'm glad for her sake," he went on, "she didn't marry Slade. I never thought she would. But I don't know what to do—what to do about it, or about her—I don't know at all. I can't help having been right; I don't feel like taking any blame for that. She *has* been wrong all this time, and there's no other way to look at it."

Argandeau gazed long and steadily at the moon. "No," he said dreamily. "No! Of course there is no other way to look at it. No other way at all. Nor can you ever change her hate for you; of course not! Still, that pigeon is a guest on your vessel. She is in your charge, even; so you might, perhaps— it is a small thought, this one, and of no value, doubtless— you might do what you could to make her feel better."

"Why," Marvin said simply, "I would! I'd be glad to! But I don't know how! She takes no pleasure in anything I do or say!"

Argandeau raised his eyebrows, a moon-struck picture of exasperation. "But there is nothing easier! Go to her and tell her!"

"Tell her what?" Marvin demanded, equally exasperated.

"Tell her you've been wrong."

Marvin just looked at him; and from his look, it was clear to Argandeau that Marvin thought him off his head.

Yet Argandeau's words recurred to Marvin in his bed that night, and he thought about them. Indeed, he lay awake, turning them this way and that in his mind; and at last he struck upon a matter concerning which he might have been at least a little wrong. He had, as he recalled it, told Corunna she would never make a proper captain of a ship. That, he admitted, might have been an overstatement; for certainly she could come as near being a proper captain as any woman could. His words, perhaps, had been a little rough, tinged with incaution. Hazily, before he slept, he knew he owed it to Corunna to explain those words.

Thus it happened that at noon the following day it was the captain himself, instead of Newton, who came to the cabin for the log book. He hesitated before the cabin door, and almost turned away; but at length he cleared his throat and knocked; then dropped his hat and fumbled for it on the floor, and was still groping for it when Victorine's voice called, *"Entrez!"* When he had found his hat, he coughed and knocked again and immediately entered.

They were at the table, both of them, engaged in unraveling the last product of Victorine's needles, and at the sight of him they stopped and stared.

"I wanted to see—that is—you know, the log book," he said with an air of choosing his words carefully.

The two women looked at each other and then back at Marvin; and it was Victorine who took the log book from the rack beside the door and placed it in his hands.

He took it gratefully. "I didn't want to disturb you," he said. "I only thought I'd get the log book." He coughed, examined the cover of the book with apparent surprise; and then, with a sudden desperation, he said to Corunna, "I've been thinking things over, and I thought I'd tell you I believe I've been wrong about—about——"

She looked at him strangely. "Wrong?" she asked. "About what?"

Unexpectedly to himself, as if by a God-given inspiration, he said the right thing. He heard himself saying, "About everything!"

At that she seemed to change before his eyes. No sailor woman stood there, hard and hating him, but a soft-eyed girl, drooping, gentle and on the point of tears.

"Ah, no!" she said in a shaking voice. "You were never wrong about anything, nor ever will be!"

Beneath the noonday sun the *True-Hearted Yankee* sliced, close-hauled, into the teeth of the northeast trades. Under the watchful eye of the Indian, Steven, two gun crews trundled the long guns toward the bow, racing, amid the hoarse exhortations of twoscore brown-clad seamen, to win the gill of rum that would reward each member of the winning crew.

On the quarter-deck, Argandeau walked twice around the cabin scuttle, staring at its shining frosted glass as if beneath it rested some rare treasure he had helped to find. As he walked, he skipped and muttered.

"What's that you say?" Newton asked.

"It should be put in the log," Argandeau declared. "In the log, certainly!"

"Not today it shouldn't," Newton said. "The captain's writing the log today. He took it to the cabin. You'll have to wait until tomorrow. Is it the race you're so anxious to get in the log, or what?"

With his thumb and forefinger, Argandeau pinched Newton's cheek ecstatically. "That I am gay once more, my small good friend! That I am gay again!"

\*　　　\*　　　\*

Below them, in the bright cabin, the captain smiled down upon the golden square of sunlight that lay across the log book's open pages. The ink was wet upon the ancient words that he had written:

*And so ends the sea day; all well on board the good brig* True-Hearted Yankee, *of Arundel. God Save the United States of America.*

**THE END**